M000035614

ARES ASCENDING | BOOK ONE

Marianne,
Thank you for being so kind and
supportive. I appreciate you so
much. I hope you enjoy your
time aboard the Ares!

STEALING ARES

KIM CONREY

Kim Conrey

www.blackrosewriting.com

Black Rose Writing | Texas

©2022 by Kim Conrey

All rights reserved. No part of this book may be reproduced, stored in a retrieval system or transmitted in any form or by any means without the prior written permission of the publishers, except by a reviewer who may quote brief passages in a review to be printed in a newspaper, magazine or journal.

The author grants the final approval for this literary material.

First printing

This is a work of fiction. Names, characters, businesses, places, events, and incidents are either the products of the author's imagination or used in a fictitious manner. Any resemblance to actual persons, living or dead, or actual events is purely coincidental.

ISBN: 978-1-68513-034-3
PUBLISHED BY BLACK ROSE WRITING
www.blackrosewriting.com

Printed in the United States of America
Suggested Retail Price (SRP) $22.95

Stealing Ares is printed in Calluna

*As a planet-friendly publisher, Black Rose Writing does its best to eliminate unnecessary waste to reduce paper usage and energy costs, while never compromising the reading experience. As a result, the final word count vs. page count may not meet common expectations.

PRAISE FOR
STEALING ARES

"*Stealing Ares* is an inventive and creative adventure that will have you thinking about the characters' plight between readings. Conrey has created a new spin on the sci-fi genre by adding innovative ideas that hard-core sci-fi fans will enjoy and tender moments that will have all readers falling in love with Harlow and Jack."

–David McDaniel, author of
The War for the Quarterstar Shards series

"An intense view of the future with an unpredictable plot and a romance stretching across a divided world. Harlow struggles with a past that never lets go and enters a relationship that rachets up the suspense of the story, making it impossible to put down. *Stealing Ares* delivers."

–Sharon Grosh, author of
Lazarus Rising and *Capturing the Butterfly*

For Sloane and Breaganna

ACKNOWLEDGEMENTS

Finally seeing a book in print is a humbling experience, especially when surrounded by so many other talented writers whose work is also worthy of the honor. Many of those writers gave of their time and talent to critique these pages and make them better. A huge thank you goes to the Atlanta Writers Club and Roswell critique group. I cannot imagine this book or any of my other work without their input. Every writer should be so lucky to be a part of a group like ours. From that group came the Wild Women Who Write and our podcast. The encouragement and support I've received from Kathy Nichols, Gaby Anderson, April Dilbeck, and Lizbeth Jones has made me a stronger writer and pushed me further in my writing journey than I would have ever gone on my own. I would like to thank my incredible husband, George Weinstein. His support is absolutely ceaseless, optimism contagious, and faith unwavering. Thank you to my ex, Sean, who believed I could do it and suffered through the cringeworthy first drafts of all my novels. And Cherie, you always believed. Mercedes, thanks for being my first fan. Thanks to David King for a gorgeous cover that I can be proud of. I'm sure I'll think of a few dozen people I should have added later, and it will never be enough. I've journeyed with beautiful souls. Thank you all.

STEALING ARES

CHAPTER 1

HARLOW

The reek of stale beer drifted down to the basement from the tavern above as Harlow Hanson sought her contact in the dim light of a single, bare bulb. "Mike?" she called into the darkness.

"Mike's late." A male voice spoke from the shadows. "Can I help you?"

The stranger's hands slid up her arms, and against her cargo pants, she felt a more persistent threat that set off warning bells in her head. She stepped to the side and drove an elbow into his face.

As his hands came up to cup his bloody nose, Harlow turned in the narrow hallway, and made sure the man stared down the barrel of her gun.

"What the hell? You broke my nose!"

Her tone was deadly as she narrowed her eyes at the stranger, just waiting for him to try something else. "Touch me again, and I'll break more than that."

Mike stepped from the darkness, laughing. His auburn hair was wild about his head, sticking up at odd angles. A cigarette dangled from his fingers. "I told you not to go screwing around with her," Mike said to the stunned young man.

Harlow didn't care for the joke or the extra company. "My business is with you, Mike. Not him."

Mike nodded and turned to his injured friend. "I'll meet you upstairs, Theo, and don't go bleeding all over my bar." Mike had the distinction of owning the only bar on the Red Planet and, as a result, knew all the gossip and most of the secrets.

Theo left, still holding his nose and cursing Harlow on his way up.

When the door at the top of the stairs clicked shut, Mike spoke. "Forgive him. He's young, stupid, and didn't think you were as badass as people say. I thought it would be a good lesson for the kid. Let him test his mettle against the best." Though most respected Harlow, and the younger ones even hero-worshipped her brand of benevolent thievery, there were some that seethed with jealousy. She looked at Mike and let out an exasperated breath as she slid her weapon back into the holster concealed under her jacket. "Do you have my info?"

"Better than that, I've got the actual blueprints." Mike pulled a camouflaged panel from the wall, reached in, and retrieved a small cube. He tapped it twice, and a two-foot tall, holographic *HMS Ares* appeared in the dim lighting. She'd been designed to defend Mars and transport the colonists and tons of mined ore back to Earth. But then a park that once attracted visitors with amusing geysers with names like Old Faithful became anything but faithful and began spewing gray lethality into the air when the caldera that was Yellowstone Park blew. Ash, hunger, and death circled the globe for a generation, and the grandest starship of all time fell silent not long after, as if in mourning. No one knew why the *Ares* wouldn't reboot. But there were people on Earth and Mars willing to buy pieces of the ship to build their own transports, not to mention the gold conducting material throughout—already refined and ready to use.

She bit her lip and studied the glowing beast before her as Mike flipped through the hologram, revealing every illuminated floor, hallway, and ventilation shaft. This was more than a challenging heist. Pulling this off could save her people. They'd been hailed as heroes decades ago, then abandoned and left to fend for themselves. They were a burden to the struggling Earth at best, and at worst, a potential slave colony. Everyone knew about their desperation for supplies and the plentiful natural resources of Mars.

Harlow watched Mike's face glow in the blue-white light of the 3D hologram as he pulled his gaze from the plans to look at her. "I have to say, I'm impressed. Everybody talks a big game about taking that ship apart, but no one has the bollocks to do something about it."

"Well, Margaret Thatcher said, '... if you want anything said, ask a man. If you want anything done, ask a woman.'"

"Pft, Thatcher. Might have been five hundred years ago, but an Irishman doesn't forget a right bags like that. Anyway, I think you might be getting a little ambitious here. You know I got your back, but this...this is huge."

"The self-replicating nanotechnology that terraformed this planet was huge. Sticking that crazy black hole at the center of Mars to control our gravity was huge. Picking off a worthless starship beneath the nose of an arrogant prince? That's nothing." She laughed and waved a dismissive hand.

"If you get caught doing this, you won't be getting another arrest warrant you can just wipe your arse on. This will get you sent to the Bastille," he said, referring to the Bastille de la Terre Rouge, the Martian prison set up by the French members of the coalition. "I've seen some of the women that came out of that place; if they come out at all, they're broken."

"I need a challenge. Besides, you helped me strip the guts out of that little RAF transport vessel they left by Elysium Mons. You know I'm fast and efficient. They never even knew we'd been there until it was too late to catch us."

Mike smiled. "Yeah, you're good, but—"

"Look, I'm tired of seeing our people suffer while that ship sits there, accomplishing nothing. Our homes are crumbling. People are dying from infections like tetanus. *Tetanus*, for God's sake! It was eradicated from Earth centuries ago. All it takes to end a life here is stepping on a rusty nail. Just last week, the Nakamuras' son died of lung congestion because we don't have the materials to make a simple inhaler. The ship has sat for twenty years containing everything we need to improve our lives. I can't believe it's taken me this long to get around to stripping that soulless behemoth. With the gold conducting material alone, we could afford to vaccinate every person here. The damn thing doesn't run anyway."

"You're preaching to the choir, woman. Just think about it a little longer, okay?"

She paid him the other half of the credits she'd promised. He shut down the hologram and gave her the cube.

Harlow winked at her friend to lighten his mood. He'd handed her the *Ares* blueprints as if they were a death sentence.

"Don't look so concerned, Irish. I'm the best," she said.

"You are. Just think about it for my sake. Please, Harlow."

"I will. I promise."

She watched as Mike sighed and shook his head. He knew her well enough to recognize she'd already decided. He took a long drag of his cigarette before speaking. "Be careful. Don't get greedy."

She gave the man a quick hug and ran back up the stairs without another word.

· · ·

Thanks to a cleverly engineered alloy, the *Ares* never rusted, and unlike everything else on Mars, it even repelled dust due to its electrostatic coating. Its visual perfection added to Harlow's annoyance—while every other thing on the planet was subject to decay and suffering, the hulking beast before her escaped the ravages of time and greedily concealed a wealth that could make life easier for them. After twenty years of silence, what more proof was needed? This leviathan would never awaken.

After weeks of studying the blueprints until she could draw them from memory and observing the security around the ship such that the timing of every guard change was fixed in her mind, Harlow was ready. But as she stood before it, she knew Mike was right: this wasn't the same as stealing a wallet off some half-drunken bureaucrat to smuggle in extra supplies for the clinic. This was the *Ares*, the prince's baby, but Harlow and her mom, Judith, were also two months behind on their rent. Judith was a waitress at the only restaurant in the village, and it paid very little.

Harlow took a deep breath. The sulfur from the mines burned her nostrils and reminded her of her mission: besides a dozen other injustices, the colony miners were dying of simple lung congestion while the Earth coalition shrugged their collective shoulders and refused to spare the needed ventilation and medication.

She walked forward with renewed purpose, pushing a big red crate bearing the coalition symbol on the side. The trolley it rode on creaked as it bumped along the path leading to the cargo entrance of the *Ares*.

On the way in, an old, sputtering buggy passed by with an elder nun at the helm. At least fuel was the one thing they didn't have to worry about. Excrement was a cheap and endless supply. Humans and animals never stopped producing it, but between the sulfur used for the mining operation and the waste treatment tanks that sat while the industrious microbes turned the sewage into methane, Mars could be a very smelly place if the winds shifted your way.

The nun's habit waved behind her in the dusty breeze. The woman glanced at Harlow as she went on her way. Though the nun's head was covered, from the neck down she was dressed like any other colonist, in an old button-down shirt and cargo pants. People from the colonies were identified the moment they landed on Earth by their practical clothing and the no-nonsense look in their eye— though most of the second-and third-generation colonists hadn't even seen Earth except in pictures, not since the *Ares* went silent. Few could afford to hire a transport, and almost none of those vessels were still available.

The *Ares* was designed to shuttle the colonists, and with a full weapons complement, it meant smaller ships dared not mess with the budding colony. But with it offline for two decades, all it now stood for was a symbol of the prince's vanity. He was like a man with an expensive toy who refused to feed his children. The story he told was that bringing the ship back online would mean defending against outside attacks and transporting large shipments of minerals to Earth for more profit, meaning more supplies, vaccines, and quality of life for the colonists. Though most suspected coalition greed was the real motivator behind the prince's determination.

Harlow made it inside without incident and rattled off a series of credential numbers to the guard on duty. He glanced at the comm panel running on auxiliary power to confirm them and waved her through with a bored expression. She would have felt a lot more secure with her sidearm, but upon boarding the ship, the *Ares* disabled all weapons without a registration chip the second they crossed the threshold. Still pushing the trolley bearing the empty crate meant to carry as much as she could stuff inside, she made it to the core. She'd heard it was well-guarded, but the two sentries stationed there were passed out cold, thanks to her paying off the guy who always delivered their lunch; she had slipped enough tranquilizers into their food to knock them out for quite some time. Everyone she saw on the way from the cargo bay to the core must have assumed she wouldn't have made it in without authorization anyway.

Still, she stepped softly. Taking the gold was pushing even her limits. She took the multi-tool from her cargo pocket and began unfastening the screws that held the large panels in place. The sheets were taller than her 5'4" frame, but she'd rehearsed it in her mind enough to know that if she just let the weight of the panels settle on her and then backed up slowly, she could let the sheets slide down her body and lower them to the ground without making any noise.

The first panel came to rest on the floor as planned. Then she began working on the second one. Moving quickly and methodically, she timed it out in her mind as she did with everything. All was going according to plan. There had been no one else around except for the slumbering guards. Hell, why would there be? After this long, it was a pipe dream for Prince Jack to keep believing the ship would magically spring to life.

She lifted the multi-tool once more then froze as a large shadow fell over her.

CHAPTER 2

JACK

Jack felt the ever-present annoyance of sweat streak down his face as he searched each wire that funneled through the floor, heading into the core. For most of his adult life, he'd dreamed of nothing but getting the sleeping *Ares* up and running.

In the wake of the gray death, the *Ares* was left silent and abandoned, when it could be so much more—the saving grace of the forgotten colonists. There was simply no logical reason the ship wouldn't come back online. It was a fascinating puzzle that no one had solved. He joined the Royal Air Force hoping to get an assignment on Mars—not a simple task with his parents, most especially the Queen Mother, blocking him at every turn.

Now he tried to solve the mystery of the sleeping *Ares* as his home planet was recovering. He had worked tirelessly to wake the ship for the better part of seven years, with no success. He rubbed his eyes and refocused on the small wires once more. That's when he spotted it, a wire hanging loose, frayed. No telling how long it had been there, years? Excitement flared in his chest. You've been here before, he chided himself. We have inspected every inch of this core. But we could have overlooked something.

He removed the frayed section and spliced in a new length of wire. *Could it be something as simple as that?* Flushing with heat and adrenaline, he walked over to the master control panel, held his breath, and then spoke his credentials. *Today could be the day. But don't get your hopes up.* The master board glowed with auxiliary power, but no code scrolled across the hologram before him. Hope had made a fool of him again. A guttural sound escaped his throat as he kicked his toolbox across the floor, scattering wrenches, meters, and the rest of the collection, complicit in his defeat.

Pull it together, Jack. A leader doesn't throw fits. He ran his hands across his face, knit his fingers together behind his head, closed his eyes, and took a deep breath. He walked over to his toolbox and began placing the tools back inside as he thought about the colonists. They had given up hope for anything more but looked happy enough gathering in the pub and enjoying the simple things. Perhaps hope was the enemy.

Jack's thoughts were interrupted when Sergeant Carlos Gonsalves came into the room. He wore the uniform of the United States Marine Corps—part of the multinational task force that made up the Mars coalition. "How's it going, Marshal?" he said, using Jack's military title.

"Same damn way it's gone for the past seven years." Jack shook his head and rubbed his eyes again. "I'm knackered."

Carlos smiled. "Thought you could use this, sir." He handed him a bottle of beer.

Jack unscrewed the cap and took a long drink. "Where's yours?"

"I'm still on duty, sir."

Jack nodded.

"Where's Daniel?" Carlos asked, referring to the chief engineer.

"He's got the day off."

"You'd be in here anyway, Marshal." Carlos said with a smile.

Jack laughed. "I don't like to ask anyone to do the work I wouldn't do myself."

Carlos nodded. "Part of why I'm still here, Marshal. Though it must be tempting sometimes to head back to the palace and be done with it."

"To leave these people with few supplies and a barely functioning legal system would be an insult of the highest order. Their great-grandparents traveled here with nothing but bravery and science in their heads. Powering up the *Ares* could ensure their work wasn't in vain." He knew his purpose for coming to the colonies had morphed into something much more important than being the hero who finally woke the *Ares*. He wanted to give the colonists the hope the *Ares* had given him. He wanted to see Air Vice-Marshal Miller fly it again. She'd refused to leave the ship, holding onto the belief that one day it would come back online. "Besides, this place is far too vulnerable."

"The Chinese outpost on Enceladus worries me, sir." Carlos said. Saturn's icy moon seemed far away, but with the right ship, it was practically a neighbor.

"You and me both, mate." Jack realized it was only a matter of time. Mars would make a perfect base for any radical group looking to take advantage of the weakened state on Earth to launch an attack. Waking the *Ares* meant they could defend their little outpost. They hadn't suffered a major attack yet—as no one on Earth had the resources to do more than send an occasional transport to steal from the ship, which had ended with them getting caught and thrown into the infamous Bastille de la Terre Rouge.

"Not only that, sir, getting her running means the colonists could move more raw material and make a true profit, not just enough to barely survive," Carlos added.

Jack smiled. "I'd love to see that."

"Well, I'll leave you to it, sir."

Jack lifted his beer in a gesture of thanks as Carlos left the room.

So many times, he felt on the verge of victory, only to realize he was hitting another dead end. He pushed away his doubts and frustration and went back to work examining the wires for a disconnect. He'd been at it for an hour when his concentration broke by the sound of someone in the core room. No one was supposed to be in there without permission. There was the nuclear component of the core to worry about but also the gold conducting material—a point of serious contention among the people, as many felt they should sell it to buy much-needed supplies. He started to call out before deciding this might be an opportunity to catch a thief among his crew.

Lying on the floor at such an angle that if anyone were heading in to strip the gold they wouldn't see him, he slowly crawled toward the intruder on the other side of the core. He knew there was the possibility that it could be his chief engineer, Daniel, but whoever was in there was being quiet on purpose.

As he crept across the floor, he thought back to the days he'd spent on riot detail during the famine in London, when they had dealt with thieves constantly. Others in his unit commented he had a remarkable amount of stealth for a 6'4" man with broad shoulders. He'd had to learn to be silent because he wasn't small enough to fade into the woodwork.

He was glad to see that it was a woman; she would be easy to take down. He was already sweating and had no urge to wrestle with anyone. She couldn't have been more than 5'4" and was as slight as most colonists. She was dressed in cargo pants, a t-shirt, and boots— standard for the colonies and on the ship. Her raven hair was tied back into a ponytail. His mind raced as he tried to figure out how she had infiltrated the *Ares*.

He rose behind her like a ghost. "Let's see your hands," he said as he pressed the cold steel of his pistol into the thief's spine. His old-fashioned weapon used actual projectiles; he preferred the solid weight of it to the pulse sidearm that most people carried.

She raised her arms slowly, multi-tool dropping to the deck.

While he was mentally assessing the ship's security, she whipped around while reaching for the barrel of the gun. As fast as she was, he was faster. He grabbed her wrist and swept her feet out from under her.

She lay on the floor, curled into a ball, gasping like a landed fish. If he hadn't hated thieves so much, he would have to admit that he actually had some admiration for her. What she was trying to do was damned ambitious.

When she finally caught her breath and rolled over to face him, wide blue eyes looked back at him, and he realized where he'd seen her. This was Harlow Hanson, the striking culprit that had taken several wallets from his crew. Petty theft was exactly that and not worth his time, and he understood, to some degree, why the colonists did it. In fact, he had more tolerance for it here than he did back home. These people had been abandoned, and unlike those on Earth, they couldn't just up and move to greener pastures if things went pear-shaped in their district. Conditions were the same everywhere on Mars, and they both knew she had just gotten caught by the one man who could make this charge—and every other warrant for her arrest—stick. He watched as defiance, anger, and then finally, resignation, settled across her face.

"Damn it," she whispered.

Jack released a breath and fought to control the volume of his voice. "I've been busting my arse here for *seven years* trying to get this bloody ship online. I won't have you taking it apart." Half his crew had lost faith in the project. Nearly all the colonists thought he was just taking a piss—Harlow's thievery drove that point home. Never mind the fact that his parents wanted him back on Earth and hassled him about it so often now that he was avoiding them.

He looked her body up and down as she crawled backward. Though he was only checking for weapons, he could tell he was succeeding at making this ballsy thief nervous. With just enough curves to be an asset or an annoyance to her, depending on who was looking, he didn't blame her for wondering about his intentions. His gaze stopped at her boot, and he guessed correctly that she had stashed a knife there. He quickly confiscated it and slid his own weapon into the holster and began patting her down in a practiced, methodical way. He reached into the cargo pocket of his pants and found the flexible plastic cuffs he always kept on him. People living in desperate circumstances had short fuses. Fights among the colonists weren't uncommon. He cuffed her quickly and was relieved that she didn't fight it.

The idea that this woman could just come in here and make an impossible job even harder grated on his nerves. Now he had to deal with her in such a way that would prove to the colonists that they couldn't screw with him and fade back into the population. However he dealt with Harlow, it had to stick. Punishing her put him in a horrible position. She was a local hero. If he punished her too harshly, they would hate him for attacking their Robin Hood. If he went easy on her, he would lose face and have every thief with the bollocks to challenge him breaking into the ship. Either way, it tipped the scales in favor of a riot, an ever-present worry.

"Get up," he said, offering no hand to help her.

"Chivalry is dead?" she asked as she stood.

He gave her an incredulous look. "You're just lucky I didn't shoot you."

Hand on her elbow, he pulled her out of the room as he called to the guards, "Naadir! Allan!" He wondered how in hell she had gotten past them. He found them around the corner, lying still.

When they didn't respond, he looked at Harlow. His tone was low, lethal, and intended to send shivers up the spine of the streetwise woman who thought she'd heard it all before. "They better not be dead, or I swear to God, I will have your head." There might not be many men that Harlow feared, but Jack intended to be one of them. He leaned over and felt both guards' pulse. They were alive. He turned to look at Harlow with raised eyebrows.

"They'll wake up in a few minutes. I only drugged them long enough to get in and out of here."

Rage blazed behind Jack's eyes.

"What? I didn't kill them!"

It had been a rubbish day. Hell, it had been a rubbish decade, and this woman wasn't making it any better. He called for the medics to come take care of the guards, then grabbed her arm and took a deep breath, forcing himself to loosen his grip as he felt his fingers digging past muscle and onto bone. Stealing was one thing; drugging his crew was quite another.

He didn't speak on the lift that took them two floors below or when he gave instructions to the guard in the hallway and shoved her into the holding cell, which was little more than a storage space with a mechanical lock on the door. With the *Ares* being offline, whatever auxiliary power that came from the sun was needed for basic ship functions. The shock fields used to keep prisoners in their cells while allowing maximum visibility drained too much power. While he knew she could pick a lock, she wouldn't be able to lift the iron bar he slid into place.

He needed time away from her to think clearly about the right course of action. He stared at her for a moment through the small window and then left without looking back.

CHAPTER 3

THE CUSSING NUN

Harlow had thought about running several times on the way down to the holding cell but knew she would only make it a few feet before the giant of a man caught her. It was Prince James; the one the colonists loved to hate, though she'd heard the women talking about how gorgeous he was with his broad shoulders, thick brown hair, and eyes "the color of sunlight filtering through amber," as she'd heard one woman describe them while Harlow rolled her own eyes. Those who knew him called him Jack. She had a feeling she wouldn't be calling him anything except "executioner."

She lay on the thin cot in the small room and felt a migraine building much quicker than usual. There was only one lamp, and she shut it off to stop the searing pain behind her eyes. Migraines had troubled her before, but this was ridiculous. She lay back and felt the room spinning beneath her as a rush of nausea hit. Harlow pressed the heels of her hands into her temples, but it didn't help.

She didn't know how long she had lain there before she heard the iron bar slide from the door, followed by the creak of it opening, sending shock waves of pain coursing through her head. "If you've come to punish me, don't bother. I'm already about to die." She squinted into the darkness finding there was just enough light to make out the figure of the nun she'd passed outside the ship earlier. She looked to be in her late sixties or maybe even seventy.

"Do you suffer from migraines often, Harlow Hanson?" The woman's voice was both rough and soft all at once.

"Sometimes, but this one is its own special hell. Do I know you?" Harlow wasn't completely surprised someone on the ship knew her. She was wanted for theft in more than one district on Mars.

The older woman spoke with amusement in her tone. "You do. I remember a beautiful little girl with thick black braids and soulful blue eyes. You tried to steal the candlesticks right out of the chapel."

Harlow could hear the smile in her voice and felt grateful for the darkness. She wrapped it around her like a security blanket, not wanting the woman to see the memory moved her. She was the Mother Superior of the only convent on Mars. Not only that, she was also the only priest on Mars. It was hard to imagine that there was ever a time in history when women weren't allowed to be priests. How could it have been that strong, wise women were denied their place as spiritual leaders?

The women at the convent had loved Harlow when she was a little girl and took every opportunity to play with her, braid her hair, and tell her she was special. That place represented order and safety. She and her mother had gone there when they were evicted from their home. The nuns were especially patient with her as she struggled to get the words out when a speech disorder that plagued her youth made her frustrated to the point of tears. As an adult, her words were mostly clear, but certain sounds still slurred, and consonants dropped into oblivion when she was particularly exhausted or stressed.

She and her mom had only stayed with the sisters a couple of months before her mother found a man. Harlow had hated the new boyfriend, Nick, from the start—he had a perpetual habit of smacking her mother on the bottom every time she entered the room. Harlow had such a hatred of the action that she had once broken a man's wrist for smacking her ass in a bar. Nick had been of some use, though. He was an excellent thief, and she couldn't help but listen with wonder to his stories of taking wallets right out of men's pockets in broad daylight and then disappearing into a crowd before anybody noticed. Once Nick realized his stories impressed her, he explained all his tricks to her. After a lifetime of being overlooked, he liked that Harlow appreciated the unseen genius in his work. He was finally getting recognition for something that he couldn't tell anyone about—anyone but a little girl fascinated by a life of crime.

It wasn't until adulthood that she understood why she hated Nick so much; he represented her mother's lack of choice. She realized her mother stayed with Nick because she felt she had no alternative. Thievery gave Harlow a choice. There were few opportunities on Mars. She was making her own—legal or not.

Harlow turned her attention back to the older woman. "I remember you, too."

• • •

Eleven-year-old Harlow carefully lifted the bottle of communion wine from the cabinet. She was told that long ago, before the gray death, they served the wine at every mass, but now it was so rare they only served it on the holiest of days. That, along with her mother telling her she was too young for alcohol, made Harlow want to try it even more. She'd lifted other things—a piece of candy from an older child who'd bullied her, credit vouchers from patrons at the restaurant where her mother worked—but she was entranced by her first real heist. Exhilaration rushed through her small body as she jiggled the scrap of metal in the lock, waiting until she felt the mechanism inside give. Finally, the cabinet popped open, and she lifted the wine with a reverence that was quickly replaced by curiosity and a desire to get her forbidden sip of alcohol, return the bottle, and get out of there.

Quiet footfalls sounded behind her only seconds before large hands grabbed her by the shoulders and the prized bottle of wine crashed to the floor. Its contents splattered across her pant legs and ran along the tiles like the blood of Christ it represented.

The stranger's breath was hot on her neck and sour in her nose. She froze in fear. He pressed her to his chest, lifted her off the floor, and squeezed until she couldn't find the air to form a scream. He made it only a few feet away before she heard a thud, and he dropped her. Her knees hit the floor painfully. She turned to see Mother Superior brandishing a candlestick as the man grabbed the side of his head for a moment. To Harlow's horror, he drew a knife as he advanced toward Mother.

"Run!" Mother commanded, but terror glued the little girl in place.

The man kept his eyes on the candlestick as he slowly stepped backwards in Harlow's direction. She watched as Mother glanced frantically from the stranger to Harlow and back again before coming at him with the candlestick once more and changing tactics mid-swing. Harlow watched Mother's habit slide from her head and steel gray ribbons of hair fell free about her face. She transformed into an avenging angel in the eyes of the little girl. As he lifted his hands to protect his head, she kicked him in the groin.

When he doubled over in pain, Mother brought the candlestick down on his head with a savage grunt. He fell to the ground and didn't move again as she confiscated his knife and yanked the tie backs off the chapel curtains to restrain his hands and feet. Other women from the order came rushing in. One of them froze as she looked at the man. Harlow thought the nun had stopped breathing.

Mother looked at the woman as some unspoken understanding passed between them. Mother said, "Maria, it's him, isn't it?"

Maria nodded.

Mother brandished the heavy candlestick once more, walked over to the man, and brought it down on each of his ankles in turn. Harlow heard two soft cracks. The man woke up, moaned, and writhed in pain. Mother responded by giving him an extra kick to the ribs. "Won't be so easy to run from your sins this time, asshole. Sister Catherine, call the bobby to come get this filth out of my abbey."

Sister Catherine nodded and Harlow noted the sister didn't seem surprised by having a criminal in the convent or Mother's actions, though they looked at Harlow with concern.

"She's okay, Sister." Mother turned to Harlow. "Aren't you, sweetie?" She held out a hand for her.

"Teach me to do that," the little girl said with slurred words, but the wide-eyed hero worship was unmistakable.

• • •

An hour later, the two sat in Mother's study with a crude holographic image of a male human body. Mother reached into the steady blue light and drew a circle between the legs. "Run first, but if you can't get away, then aim here."

"You went for his balls!" eleven-year-old, Harlow said, accusingly.

"Well, yes."

"My friend Sanjay says going for the balls is a cheap shot."

"He says that because he has balls. If you don't have them, then you may kick them if you need to."

"My mom says *you* have them!"

Mother threw her head back and laughed loudly.

Harlow had never seen anyone do that. It made her curious. "Are you happy?" she asked quietly. Her own mother never answered such inquiries. She said it was a silly question.

Mother stopped and considered for a moment. "Happy is fleeting, subject to shifting moods and circumstance...I'm joyful."

Harlow looked at her, perplexed.

Mother got up and walked over to the cabinet containing one of the rare copies of scripture. She removed a key attached to a cord around her neck and opened the glass case. Harlow gasped as Mother tore half a page from the book. Not only was it scripture, it was *paper*, a rarity on Mars. She sat down at her desk opposite Harlow, wrote something down, and slid it across the table to her.

"But this is...holy," Harlow said.

Mother waved a hand. "Oh, don't worry. I tore it from one of the so-and-so begat so-and-so pages."

Harlow laughed.

"I know you don't have a comm device. Besides, no book is ever more important than the people it was written for. *You* are important, my girl."

Harlow read the larger words written by Kahlil Gibran, atop the much smaller scripture in the background. *The deeper that sorrow carves into your being, the more joy you can contain.*

Harlow looked up at Mother and saw a gentle smile on her face as the older woman spoke. "You may not understand it yet, but one day you will."

• • •

Harlow sat up on the thin cot and felt the same piece of paper, now wrapped in flexmat to preserve the words, shift in her cargo pocket. She hadn't thought about it at the time but realized later that Mother knew writing something down, instead of vocalizing it, was a kindness for Harlow. Thanks to her speech and language disorder, the time it took to process what was being said to her had become a source of embarrassment as a child; reading it was easier. If someone was speaking directly to you, they were looking at you, waiting for your reply. It was too much pressure. The language processing part of her brain had caught up as she grew older, but fifteen years later, she continued to unravel the meaning of the words written on the paper. Life carved deeper and took a little more every day, but she was still waiting for the joy.

The woman before her now had a few more lines on her face but looked every bit as formidable as Harlow remembered. "I won't see you in Bastille de la Terre Rouge, Harlow. You may be streetwise and think you're tougher than iron ore, but you've never seen the inside of that place."

"How do you know I haven't?" Harlow asked. The throbbing in her head was getting worse by the moment. Her words had slurred a little.

The older woman looked sharply at her through the dim lighting coming from the hall before she spoke. "I know because I still see light in your eyes and hear defiance in your voice. You aren't broken yet."

"I don't think His Highness will let me go so easy. He was beyond angry when he found out I drugged his guards. I don't know why he's making such a big deal out of it. I didn't kill them, for God's sake." The talking was making her head slam with every word. She covered her eyes to block out what little light funneled in from the hall.

"Harlow, his wife and unborn child were killed when an assassin poisoned them. He despises the insidious nature of poisoning someone. If you wanted to piss him off in the worst way possible, you succeeded." The woman was just as direct—and delightfully irreverent for a nun—as she'd remembered.

"I didn't know that, but it was only sedatives, not poison." Still, she knew it wouldn't have changed anything. Drugging them was the best option a woman of her size had, no matter how skilled in fighting.

"I will speak with him about bringing you to the convent."

Harlow said nothing. There was nothing left to say, but she also wasn't sure she could speak past the pain in her head anyway. The effort of keeping her words intelligible as the ice pick relentlessly chipped away at her skull had become a herculean effort she couldn't maintain. She began to think she must have damaged her brain when the prince had knocked her off her feet earlier.

CHAPTER 4

LET MY PEOPLE GO

Jack sat poring over the ship's blueprints again—the action helped clear his mind. All that logic and planning woven together into a blessed cohesion was a balm for his scattered thoughts. People were a hell of a lot messier. He was avoiding the Harlow issue—knowing it was going to create a shit storm for him. He still couldn't believe the woman snaked her way past all the guards. Not only had they been stationed outside the entrance to the core, but there were also a dozen patrolling outside the ship. As much as she angered him for trying to steal from him, he appreciated her ingenuity.

But what happened today was a low point. He'd busted his arse year after year on the damn ship. Now today, his worst fears seemed to come to life. The people were getting bolder with the *Ares*. They felt the massive starship was a vanity on his part. For the first time, he was thinking they might be right. A knock at the door snapped him out of his spiral.

"Come in."

He looked up to see Mother Superior, his aunt, standing in the doorway. He'd forgotten to mask the defeat in his voice, and he knew it wasn't lost on the wise woman that walked into his office.

"Rough day, Jack," she said.

He scrubbed his large hands across his face to clear the fatigue. Half emotional, half physical. "Yeah."

No one else would have walked in and sat down in the prince's office without being asked to do so. No one else got away with calling him Jack either, but he never corrected her. Her presence grounded him.

"I wish there was a better time to talk to you about this, but I need a favor."

She rarely asked him for anything and certainly nothing for herself. Despite his exhaustion, he listened.

"Please don't send Harlow to prison."

"I can't abide thieves, Mother. I cannot let the colonists think it's okay to take this ship apart."

"Then allow me to take her back to the convent. It's an excellent compromise. She doesn't go to prison, but she doesn't go free either. Most people would consider a convent a type of prison anyway, right?"

Jack gave a tired laugh. "Most would, but you live it as freedom." He looked up, beyond his aunt, trying to clear his mental exhaustion long enough to consider her idea. "You've seen her kind before. Everyone must fight to survive. Thievery is the lazy way out," he argued.

"Maybe, but it is how *she* survives. She doesn't know another way. Please, Jack."

His younger days of trying to quell riots while in the service sprang to mind again. Losing lives, the scars that would never heal. Letting Mother escort the people's hero away from the *Ares* might pacify them—at least temporarily.

He exhaled, releasing his frustration. "Fine. Get her out of here. I'll walk you back to her cell. I want to make sure she knows there won't be a reprieve next time."

Jack watched his aunt smile in triumph, causing the corners of her green eyes to crinkle like rays of sun bursting through the clouds.

• • •

After the guard opened the door of Harlow's cell, they heard the distinct sounds of vomiting. Harlow was hunched over a bucket, dry heaving before she fell onto the ground. Her body was drenched in a cold sweat, and her dark hair lay plastered to her cheeks. Jack looked at her with sympathy for the first time. From where he stood, she no longer looked so properly chuffed to have made it on his ship, and yet he couldn't ignore the anger that still flared in his gut.

His aunt placed a hand on his forearm. "It's a migraine. At least send her to sick bay until the headache passes. She can't travel like this. She needs compassion."

"I'm not sure I have any, Mother. Besides, what's happened to you? You've always been the toughest old broad I know."

"Birds of a feather," she said, pointing at Harlow and smiling. "Please, for me?"

Jack rolled his eyes, let out a low growl, and walked over to where Harlow lay on the cold floor. He pondered the irony that an old lady and a thief had talked him out of his plans to keep this woman in jail. Despite his anger, he picked her up gently. She made a soft, pained sound. She was light in his arms, and it made him wonder how someone so small could create so much trouble.

As he stepped out, the constabulary stationed outside her cell stepped forward. "May I call medical, sir?"

"I'll be up there quicker than they can make it down here."

"I'll have a guard posted at medical then?"

"Thank you," Jack called over his shoulder as he entered the lift with Harlow in his arms and Mother by their side.

When they reached the infirmary, Jack laid her down on the nearest lifecomm bed. "Hey, Doc, can you see what you can do for her?"

The doctor shoved his glasses farther up his nose and looked at Harlow warily. "Is she sick?"

Jack didn't miss Doctor Seamus Hagen looking down at her with suspicious eyes. He couldn't blame him. He knew there were many in the colonies who had received no vaccinations, and he also knew, as a little boy, Doc had watched helplessly as a quarter of County Carlow, Ireland—those that famine and the ash clotting the skies hadn't already taken—died of diseases that earlier generations would have found archaic. Though Jack had made sure everyone on his crew were vaccinated years ago, new viruses sprung up all the time.

"It is just a severe migraine," Mother answered.

Jack could tell his aunt was trying to hide her annoyance at the doctor's hesitation, but various epidemics had left a permanent mark on all of them, albeit an emotional one for the survivors.

Mother walked over to the sink, wet a cloth, and returned to Harlow to wipe her face as she called her name.

Harlow began to shake violently.

The lights on the *Ares* flickered, and the dormant screens in the infirmary, which had been dark for twenty years, lit up as code scrolled.

"Shit!" the doctor called out. "She's seizing!" He reached into a nearby cabinet and pulled out a Rescue Wave, tapped in a combination of numbers as Mother held Harlow's head down to stop the trembling long enough for Doc to administer the correct frequency to stop the seizure.

Harlow's seizure subsided mere seconds later.

"Marshal!" Sgt. Gonsalves rushed into the room.

Jack looked at the man to confirm what he was seeing. "Carlos, is this—?" Jack asked, unable to finish a sentence as he pointed to the screens.

Carlos smiled. "That isn't the auxiliary power, sir. The core is coming online!"

Jack tried to process what was going on. After seven years of trying everything he could think of, it was finally happening and damned if he knew why.

Jack noticed Harlow had stopped seizing but still squeezed her eyes shut against the pain. She sat up and gave one sharp cry as the floor shook beneath their feet—the telltale sign the core wasn't just powered up, but the gigantic oscillating disks inside it were rotating. Jack, Doc, the guard, and Mother all looked at each other, speechless.

Doc looked at the Rescue Wave in his hand. "Well, it works, but it doesn't do that!"

• • •

Jack and Carlos left the infirmary and ran straight to the core. "Was Daniel working in here again?" Jack inquired.

"Not that I know of, sir," Carlos replied.

As they rounded the corner, they saw Allan and Naadir—recovered from their earlier bout with Harlow's tranquilizers—back on duty. "Nice job, sir!" Allan said with a broad grin.

"Thanks, but I'm not sure it was me."

Once inside, Jack and Carlos found the room empty, with the large panels still lying on the floor where Harlow had placed them, along with her trolley and crate meant for carrying out whatever she'd planned to pilfer. Jack thought surely there must have been something she had done that he hadn't thought of, but for the life of him, he couldn't figure it out. She hadn't been in there more than a minute or two at most—and her intention had been to steal, not repair.

. . .

Later that evening, Jack was still trying to work it out when Mother stopped at his office with Harlow. "I just wanted to say goodbye, Jack. If we don't get going now, we won't make it back to the convent before nightfall."

Jack looked up and saw Harlow standing beside his aunt with her arms crossed. She appeared to have recovered from her earlier illness, though he noted the purple smudges beneath her eyes. Surely, she didn't have seizures with every migraine. Though she was no longer his problem, he still wasn't sure he was making the right decision to send her to the convent. Although his instincts told him he need not worry about his aunt with Harlow, another part of him knew exactly how desperate many of the colonists were, and it caused them to make poor decisions they wouldn't normally make—sometimes with deadly results. He got up and walked around his desk to face Harlow. "Don't make me regret letting you go," Jack said as he locked eyes with her.

"You need not worry about your aunt. I owe her."

"You would be in prison if it weren't for her. She saved you."

"More than once," Harlow answered.

Jack held her eyes for a moment longer, searching for it, that wave of uneasiness that would tell him he was making a mistake. He'd learned the price of ignoring it. He found no malice, but he found unease—his own. While he was reading her, he got the feeling she'd begun reading him right back. He looked away. Mother walked up, hugged him, and whispered into his ear, "Thank you, Jack."

He nodded and walked back around to sit at his desk as they left the room.

He couldn't remember the last time he'd felt so rattled.

CHAPTER 5

SECRETS ON STONE LIPS

Harlow and Mother walked into the late afternoon sunlight, and Mother fired up the ancient buggy that sputtered every few feet but got the job done. They rode in silence for a while. The older woman spoke first. "How is your mother? Is she still...?"

"Alive? Yes. She lives alone now. Her boyfriend got shot. Died a few years back."

"Stealing?" she asked.

"Yes."

"You are such a smart woman. You don't want to go like that. Just because that's all you were ever taught—"

Harlow found herself irritated by the lecture. "Remember, Mother, I was stealing the candlesticks out of the chapel before my mother met him. Maybe my gift is innate."

Mother laughed softly. "Yes, that you were, but everything has a flip side, Harlow. If you are clever enough to become adept at stealing, then you are clever enough to make a real difference in your world. I'm willing to bet you fenced half the things you stole, right? You could be one damn fine businesswoman."

Harlow spoke with an exaggerated tone of scandal. "Nuns aren't supposed to cuss!"

"Yeah, well, I've been on this orange hellhole for far too long. Don't judge." She smacked Harlow playfully on the arm.

"Couldn't you request the Church send you back to London?"

"I could, and they just might honor that request at my age. But I've grown to love these people, and I won't go back there and leave Jack alone."

"Who is he to you?"

"He's my nephew."

"Oh." Harlow had no idea. She didn't remember anyone mentioning it at the convent.

"I take it you don't like him very much."

"It doesn't matter what I think. He's the prince, and he hates my ass."

"Well, you were trying to steal his life's work."

"Maybe he's too old or out of touch to understand how hard it is for us. He's a prince."

"He's not that much older than you, only thirty-three, and he gets nothing from home to live on. He's not just some nob. His parents want him to come back to London, so they refuse to make his life here comfortable. He gives up a lot by staying. It would be so easy for him to just call a transport, leave, and forget about these people, but he stays. He has honor in his heart, the likes of which I have never seen."

Harlow turned to look at the older woman's profile in the fading light. She was part of the royal family. She could have had a much easier life than this, yet she stayed. Steel gray threads of hair blew free of the woman's habit.

"I've seen it," Harlow said quietly.

• • •

Harlow slept better that night than she had in years. After a quiet breakfast with the sisters, she and Mother walked the grounds of the convent as Harlow studied the statues: the Virgin Mary, St. Anne, and St. Francis. When she was a little girl, they seemed to loom before her, full of mystery and magic—as if they held secrets behind their stone lips that they refused to share with her. Now that she was older, they didn't strike her as being that large, and she no longer felt they held a secret, just a struggle. Everyone struggled. The thought struck her as both refreshing and frightening. It was easier to believe they had some knowledge that, once spoken, worked like a magic key. Instead, she was left with the unsettling notion that if there was a key to be found, she had to forge it herself; or perhaps, find out who had it and steal it.

They had reached the front of the building when a vehicle came rolling across the dusty terrain in the distance. Mother raised a weathered hand to shield her eyes and squinted. "It's my nephew."

Harlow's heart started racing. She wasn't looking forward to seeing him again and assumed she wouldn't. She watched as Jack pull up and got out of the buggy with a spring in his step and fairly hummed with...excitement or joy? Harlow couldn't tell. It was confusing. He was supposed to be angry at her. He might just be happy the core was back online.

Stupid ship.

The Marine they called Carlos had come along with him. Harlow noticed he looked at Jack with amusement and surprise. She assumed Jack wasn't always this jovial. *That* she believed. Then again, her only interactions with him were after trying to steal something he had worked on nonstop for seven years.

"Good morning, Mother!" Jack said with a smile.

"Good morning, sweetheart. I didn't expect to see you for a while yet."

"I'll just get going so you two can talk," Harlow said, hoping to make a hasty retreat before he changed his mind and hauled her off to prison.

He turned to look at Harlow. "I'm actually here to speak with *you*."

Harlow felt Mother stiffen beside her. "Why?" she asked.

She almost laughed out loud when Mother stepped in front of her protectively.

"Don't worry. I'm not here to go all argy-bargy on your star pupil. In fact, I just may have a job for her."

Mother stepped out of the way but made no move to leave.

They all stood in the courtyard in what felt like a type of standoff. Jack smiled at his aunt. "She'll be fine. I wouldn't take her without telling you."

Mother gently touched Harlow's shoulder. "I'll be in my office when you're done," she said, before turning to leave. Harlow watched Carlos walk to the other side of the courtyard. She assumed to give her and Jack some privacy to talk, though she would've preferred that he stayed.

"Why are you here, Highness? Did you come to arrest me anyway?"

"No, but I wouldn't be wrong if I did. I caught you bang to rights, and you've got more than a few warrants."

Harlow simply nodded.

"Then what can I do for you?" She made a conscious effort not to be a smart ass. He'd earned a little respect; he could have sent her to prison.

"I kept going over in my head what might have brought the ship back online. I've been working on it for years, so it's hard to admit this, but it wasn't anything I did." He began pacing back and forth in front of her. "I fell asleep looking at the blueprints, the logs of all the different ways I've gone about this for the last seven years. Anyway, I drifted off and dreamed of you and—"

Harlow laughed. "Did you now?" she said in a teasing voice.

"No, not like that! Look, here's why I'm really here. I'm here because of Colonel Michael Hanson."

When Harlow heard her father's name, she felt hot tears burn the backs of her eyes and blinked quickly, hoping Jack wouldn't notice. "The pipe dream of this place took him away from us." She always believed his death was the root of all of her and her mother's troubles. It was why she had little conscience about stealing; she only took from the officials she thought responsible for everyone's problems; officials like the prince. "I don't carry the same sense of duty to keeping the Mars mission alive. The Mars dream ruined many families, not just mine."

"I hear where you're coming from. But he was protecting these people that you go to such lengths to help. You risk jail time for your people. He just helped them in a different, more legal way," Jack said with a smile. "He piloted the *Ares*. Not only that, but he was one of the chief designers of the new system, wasn't he? He also had a degree in engineering. When the colonies were attacked by the Brotherhood, I believe he created a lock so that no one could ever get it online again without the key. He knew once they had that ship, it would all be over for the colonists and Earth as well. He put it somewhere no one would guess." Jack lifted his eyebrows and looked at Harlow. "The only problem is, he was killed before he could let anyone know where he hid the key. Or, just maybe, the life he wanted for you was on the *Ares*, and this was his way of ensuring the ship never left port without you." Jack gave her a moment to let it all sink in.

His theory about locking down the ship from the Brotherhood wasn't completely without merit. In the beginning, the Brotherhood had been a group of religious zealots with roots in the terrorism that plagued the twenty-first century. Over the years, it had morphed into a haven for anyone disgruntled by governments that had lost touch with their people. The handling of the gray death had only added fuel to an already well-lit fire. Many thought the wealthier countries and corporations had favored some groups with the nanobot technology to make the air breathable, which led to repairing the atmosphere and being able to grow some crops again while allowing others to die.

The Brotherhood had attacked before, and it could happen again. Earth sent coalition troops on small transports and subdued the plot within a few days. Even though Harlow had been a little girl at the time, she remembered it well. But everyone knew the coalition help sent from Earth had less to do with protecting the people of Mars and more to do with keeping their own asses safe from an off-world terrorist group that would quickly grow out of control. As the years went on and the small ships on Earth fell apart, there were fewer resources available to repair them. Even though Earth was recovering, the resources went into food, water, and more immediate necessities.

If the Brotherhood attacked again, it wouldn't take much to bring down the small population on Mars. Once they took over the *Ares*, the coalition wouldn't have the resources to fight them again, as they were still trying to recover from the gray death. They could use the *Ares* to terrorize Earth. They weren't wrong in thinking they could bring the vulnerable Earth to its knees and Mars would end up being the ultimate terrorist headquarters, but even when the Brotherhood had infiltrated the ship, they couldn't get it online. But now....

"Look, I get what you're saying, but how could I have the key?" Harlow replied.

"Just humor me a moment." Jack pulled a chip reader out of the duffel bag he had slung over his shoulder. "Hold still." He ran the device over her head, and it beeped.

"What the hell is going on?"

Jack spoke with fascination in his voice. "I knew it. You have a type of 'key' in your brain. You're the reason the *Ares* finally started up again after all these years. I believe your head began hurting as soon as the ship started communicating with that chip. As it started reading the information to power the ship up again, your headache started. The more information it read, the more excited your brain became until you ended up with one hell of a migraine-seizure combo. Your head must have felt like it was about to explode. I can't imagine. I would have been a lot more sympathetic had I known what that thing was doing. I'm sorry. I thought maybe you were..."

"Faking it to get out of going to prison? Sounds about right for a thief." Harlow laughed. "But getting back to me having something in my head that I haven't known about for twenty-six years..."

"It isn't that unusual. Before Yellowstone blew and the gray death took hold, people could afford technology in their heads to do everything from starting their car to their washing machine."

"But an entire starship?"

"I don't think your father would have put something in your head that would hurt you."

She nodded. She remembered little about her father but knew enough to believe that much.

"Come back to the ship with me, Harlow."

She looked at him in shock. "First, why would you want a thief on your ship? I think you made it clear yesterday you couldn't bear to look at me. Second, I've got no urge for another migraine. I've never experienced anything like that in my life and don't want to again."

"Fair enough, but I don't think it will give you a headache now that the ship is back online. And no, I don't want people stealing from me, but I know why you did it." Jack crossed his arms and leaned against one of the columns in the garden. "I know the people here resent me. I can't blame them. They think I'm holding on to that ship for pure vanity and pride keeps me from selling it off in pieces to fund a better life for everyone. But I believe a starship of that magnitude says something important to the rest of the solar system. Something you would definitely understand."

This ought to be good, she thought. More bureaucratic bullshit. "What does it say, Jack?"

He grinned. "It says, 'Don't fuck with me.'"

She laughed. "I've never told you that."

"You say it constantly. It comes off you in waves. Listen, it's just a matter of time before someone out there takes advantage of how vulnerable we are and comes to take what little we have here and enslaves or kills us. I believe you have information in your head that could help protect everyone. Come back with me—you were meant to be on the *Ares*. I just know it. I did some research, and you were even born on that ship."

Harlow raised her eyebrows. Her mother had never told her that. "You know I have zero flight skills, right? My dad might have been a pilot, but I am, sadly, untrained."

A board grin spread across his tanned face as he laughed at the idea.

"Even I don't fly the *Ares*. Air Vice-Marshal Miller does that. She flew with your father two decades ago. That woman won't be letting either of us near her chair."

Harlow laughed, but there were some genuine issues. She knew coming back with him might be a power struggle. They both had strong personalities.

He continued. "If you stay here, you only get a quiet life of celibacy. No adventures, no risks or challenges." He grinned and scratched at the stubble on his chin.

"Not exactly looking forward to that," she said with a laugh.

"I wouldn't be, no. Come on. Let's go tell my aunt goodbye."

He gave her a good-natured smack on the shoulder, and they went to go say goodbye to Mother.

CHAPTER 6

VOICES OF THE PAST

When Jack, Harlow, and Carlos arrived at the ship, the overwhelming presence of the vessel struck her. Like most people in the colonies, she had gotten used to seeing it until it became part of the landscape, but now that she was to board it as a crewmember, she struggled to place what it meant to her. It was a painful memory, not just because of the nightmarish migraine, but also because it brought all the resentment and grief of growing up without her father racing back to her. But for the first time, she glimpsed what Jack must have felt when he saw it: potential, responsibility, a challenge.

"You all right?" Jack asked.

"Yeah, I'm good."

They walked inside and Jack pointed at various objects, saying, "Don't steal that. It's my favorite." He grinned every time, but Harlow still wanted to smack him.

"Come on. I'll take you to the bridge," he said.

Despite her annoyance at helping forward the Mars dream, she also knew Jack had a point. The Mars outpost was beyond vulnerable, and she did like the idea of the people she cared about being protected. She had to admit the ship was impressive—now that she wasn't just looking at it in terms of what she could take.

As they stepped on the bridge, Harlow counted seven at their duty stations. Several uniformed RAF members saluted, fingers on their forehead with palm facing out. Harlow had noticed this palm-out distinction from the American soldiers when one Airman and Marine saluted as well. A British civilian bowed to Jack. All went back to their stations after a quick glance her way. She had the impression word had gotten out. They were all looking without looking. Or trying to. *Obvious. A thief could teach them to do it better.*

One didn't hide her curiosity or appraisal. A woman who appeared to be in her fifties rose from the command chair while keeping a keen yet kind eye on Harlow. "Welcome aboard. I'd love to speak with you once you settle in."

"Of course." She wasn't sure whether the woman wanted to give her an ass-kicking for stealing from the ship or thank her for getting the thing online. She searched her face, but try as she might, she couldn't get a lock on one emotion or the other.

The woman's face became blurry, and Harlow felt herself start to zone out. She shook her head to clear it. It wasn't unlike the feeling she had gotten in the infirmary before the ship came online, except this time, her head wasn't about to explode.

Jack was in front of her with his mouth moving, but she couldn't hear what he was saying. He put his hands on either side of her face and lifted an eyelid with one of his thumbs. "Hey, you in there? Harlow?"

She watched Jack's head whip around as the large screen above the console came to life, and a man that looked familiar to her began speaking.

"Colonel Michael Hanson," the man on the screen said, followed by a series of numbers that Harlow assumed said something about what he did in the Air Force. His face blurred as tears sprang to her eyes when she realized it was her father. She had never known just how much she favored him. She only remembered fragments here and there when she was seven. He had the same dark hair and blue eyes, the same nose, even his hair parted on the same side as hers.

"Hello, Harlow. If you are seeing this message, it means you've made it back to the *Ares*, where you belong. I'm heading out to do some reconnaissance in a few days, and I have a feeling I'm not coming back."

His words were somber but not overly sad. She felt Jack looking at her and wanted to move closer to him. She hated the feeling of her own vulnerability.

The seven crew members on the bridge were all either looking at her or transfixed by the screen and the technology they knew was in her skull and responsible for the ship powering up. She knew they couldn't help but wonder what else might happen now that she was back onboard. More than a few of the scientists might want a look inside her brain as well, but she realized her dad might have been right in putting the information in her head. She wouldn't hesitate to tell anyone to back off, and she couldn't be ordered to do anything either, as she wasn't a member of the military or the coalition.

Her father continued speaking. "I don't know how old you are now. Whether you are ten or thirty, I'm giving my letter of recommendation. When you were little, you took apart every gadget you could find so that you could figure out how it worked. A few days ago, you grabbed a baseball bat and stood by the back door. When I asked you what you were doing, you said that you were 'guarding the house in case of robbers.'"

His story made her smile. Her mother rarely spoke of their life before her father died, and she hadn't remembered that incident.

Her father continued, "You are seven at the time of this recording. I have hope that you will remember me, but if you don't, that's okay. You will see me every day when you look in the mirror. I will be in your heart, and I will watch over you. I don't know what course your life will take, but I know you are brilliant and capable of great things. Be strong, be brave, and protect the information I've entrusted to you. I love you." With that, he looked directly into the camera for a few seconds more before giving the command to end the recording.

Everyone was silent, frozen in place as the symbol for the Mars coalition that bore flags of several nations on a background of orange replaced his image. Until then, Harlow had never felt a sense of embarrassment or shame over what she did. She'd been proud of her skills for thievery and stealth; they'd served her well. But seeing her dad on the screen, believing in her, made her judge her own life compared to his, and it disturbed and angered her. It wasn't her fault he'd died for a lost cause. It wasn't her fault that Mother Nature had given them all the finger and let a part of the Earth explode and rain gray death from the sky.

Jack stepped in close enough to whisper. "You okay?"

"No," Harlow answered in a clipped voice, afraid to move.

Jack took her by the elbow to guide her off the deck as Air Vice-Marshal Miller spoke to the crew. "All right. Lots to do here. Airman, see if you can find a replacement for that burned coil in the console."

With that, everyone got the cue that they were to disperse and stop staring at Harlow.

"Come on, I'll show you to your quarters," Jack said. He placed his hand on the small of her back as they left the bridge, walking in silence until they reached a row of rooms around the corner.

Jack tapped a silver plate next to the door before them. "Check this out."

Harlow read the inscription engraved on the shiny metal: *Colonel Michael Hanson.* "You've got to be kidding me." It filled her with a sense of wonder. For 26 years, Harlow had thought nothing could rattle her. She'd seen or stole it all in her time, but the last forty-eight hours were quickly threatening to overwhelm her. It wasn't the chip in her head that had her reeling, either. It was challenging to the life she stubbornly defended, and her very identity being turned on its ear. She reached out and ran shaky fingers over the inscription. "How is it still here? I would have thought someone would've removed it by now."

"I asked that it be left where it is," Jack replied. "It seemed wrong to remove it, especially because the *Ares* went to sleep when he did, I guess you would say. I figured if we ever got the ship up and running, we could always put another nameplate under it—maybe yours."

Harlow nodded. She had to admit Jack was making it hard not to like him. She loathed wasting her time, and she had invested a lot of it in resenting this guy.

When Harlow walked into her room, she marveled at her surroundings but tried to hide it. It had its own bathroom. She couldn't imagine such a thing.

"My room is across the hall," Jack said.

Harlow needed to feel comfortable in her own skin again. She switched into the sarcastic language that had guarded her well for as long as she could remember. "Is that a warning that you'll be watching for me to steal something?"

Jack laughed. "No. I was letting you know your room is in the same area with the other bridge crew. Support staff is on deck two. I want you to know that this is your job now. You're an essential part of the crew. Besides, it was your dad's room. It's only right you should have it."

"I'm part of the crew because I have all this stuff in my head. I have no skills useful to this ship."

"You've got a keen shite detector, and I wouldn't try to pull anything over on you. Yes, we need the information in your head, but I also believe your father is right. You're brilliant. How you've managed to escape capture all these years and get on a ship as heavily guarded as this one—into the core no less—is the kind of genius that could benefit our mission to make life better for everyone in the colonies. I want you to be my personal advisor. I need someone that thinks like—"

"A criminal?" Harlow asked with a twinkle in her eye.

"No, a brilliant tactician. You've only been using it to be a criminal." Jack smiled.

Harlow narrowed her eyes and looked at him for a moment. "I'll need to let my mother know where she can find me."

Jack narrowed his eyes right back at her. "Well, bugger me! You're going to run."

"Now, why would I do that?"

He answered without pause. "Because you're scared."

"You don't know what I am!" But he did, and she knew it, which made her want to run even more.

"I've seen that look before."

"Where would a prince find such a look?"

"In the mirror, love. But that isn't important. This is bigger than you, Harlow. Think of what can be done with this ship. I know what you've done with all the things you've stolen. I've followed the trail. It all leads back to you, but I know you've used it to buy things, or smuggle supplies in, for the kids and the sick. You've kept very little for yourself."

Though his scrutiny was in her favor, Harlow squirmed beneath it and needed to deflect some of it immediately. "Yes, I've kept a little. My boots are kick ass. These were for me." She looked down, admiring them.

"They are nice, yes. I also think Janet in engineering might like them too. You know, since they're hers. You've been going through the cargo at the dock before it even gets transported onto the *Ares*, right? There's a tiny emblem on the back of the heel." He laughed. "Anyway, I think you get my meaning. The *Ares* could transport enough gold and other raw materials off this planet to make some serious money for these people and build the world your father dreamed of. Besides, I'll pardon all the warrants for your arrest, but you have to agree to stay here."

She wasn't that worried about the warrants—though he didn't need to know that. But she knew he wasn't wrong about the ship. Having just a few small transport vessels, they could only sell a fraction of the hematite, gold, and other raw materials they mined. Ferrying it back and forth took months, and the heavy equipment they needed came in piece by piece for the same reason. Production crawled.

Harlow stuck her hand out. Jack shook it.

It wasn't lost on her how warm his hand was or how soft his gaze could be—that is, when he wasn't about to throw her in prison.

CHAPTER 7

A VISIT TOO FAR

Jack had agreed to let Harlow inform her mother where she was, but he refused to let her go alone. He walked beside her as his guards from the British Special Air Service, Devante McNamara and Evelyn Chuang, followed. Harlow had cared little about their ranks but knew their names from the time they spent at O'Malley's Pub when they were off duty. The guards were sent to the outpost with the prince seven years ago. Devante had married a village girl, and Evelyn had a girlfriend Harlow had seen her with at the pub. She often wondered what they would do if they were sent back to London. Being part of a small colony where they learned to rely on each other and think in terms of what's best for the village probably wouldn't translate well if they returned to Earth.

"Harlow!" came a voice from above them.

She looked up and noticed the seven-year-old girl with the head full of braids, dark skin, and golden eyes—a mutation that was popping up in the few children being born on Mars. There weren't many, though. Even though the controlled black hole deep within the center of the planet made the gravity similar to that of Earth, it fluctuated slightly, and was suspect for making infertility more common.

The girl jumped down from the tree. They designed each village within the colony with a little green space in the center of town. The grass was patchy, and the park benches were faded—the gray death that had killed half the population on Earth meant supplies were rare, and there were certainly no upgrades or improvements forthcoming, but the people still took pride in their little park.

The girl smiled at Harlow. Clad in black from head to toe, Harlow's sleek black ponytail and cat-like movements made her intimidating to some, but the kids in the colony knew her well enough to understand she was their friend.

"Hi, Piper!" Harlow said.

Before responding, the little girl looked at Jack, and the guards following, with suspicion before eyeballing Harlow's pockets.

"Sorry, Pipes. No candy today," she said with mock sorrow.

Piper looked at the ground. "Oh."

"Just kidding." Harlow grabbed two lollipops from her pockets as if she were drawing weapons from holsters. "Pew, pew!" She twirled them between her fingers before handing them to Piper with a flourish.

"Thanks, Harlow." Piper left, giggling.

"You have to give one to your brother!" Harlow called.

"Damn it!" Piper said, as she rounded the corner.

Harlow tried not to laugh but failed. "Language!"

She heard Jack chuckling beside her.

They walked to a small row house at the edge of the village. Harlow walked in without knocking. It was sparsely decorated and too cold to be comfortable. There were restrictions on power usage in the colonies.

"Mom!" Harlow called.

"In here!"

She walked into the kitchen to find her mom, Judith, bundled in a well-worn green sweater with a hole in the elbow. Her shoulder-length red hair made a sharp contrast to the green wool, but her mother's eyes matched the sweater almost perfectly. Though Harlow had her father's coloring, she and her mother had the same bone structure.

Judith spotted the prince and narrowed her eyes. "What's *he* doing here?" she whispered.

"Mom, this is Prince James. This is my mother, Judith."

Jack stood at the entrance to the small kitchen and inclined his head with respect. "Pleased to meet you."

"Hello," Judith said, with a look that suggested he was something to be scraped off her shoe.

Harlow cringed but noticed Jack didn't react to Judith's expression.

"I'll give you two a minute," he said, then turned to wait in the small living room.

"What's he doing here?" Judith whispered again to her daughter. Harlow knew her mother thought he was there to enforce all the warrants Harlow had accrued—the ones they had spent their evenings laughing about.

"Mom, I'm going to go work on the *Ares.*" It came out in a rush. Harlow hadn't realized, until that moment, how much she feared telling her. Judith resented everything about the ship. After seeing her father's image on the screen that morning, Harlow felt closer to the *Ares*, not further—though in some ways she felt a conflicting sense of betrayal. Whether the betrayal was toward the people in the village or her mother, she couldn't tell. She just knew that it felt as if she was suddenly on the other side of a gap that separated her from her family and friends. But her father had been on the *Ares.* So, it was part of her, wasn't it?

The look of shock on Judith's face felt like a dagger in Harlow's gut.

"I heard that damn thing was back online. It's all anyone wants to talk about. I thought you were going to strip it, not join the crew."

"Mom, I didn't go there to join. The prince was in the core, and he caught me. If it weren't for his aunt, I would have gone to prison."

"Mother Superior?" Judith asked softly as a light sheen of tears was quickly blinked away. She and Harlow both shared a hatred of appearing vulnerable—not just to the rest of the world but with each other as well.

"Yes, she remembered me and talked the prince out of sending me to the Bastille de la Terre Rouge. She took me back to the convent with her. That was the deal, but while I was on the ship, it came online and Jack, I mean, the prince..."

Judith locked eyes with her daughter and gave her a sharp look.

"Anyway, he figured out that I have a chip in my head that communicates with the ship. He needs me there, and I get to stay out of prison. He is also pardoning all my warrants."

"And he's *using* you," Judith said with venom.

Though her mother's statement settled on her like a cold rain, she knew she was right, to some degree. Harlow took a deep breath before continuing slowly, unwilling to let her mother hear her stumble over her words—the telltale sign she was stressed, the giveaway that she couldn't hide. "Yeah, but Dad put this in my head. He left me a message. I actually saw him, Mom." Despite her best efforts, Harlow choked up as she told her mother about seeing her father. "He said I belong there."

"He was obsessed with that damn ship. Now I will lose you to it as well. Prison might be better than that soul-sucking hunk of metal!"

"What?" She understood where her mother was coming from, but her contact at the tavern, Mike O'Malley, had shown more concern for her well-being and keeping her out of prison than her mom had.

Judith continued. "We were happy. He was my world. But he had no business putting that chip in your head. You were a little girl, not a science experiment."

"You knew about it and didn't tell me?"

"Why tell you? So this can happen? Exactly *this!*" She threw her hands in the air. "The damn thing is taking my daughter now. I had no idea just boarding the ship would activate that chip in your brain, or I would have never let you go."

"Mom, I don't want to go to jail, and maybe this is my chance to do something with my life, and I—" If she didn't slow down her speech, she wouldn't be able to speak clearly. But if she paused, her mother used the opportunity to attack.

As a child, it made Harlow want to scream, cry, or both. After her dad died, she remembered asking her mother where he was. She simply told her he was dead and "that stupid ship" was to blame. Years went by, and he was never spoken of again. It felt to Harlow as if he'd never existed at all.

Once, not long after her tenth birthday, she had stood frozen, looking out the window, as a dust storm came rolling in from the desert. Though the planet was terraformed, there were still areas with very little vegetation. She'd heard that before terraforming, the storms were much heavier and lasted longer, but she couldn't imagine them being worse. As dust and small rocks pelted their home, Harlow lay on the floor, screaming. Her mother had hugged her close and explained, again, that they were just more of a nuisance than anything else, but the dust wasn't the problem. Night after night, she was tormented by nightmares of being swallowed up by the storm. She'd become a ghost, walking through the village and feeling as if she had never been there at all. She watched her mother at work, and her mother wouldn't speak of her. You not speaking of someone after they died scared her more than death itself. It was only later that she learned her mother was the only one who didn't speak of Michael Hanson.

"Why does the storm frighten you so much?" her mother had said to ten-year-old Harlow. She struggled to get the words out. Judith waited. Inside her brain, Harlow fought for tone, syllable, noun, and verb, but between the storm and Judith's disapproval of what she wanted to talk about, the words came out in a garbled rush. "Dad'll did die, not to speak and I die and gone forward ever."

More than anything she needed her mother to reassure her that if she died, she'd still acknowledge her, still care about her, but she feared she'd fade away just as her father had, with no one to remember her, as if she had never even existed, but the moment Judith heard she wished to talk about her dad, she shut down.

"You're fine," she said to Harlow as she gave her two swift, matter-of-fact pats on the back before turning to walk away.

Harlow fought to get more words out, determined, this time, to have a conversation about her father, but when she opened her mouth, speech abandoned her entirely and a sob escaped, sounding nothing like the word in her head: Dad.

Judith's dismissal hurt her as a child, but as a twenty-six-year-old woman, it made her want to shut down entirely.

Like usual, her mother now continued talking before Harlow could gather her thoughts. "You *have* been doing something with your life. Don't you see how these kids look up to you? The entire village loves you."

Harlow spoke in a small voice. "Would it be wrong if I wanted to be something other than a thief?"

"That *ship* is a thief, Harlow. Don't become one of them."

"Mom, do you know me at all?"

"There's no sense in discussing this any further. You've clearly made your decision."

"I've been with you my whole life. It's *me*." All their lives, it had been Harlow and her mom against the world. Now, in the span of five minutes, her mother had turned her into an outsider.

"I thought I knew you. Now you're leaving me for that ship just like your father did."

"Mom..." Harlow swallowed against the lump in her throat. "Okay, well, I'll get money for the rent just as soon as I can."

"Don't bother. It's already taken care of."

"How? Who?"

Judith pointed into the living room where the prince sat on her couch moving things around on a page of schematics projected as a hologram in front of him from a pair of glasses he wore. "I suspect he made the payment. I'll take it. God knows they've taken enough from me over the years."

"I'll grab some clothes and be on my way then." She looked back to tell her mom that she loved her, but her mother was looking at her with annoyance.

"Harlow?" she said suddenly.

"Yeah?"

"In case you haven't figured it out, he only wants that ship for vengeance." She spoke barely above a whisper, as if fearing the prince could hear much of what they were saying.

"What?" Harlow mouthed as she moved in closer to hear her.

"Mark my words, the first thing he will do is take that ship to Enceladus. Rumor has it the assassin who killed his wife and child was offered sanctuary there."

"Why would they hide a murderer?"

"I don't know. Just be careful that his vengeance doesn't destroy you." Judith turned around, picked up a scrub brush from the sink and went to work on a dirty plate.

Harlow knew when her mother had reached the point of shut down. She tried no further but went to her room, gathered what few things she had, and threw them into a bag.

She walked back into the kitchen with her duffle slung over her shoulder, her heart thundering. Her mother sat at the table with a holo book and a cup of coffee.

"Well, I guess I'll be going now. If you need me, you know where to find me."

Judith grunted. "I won't be stepping foot back on that ship...for any reason."

Tears gathered at the backs of Harlow's eyes, but she refused to let her mother see that she was affecting her. She turned her head to the side and began adjusting a strap on her bag that didn't need it. "I'll be back by as soon as I can."

"No need," Judith said without looking back up from her book. "I'm fine here by myself. Besides, you won't be back. That ship will swallow you up."

"Mom," she began, but realized there was nothing she could say that would make any difference now.

CHAPTER 8

THE TENACITY OF JUDE

When the buggy pulled back into the garage alongside the *Ares*, Harlow saw AVM Miller leaning against the giant frames that housed the hydraulics for the boarding hatches. Harlow couldn't help but admire that a woman in her mid-fifties looked as formidable as Miller did. She was roughly 5'7", lean and muscular, with cropped brown hair bearing strands of silver. She had changed into the charcoal-colored flight skin Harlow had seen images of. This woman was ready to fly. For the first time, Harlow imagined what it must have been like for someone like Miller to wait twenty years for their life's purpose to come back online.

The woman didn't budge as Harlow walked up the ramp toward her. Jack and his guards had departed the buggy and headed off in a different direction.

"How's Judith?"

"Oh, uh. She's..." Harlow did not know how to answer that one. Honesty would completely offend the woman. She was sure of it. It hadn't even occurred to her that Miller would know her mother. Then again, if the AVM worked with her father, she and Judith might have known each other.

Miller gave a sad smile and nodded. "I get it. I do." She crossed her arms over her chest and looked over Harlow's head into the horizon for a moment before turning back to face her. "Have a drink with me, Harlow Hanson."

Harlow could certainly use a drink after visiting with her mother. They walked a few steps before a thought occurred to her that made her nervous, happy, and terrified all at once. She stopped walking, and Harlow turned to look at Miller.

"Can you tell me about my dad?"

"Everything I know. Open book."

Harlow started to reply but felt a sob building in her throat, so she swallowed hard, nodded, and smiled.

• • •

Harlow sat on the bridge as the ship left the Martian atmosphere, taking her into space for the first time. After talking to Miller, she felt like she understood what this moment would have meant to her father and why it meant something to the crew, despite her mother's resentment. The crewmembers had been family. All these years, had she known there was family on board the *Ares* mourning her father, she wouldn't have hated it so much.

They were headed to Earth to drop off tons of raw materials that had been sitting in broken cargo ships and doing the suffering colonists no good. The people of Mars were grudgingly excited. In Mike O'Malley's pub, they agreed they'd celebrate when their fair share of supplies made it back in exchange for the years of hard work the mined materials represented. Jack swore it would.

The list of items the colonists requested her to bring back personally intimidated Harlow. She knew she had to be careful about falling into a "loyalty trap," in which she'd damn near sell her soul to fulfill their requests since many of them were already looking at her as a traitor for working on the *Ares*. They didn't want her on the ship, but "Hey since you're headed to Earth anyway..." She understood. Years of doing without created desperation.

In honor of their departure, someone, likely Jack or Miller, had put a picture of her father on the huge screen where he'd appeared before. Instead of cheering the ship heading into space for the first time in twenty years, a hush fell over the crew as they left the atmosphere. Waves of pain wrapped around Harlow's head. She gripped the chair as beads of sweat popped out on her scalp and ran down her face. Out of her periphery, she noticed Doc nearby, looking at her. *Breathe.* This was a momentous occasion, and the last thing she wanted was to have the entire crew staring at her. She squeezed her eyes shut but heard the rustle of clothing as someone knelt beside her; she assumed it was Doc.

"You're not okay," Jack whispered.

"Please don't say anything."

"Follow Doc to the infirmary."

She looked up to find that Air Vice-Marshal Miller and everyone else were so busy monitoring their stations she got only a couple glances as she left.

When she reached the infirmary, she grabbed a bucket and vomited from the violence of the headache. Doc quickly placed the Rescue Wave around her neck and pressed a few buttons. "This should get your pain under control in a few seconds."

The ship lurched forward as Harlow's headache subsided.

"I remember that feeling," Doc said. "The bubble is collapsing."

Harlow had studied the electromagnetic bubble that ships like the *Ares* used to travel vast distances. If a bubble could be maintained, then space-time would flow around the ship, leaving them free of the usual time and distance constraints, shortening trips significantly.

"Turn it off," Harlow said.

Doc pressed the Rescue Wave keypad again, and the ship resumed its smooth travel as before, but the migraine returned. Harlow told him, "Leave it off, but don't tell Jack about this."

"I can't keep something like this from him, or AVM Miller for that matter. You and this ship are far more connected than any of us realized. This is information that could affect all of us if something happened to you mid-flight."

She looked at him and knew she wouldn't get past the resolve she saw in his eyes. "Let me be there when you tell them. Please,"

"Okay," Doc said as he walked over to the cabinet and grabbed a syringe and rifled through several vials. "This should take the edge off but won't work as well."

"It's fine."

As Doc emptied the syringe into her arm, she relaxed a little.

"I'll turn the lights off for you. Lie here a while." Doc patted her shoulder before taking the offensive-smelling wastebasket from the room. "I'll be back to check on you in a few minutes."

By day two, her headache had gone, and she assumed her brain had adjusted to whatever the ship needed to do to get going. She just prayed it wouldn't happen every time. She and Doc had not told Jack about the fluctuation in the EM bubble and its connection to her migraine. It was as if they were both in an unspoken agreement to get to Earth and back before mentioning it to Jack.

The rattle and rock of leaving the atmosphere, despite the dampeners, had meant that anything grown brittle with time—such as plumbing or dry-rotted cargo tie-down straps—created no shortage of work for the crew as pipes burst and crates fell and scattered across the floor. Harlow had never been one for sitting around and living on Mars with no supplies coming in meant you fixed what you already had with what you had. It turned out the *Ares* was no different.

"Seraph, let me help you with that," Harlow said, as she ran over to lift one of the heavy containers.

Seraph was a muscular addition to the crew and also the girlfriend of one of Jack's guards, Evelyn, who didn't want to leave port without her and had convinced Jack to hire her.

"Thanks. So, what brings you to storage?" She noticed Seraph fighting to contain a smile, and Harlow could guess why. Seraph was a native Martian, like herself, and knew Harlow was familiar with the *Ares* cargo because she'd been going through it for so long.

Harlow laughed. "I'm not here to steal it, if that's what you mean."

"It's exactly what I mean!" she said with a broad smile. "Hell, you used to take orders and show up with a list." Seraph leaned over and picked up the thick straps that had given way and caused the cargo to scatter.

"Dry rot?" Harlow asked, as Seraph turned them over in her hand to examine them.

"No, some thief looks to have cut about three quarters of the way through this one before giving up."

Harlow smiled. "Well, I said I'd never gotten caught—though I came close a few times. It's a miracle I didn't. I mean, I'm good, but... Guess it's a good thing I'm helping, since it's my fault."

"Oh, you got caught, all right."

"Yeah, going into the core was a bit too ambitious, even for me."

"That's not what I mean," she said as she picked up and stacked scattered boxes of gauze and other medical supplies back into the larger container.

"What?" Harlow asked as she flattened herself against the floor and stretched an arm underneath a row of shelving to grab what looked like a spool of tape.

"Jack knew," Seraph said simply. "Evelyn was with Jack when they caught you going through the cargo containers waiting to be loaded onto the *Ares*. She was about to come arrest you when Jack told her to let it go."

"Shit!" Harlow cursed as she cracked her head on the shelf while trying to stand.

Seraph laughed loud and hard.

Harlow shot her a dirty look.

"Sorry, I've just never seen you rattled before."

Harlow rubbed the knot forming on the back of her skull. "I don't need him patronizing me!"

The smile left Seraph's face. "He knows how things are in the colonies. You're angry at him for being an understanding person?"

"Yes! I mean, no. I don't know what I am."

Seraph nodded. "You're conflicted. I was, too. My parents didn't like me coming to work on this ship. It's an us and them thing. They had just grudgingly accepted Evelyn, Jack's personal guard—" Seraph made a face of shock for Harlow, showing her parents' reaction "—much less me heading to Earth with her."

"I can imagine."

They worked in silence until the crate was full and back on the proper shelf. The two dusted off their clothes as Seraph broke the silence. "I didn't mean to upset you."

"You didn't. It's fine."

She nodded. "I get it. Well, I've got another storage room to check."

"I'll come help."

Seraph gave a broad smile. "You didn't bring a shopping list, I hope."

Harlow sighed and shook her head while Seraph laughed again.

The smell of acrid metal hung in the air.

Harlow watched as Jack soldered the tiny amplifier back together with his large hands. He came to get her regularly to show her how the ship worked and even small things like mending an amplifier. She asked, "Where is it going?"

"Inside this old radio. We can use it to communicate with the ship even if the core goes offline." She got the idea he was preparing for more than he was sharing.

They had already traveled to London with a huge load of hematite and gold that had been waiting on the small, broken transports for over a year—and not making anyone any money. Though everyone seemed excited to be returning to Earth, after having gone, Harlow didn't get what all the fuss was about. She felt that some of the colonists were being a little disloyal to the Martian home world and their solidarity as a colony, to make such a big deal over Earth. She'd collected much of what was on her list of requests from the colonists. Most were grateful for her efforts, some seemed to believe she owed it to them, a couple were downright angry that she didn't return with the requested items. All complained to her that the ore didn't fetch a higher price, though Harlow was surprised the coalition representatives got as much as they did. She saw Jack board the ship every evening that they were there frustrated and exhausted after sitting in on the talks between the Martian representatives and the coalition.

At any rate, there had certainly been no need for emergency communication in London.

Harlow felt suspicion coil within her. "Where will we be that we might need an alternate means of communication? Are we going somewhere?"

"Enceladus."

Harlow's gut twisted when he mentioned the icy moon. "What's there?" She tried to remain cool, but her heart slammed inside her chest as she remembered her mother's warning.

Jack laughed. "Mostly a whole lot of nothing, ice, and more nothing. I want to make our presence known, though. I suspect we are vulnerable to China. There's a man there working with them who I know to be a spy. He's capable of anything."

Harlow wondered if it was the same man who had killed his wife and child. Besides being an assassin, he could have been a spy as well, she guessed, or it could've been a cover story, so Jack wouldn't have to come right out and say he was seeking vengeance. "Won't that be interpreted as an act of aggression?"

"Not at all. We've an open invitation to work with them at their science outpost. I'm just going to offer a peaceful exchange of knowledge."

"Really?"

"Yeah," he said without elaborating or taking his eyes off his work.

Harlow left him to it and made her way back to her room. Nothing about Jack appeared duplicitous. He was straightforward about everything, but she supposed once someone murdered your family, all bets might be off. She was shocked to find herself in Jack's corner so quickly, but he had been the first person to believe she could be something different, perhaps better, and whether or not her mother liked it, she wanted it, too.

. . .

Jack had eaten with the crew often. A stranger would have never guessed he was royalty. But as they neared Enceladus, he became more distant. He took more of his meals in his room and much of his playful banter had disappeared.

Harlow sat down, alone, to eat her meal. She nodded at the Marine, Carlos, and he smiled. Jack usually sat with her, but he wasn't there today. Carlos left his group and came over.

"Hi, how's life on the ship treating you?" he asked, as he sat down next to her.

"It's different. Takes some getting used to."

"I'm sure. Well, I'm glad you're here."

"You are? Might I ask why?" Carlos had always been friendly, but she assumed he was just being nice. She didn't truly believe anyone wanted her there, except Jack. Not that she didn't think she could be an asset she just knew that she had a reputation as a thief, and she was sure they all had to be wondering why she was there.

"Many reasons. I hope it will help bridge the gap between those of us on the ship and the people in the village. I know they don't believe it, but Jack truly has their best interest at heart. What they don't understand is we've been abandoned just as they have. I haven't been promoted since I arrived here. Most of my friends back home have already advanced three ranks. I chose to stay here, and they let me because a certain number of Marines were promised to the mission long ago, but they have no more interest in it and simply...forgot about us. I still get paid, but that's it. No one in the military wants to stall out like this."

"Then why would you stay?"

"I stay because Jack is a good man and a good leader. I've rarely seen such persistence either. I knew he would get this ship back online. Of course, you are the one that eventually did it, but the point is, he made me a believer. He got me envisioning myself on this starship—a *working* starship, so that even after seven years of nothing, I *still* believed. If that isn't an extraordinary leader, then I don't know what is. Check this out." He pulled a saint's medallion from under his uniform shirt. "Do you know who this is?"

Harlow shook her head.

"It's Saint Jude. He's the patron saint of lost causes. My mother sent it to me after I had been here for three years. It's hard to believe in something when it's taking that long but look where we are now: on the way to one of Saturn's moons. It's the tenacity and challenge that I've always wanted to be part of."

"I can see that," Harlow said.

"Of course you can. Most everyone in the colony is descended from someone who took a deep breath, swallowed their fears, and marched forward onto a ship with a rocket strapped to their ass. *That's* who you are."

"Thank you, Carlos." She absently pushed around a few green peas with her fork before asking him what she had been wondering. "Do the rest of them resent me?"

He laughed. "You get right to the point. I like that. Listen, they just don't know you yet."

"Neither did you."

His smile was bright against his tan skin. "Like I said, when Jack gets a vision, it tends to be pretty infectious; he believes in you."

"Yeah, he's Marshal of the Royal Air Force, but isn't that just a title that they give to royalty?"

Carlos smiled. "It can be, yes, but there's one important difference."

"What's that?"

"He earned it."

Harlow was happy to have a lunch companion. She liked Carlos. He was genuine, and nothing pleased her more. They talked easily until it was time for him to return to work. Still, she was curious about Jack, and truth be told, she missed seeing him at mealtime.

The day before their arrival on Enceladus, she found the courage to knock on his door.

"Come in."

She walked in to find him sitting at his desk. It was the first time she had been in his quarters, and her own curiosity shocked her as she looked around. It was clean and neat. No surprise there. She thought she would see a tray in his room as they had all just finished dinner, but it appeared as if he hadn't eaten that evening.

He looked up at her and smiled. "What can I do for you?"

"Sorry to disturb you. I was just wondering if everything is okay?"

"Yeah, things are fine. Just going over some protocol for tomorrow. Is something the matter?"

"No, I just..." she bit her bottom lip trying to figure out where to go with it.

He rescued her from the awkwardness. "Listen, I've been meaning to talk to you. I know you aren't used to working under a command structure. You definitely aren't used to taking orders. So, if things go pear-shaped, at any point, you have to follow orders. I mean it, Harlow. No going rogue. It isn't just your life at stake but the entire crew's. Do you understand?"

She knew he was bossing her for a good reason, and she respected that. "I understand. I really do, but why would there be an issue if we are only there on a science protocol meet and greet?"

"You never know, especially since they've let Mikhail hide there," Jack said.

"He's the spy you told me about?"

"Yeah."

"Hmm." Harlow nodded.

Jack got up from his chair and walked around to the front of his desk, rested his backside on it, and crossed his arms across his chest. "If you've got something to say, say it."

Harlow's mind reeled. She knew she was sticking her nose where it didn't belong. He stared at her, as if daring her to say it, and she thought they would be locked there in a stare off with his damn eyebrows raised at her for the next year. She wanted to ask, to just blurt it out. If he was headed to Enceladus for vengeance, she couldn't blame him. She knew she would likely do the same.

Jack was the first to speak. "I have excellent hearing, Harlow. I know what your mother said to you when we went to see her. She isn't completely wrong. Mikhail *is* part of the reason I'm going to Enceladus and make no mistake: I intend to beat him within an inch of his life. After that, I will bring him back here and throw that minging piece of shite in the Bastille while he awaits trial. He will die for his crime, but it won't be by my hands. If I kill him, word will spread that I'm the dictator of the colonies and even though I might be completely justified, and I am, it will plant the seeds of revolt for those who are looking for a reason."

Harlow nodded. Many people resented him. She had been one of them.

Jack continued. "Even if I didn't want to kill him, he's conspiring with the Chinese. The colonies are vulnerable. The last surveillance satellite we had circling Enceladus went offline last week; we're too skint to send another. We've got to get out there and make them think twice before the colonists wake up one morning with guns in our faces as we are marched into either slavery or a mass grave."

His logic was sound and sobering. "All right. What can I do?"

"You can learn to trust me."

She exhaled and nodded. "I'm trying. I really am. I'll let you get back to your work." She turned and headed for the door.

"Harlow?" Jack called. "Your mother was partially right about me going to Enceladus, but she was completely wrong about you. You don't belong in prison, and there's a hell of a lot more you can do with your life than steal."

She mumbled, "Thanks," as she left the room. As soon as she walked into the hallway, Chief Science Officer Aldric Perthshire was there with Doc.

"Just the gal we are looking for," Aldric said.

"Oh, yeah?"

"Yep, we need your help with an idea we've been kicking around," Doc said.

Harlow remembered what Jack had said, just moments earlier, about her having something to offer. It had been her experience that people usually had motives within motives, but she knew she had to take a step forward at some point.

"Okay, I'll help," she said as Aldric motioned for her to follow him and Doc.

Once they were in the lab, they explained their idea. Aldric spoke first. "You already know Doc's specialty—mine is a little broader, but one thing I'm interested in is bridging a link between biology and technology. Having a chip in one's head is nothing new but having a link between a human brain and the type and size of technology this ship is... well, that's nothing short of groundbreaking. Your father was a true genius to store the information in such a way that it could be read without exploding your head. I mean, the amount of buffering, the breaks between the download offering your brain a chance to cool down and catch up...I've seen nothing like it." The more he talked, the more animated he became. His hands were flying, and he had even begun pacing and losing eye contact as he delved more and more into his own thoughts.

Doc watched him with amusement. "What my excited colleague is getting at is that we would love to run some tests. We swear to you it won't be anything that would damage you in any way. We think we might be on the verge of creating a serum that could get your brain into a theta state and keep it there long enough to make it easier for the ship to communicate with the chip without giving you blinding migraines or worse. As great and revolutionary as your dad's work was, we still think we could protect your brain better and make communication more effortless for both you and the ship."

"Well, it sounds like a good idea," she said cautiously. The whole thing screamed red flag, but her urge to help was overriding her caution—as was the memories of blinding headaches.

Aldric chimed in again. "It won't be anything you haven't experienced before. We all produce theta waves during daydreams and sleep. What we are suggesting is that we could induce this state and bring you in or out of it whenever needed. We have equipment that can produce such a state. It's all just electrical currents. Theta waves move at between four and eight hertz. We could produce this outside the brain with a tool we literally point at the head until the brain syncs up, but we feel this might actually interfere with the ship being able to communicate with the chip. So, we are thinking an injectable might be a better idea."

"You used a device to stop the seizures the first day I was on the *Ares*."

"Right," Doc said. "The ship was only trying to come online. I believe it had already gotten what it needed to power up by the time I stopped your seizures."

As she listened to them talk, she couldn't deny that it sounded like a good idea. She liked that she might be useful on the ship, but she couldn't shake the feeling that having her head messed with was dangerous. How well did she know these men anyway? She did trust Jack though, and if he had them on his crew, then surely, she could trust them, too.

"Yeah, I'll help." She thought about the people from her village and liked that there might be more in her head that could make their lives easier. "When do you want to try it?"

Aldric and Doc looked at each other and seemed in agreement. "Well, how about now?" Doc said. "It's after our regular work hours, so we shouldn't be disturbed."

She sat in a comfortable chair, and they explained what would happen. Aldric spoke first. "The instances that we know for sure you've linked with the ship would be when it came online, when your father's message came through, and when it needs to maintain its EM bubble. Those instances were involuntary. We think he programmed the chip to activate when you are within a close enough proximity. What we would like to create is a situation in which you or we can communicate with the ship when we want, not just when a program is running on auto. What we hope is to create an interface between what's in your head and the ship. If we are successful, we should be able to see it on this screen. Once we can see it here," he said, tapping the glass, "we can open files that are embedded on the chip."

"Wow!" Harlow said. It was all very fascinating but a little strange as well. Strange that there might be secrets in her head but also worrisome that someone would take something from her that her father had entrusted to her. Then again, she realized that if she couldn't access it, then it wouldn't do anyone any good. That alone propelled her forward.

Doc put a hand on her shoulder. "You look a bit rattled."

His concern was sweet, but she also disliked him for it. She didn't care for being read so easily; it was too personal. "There's a lot to absorb."

"True. It's totally your choice whether or not you wish to continue."

She looked up at the two men just in time to see a look of annoyance pass across Aldric's face and then dissipate quickly when he realized she'd seen it. She got the idea he was excited about all the possibilities before him and didn't appreciate Doc stopping to consider her feelings. "Yeah, of course, if you need some time..." Aldric said in a rush.

Harlow held Aldric's eyes a moment. "No, I'm good."

Doc walked over to a locked cabinet, looked into a retinal scanner, and retrieved a syringe with blue liquid in it. "This is technically only a simple depressant. It will put you in a very relaxed state: you may daydream or even fall asleep. In optimal amounts, it's helpful for creativity, intuition, and restorative sleep. Everyone has a tailored amount that's right for them so if you feel depressed, a little hyper, or have a hard time paying attention, then we know that we need to make the serum less potent. It's important to make us aware of what you're feeling."

Doc pushed a button that tilted the chair back until she was almost lying down. He pulled her shirtsleeve up, swabbed her skin with alcohol, and emptied the syringe into her arm. Moments later she felt deep relaxation. Her eyes grew heavy, and as she slipped into sleep, her body jerked, and she began to see ones and zeros behind her eyelids as if they were projected on a screen. They started moving faster and faster. The passage of time faded. Her dad's face flashed before her once, and she tried to hold on to it, but it was absorbed by the ones and zeros again. She wondered briefly if her mind could interpret the numbers or was learning the language so she could convert them herself. Soon she started shaking and heard loud voices breaking into her thoughts.

"No, damn it! I'm waking her up!" an angry voice said.

She inhaled sharply and looked around. "What the hell?" Her face felt hot. She reached up and found that her eyes had been watering. "What happened? Was there a quake?" She was having a hard time focusing. "Was there an explosion in the mine?"

"No," Doc said as he wiped her face with a wet cloth. "Just relax."

Across the room, she noticed Aldric was staring at a screen muttering, "Fascinating. Just fascinating."

Harlow sniffed and wiped her nose on her sleeve as she thought of all the people she needed to check on. "If there was an explosion, then I need to see about my mother." She tried to get up, but Doc placed a hand on her shoulder.

"Doc come look at this!" Aldric called. "This is exactly the kind of thing we hoped to retrieve."

Doc ignored him and kept his attention on Harlow. "You'll be fine. Let me help you back to your room. We need to tweak the dose; that's why you were shaking. There is no quake. We are on the *Ares* on the way to Enceladus. Remember?"

Everything came rushing back to her. "Yeah, I remember."

"I think next time it will be no problem, now that we know to lower the dosage."

"Did it work? Did you find anything?" she asked.

Aldric called from across the room, "We did!"

Harlow got up on shaky legs and walked over to the screen. She stood on the side opposite Aldric and read about the ship. There were notations about things her father had been working on: improvements and upgrades her dad wanted to make to the weapons systems. "Is this everything?" she asked.

"Oh gosh, no. See down here on the lower right? Look how large the file is. We only have about a quarter of it," Aldric said.

"It looks like pretty standard stuff. Why bother with it? The ship is online now. I got my message from my dad. Why would there be anything else of interest in there?"

"Well, your father was a brilliant engineer. Wouldn't you want his work to live on? There are unfinished projects in here. Things that will help the colonists."

Harlow nodded as a strange mix of exhaustion and hyperactivity set in all at once. She suddenly felt like she had to get out of there.

"How are you feeling?" Doc placed a hand under her chin, tilted her head, and looked into her eyes. Seeming satisfied with what he saw, he reached for her wrist to feel her pulse.

"I'm okay. Just tired. I'm going to head to my room."

Doc nodded. "At least let me walk you back."

"No, it's fine. I would prefer to be alone. I have a lot to think about." She felt strange all over and couldn't seem to shake it.

"Of course. Whenever you're up to it, I would like to ask you about your perception while you were online," Doc said.

Aldric chimed in. "She really needs to speak to that right now, while it's still fresh."

Harlow felt a wall come up at his words. "I'm tired. I'm going." She turned and left the room as Aldric grumbled under his breath.

• • • • •

Splashing cold water on her face helped some of the groggy feeling pass. Looking at herself in the mirror, she almost expected to see the ones and zeros racing across her pupils. But she looked the same, except for the dark circles under her eyes. She walked over to her bed and laid down, but despite the exhaustion, sleep eluded her. Finally, she gave up and left her room.

Without thinking about it, she walked to the observation deck. They kept the lighting in the room dim to not interfere with viewing the stars. It was quiet, cool, and empty. Because the ship was carrying no guest passengers, only crew, there was no one on the deck—everyone was preparing for the landing on Enceladus.

She felt odd. Other than that, it was hard to pin down any single emotion. She wanted to jump out of her skin, sit on the floor and cry, throw something, but was having a hard time focusing on any of those things. Sitting down on one of the many benches that lined the walls beneath the large floor-to-ceiling windows that tilted at an angle above the viewer, so that one could feel as if they were looking up at the night sky, she gazed out at the stars. A sense of loneliness sank through layers of her being: past her body, her mind, her emotions, spirit, and into her very soul. She tried to snap out of it, telling herself it was simply the aftereffects of the experimental drugs she'd been given. But she couldn't help but wonder if it were only bringing to light what was already there, just waiting to be acknowledged.

For the first time in a long while, or perhaps ever, she had an urge to talk to someone. Her father was gone, her mother was lost in a sea of bitterness, and the colonists saw her as their own personal Robin Hood—which, truth be told, made her proud—but it meant she was only there for them, not the other way around. The crew of the ship either thought of her as a science project or the prince's charity case. The idea of going back to Mars and just being what she had been for years sounded good, easy. Her place there was simple. She was loved and respected. Most of all, she wasn't sitting in a corner somewhere on the verge of tears. She wasn't vulnerable there, and that part she hated most.

"Damn it!" She cursed into the silence and pulled her knees up to her chest, hung her head, and wept—grateful no one was around.

A soft male voice called from the doorway. "Harlow?"

"Shit," she whispered without lifting her head. It was Jack.

He walked over to her, and, without another word, he wrapped his arms around her. Despite everything telling her to shove him away, she couldn't. Her emotions were too raw. There was an abyss threatening to swallow her up, and it was the first time ever that anyone had been there solely for her. She leaned into him and let herself go for a strange, sweet moment.

Jack stroked the back of her head. His hand was warm. She began to pull away and found herself startled that she already mourned the loss of his touch. As she sat up straight again, he looked at her intently and cupped her cheek. He seemed to hold his breath—it was a touching show of vulnerability, and she doubted he knew he was even doing it. She thought it likely he knew she was the type who might pull away from him. He exhaled as she leaned into his touch for a moment. "What happened to you?" he asked, as his thumb brushed a tear from her face.

She started to tell him she was fine, but her words came out slurred.

Jack's brows knit together. "Are you okay?"

Embarrassment washed over her when she realized he had noticed her having a hard time speaking. "Yeah, I had a speech disorder when I was a kid. It's fine now unless I get exhausted or nervous."

"I didn't know that," he said softly.

"Yeah. Some of the kids thought I wasn't smart because of it. You wouldn't think it now, but I did really well in school."

"I *would* think it."

She wished she could see herself through his eyes for a moment. "Anyway, I'm okay."

"Liar," he said with a gentle smile. "I'm your Marshal; you have to tell me what's wrong."

"No, I don't." She playfully swatted at his hand and sat in silence with him for a moment before speaking. Logic was finally taking over, and she had questions for him. "Did you pick this crew yourself?"

"Half were here before I arrived. I handpicked the rest. Why do you ask?"

"I was helping Doc and Aldric with a serum they were working on to make it easier for the ship to speak with the chip in my head. When we were on the way to Earth for the first time and the EM bubble collapsed, it was because Doc was using the Rescue Wave to get rid of the migraine. The serum wouldn't interfere like that. They thought there might also be unfinished projects in there. You know, stuff that would help the colonists or new technology."

He narrowed his eyes and tilted his head. "What did they ask you to do?"

"They gave me a drug that slowed my brain waves so that my conscious mind would stay out of the way to make access easier and subvert the migraines, but I feel a little strange about it. It sort of... messed with me or something. My emotions are all over the place."

"Bloody hell! They aren't doing that on my ship!" He grabbed Harlow's hand and rose to his feet, bringing her upright with him.

Worrying she had done something wrong, she took a deep breath, knowing her nerves, coupled with her speech disorder, would make it hard to speak clearly. "Did I mess up? I thought it might help."

"You didn't do anything wrong. It's my crew who ought to know better!" He said nothing else as he took her hand and led her out the door.

"Where are we going?" she asked.

"To have a word with my science officer and doctor."

He kept hold of her hand, and she had to practically run to keep up with his purposeful stride. She felt a little off because of the experiment but didn't realize until now it was something that angered him. She was glad he had clarified that he wasn't mad at her.

He stormed into the lab with Harlow in tow. Aldric and Doc stood by the display, studying the results. Both men had saucer-round eyes when they saw Jack.

"Highness," they both said.

"What the hell did you do?" he asked in a tone that brokered no bullshit.

Harlow felt a little embarrassed. She consented to the experiment, and now it would look as if she had tattled on the two men.

"I agreed to the experiment," Harlow offered. "They didn't make me."

"No. They know better."

He clearly wanted to handle this his way. She knew she didn't understand ship protocol and kept quiet.

"I want to see the record of the experiment and everything you downloaded. Now!" he roared at the two men.

Aldric and Doc said nothing but scrambled to bring up their findings. Doc stepped to the side so Jack could read the report. Harlow looked at the portion she could see beyond Jack's large shoulders and realized that it was basically a play-by-play of what Doc had done and her reaction to it.

"Seizures? Hell, no! Not on my ship. We aren't doing the whole mad scientist thing, not here!"

Harlow was stunned. Doc hadn't exactly lied to her, but when she'd asked about the "quake" that she thought had occurred, he had told her she was "shaking," but that was a lot different from letting her know she was having seizures.

"This cannot happen. You could have caused her brain damage. I've seen this shite before. You people get knowledge fever and end up hurting someone in the name of science. Just like all those inmates that were experimented on in prison during the last century. It's barbaric shambolics. They had seizures until their brains fried. I will not have it on my ship. She is not your fucking guinea pig. Do you understand me?"

"Aye, Marshal," Doc said softly.

Aldric remained silent. Harlow watched the muscles in his jaws tighten as if he were grinding his teeth or, she guessed, biting back what he really wanted to say.

Jack stomped over to him so fast everyone in the room jumped. "I'll throw your arse out the airlock if you ever do this again."

"Aye, Marshal," Aldric said tightly.

Harlow wondered if it was as clear to Jack as it was to her that Aldric didn't like him. She remembered that Doc had told her theta waves could increase intuition. Then again maybe those two had a history, and it would have been clear to anyone.

"For the record, Harlow didn't come to me about this. I found her falling apart on the observation deck. Someone having seizures shouldn't be sent off by themselves." He pointed at Doc. "You should know better."

"Yes, I should." Doc turned to look at her. "I apologize, Harlow. I wasn't completely honest with you. I've failed you as a physician, and it won't happen again."

She nodded.

"You also had a responsibility to tell me and AVM Miller that the EM bubble collapsed when you tried to treat Harlow, but you kept that from me too. I can't have that. I don't know what's gotten into you, but it better stop, and I mean now."

"Absolutely, sir. I apologize."

Jack started to leave the room with her but turned back around and walked over to the display containing the files they had extracted. Jack tapped the screen once, stated his name, and then began reading off a series of numbers. "Lock this file and any copies. They are to be read only by me."

"Aye, aye, Marshal," the ship's AI voice said.

Harlow saw Aldric's hands clench into fists as Jack locked him out of the files. "Excuse me, Highness, but I worked with her father on many projects. If anyone is to understand and know how to interpret and honor his work, it would be me. I beg you to reconsider my access." Harlow watched his mouth twist on the word "beg" as if it were sour.

"Yeah, you worked with him. That's exactly why you should have had more regard for his daughter's wellbeing. If you don't like my decision, you can go back to London and find another job."

"Sir, I've dedicated twenty years of my life to this minging, orange shite hole. If I haven't proven myself by now, I never will."

Harlow felt her anger spike, and she wanted to throw the man out the airlock herself. He had no right to speak about her home like that. He didn't live among the people. He lived on the ship. Mars could be an annoying, isolating place but this was her home. "Screw you!" was on the tip of her tongue but Jack spoke to him first. He pointed at Aldric, and Harlow had a feeling Jack *knew* the pointing would piss the man off.

"You and I will discuss this more tomorrow." Jack's voice was clipped. He was clearly done dealing with it for now.

He turned to Harlow. "Come on, you need to rest." He placed his hand on her back, and they left the room.

Once they were in the hallway he softened. "Do you think you could sleep now?"

"After all that back there? No. I'm exhausted but wired. It's frustrating," she said.

Jack smiled. "Yeah, exhausted but wired. I'm way too familiar with that scenario. I have an idea."

"What?"

He smiled. "Follow me."

The two walked down a long hallway to a kitchen, much smaller than the one attached to the mess hall, and Jack began rummaging in the refrigerator until he found what he was looking for.

"Blinding! Right?" He turned around proudly, holding an entire chocolate cake.

Harlow gasped. Sugar cane plants were not a priority in the colonies. Most things were grown in greenhouses or small hydroponic gardens inside homes to protect the plants from dust storms. Dessert was rare. "How?"

"When we took the ship to London, I picked it up to celebrate our trip to Enceladus. We wouldn't be going without you, though. You should have it." He raised one eyebrow before asking, "What do you think?"

"I'm thinking I need a fork. A big one," she said.

After retrieving two forks, she followed him to a massive room close to the kitchen. When they opened the door, she heard running water and smelled vegetation.

"Have you ever been in here before?" he asked.

"No." She looked around for the source of the water. It cascaded down a stone wall and hit several ledges before emptying into a pool at the bottom. She saw plants growing up the sides of trellises; some had bean pods hanging off them. Others had blooms that looked as if they would eventually turn into something edible, but she wasn't sure what.

Jack sat the cake down on a table that was about knee height and fished out two long mats from a storage cabinet. "The botanists use these when they are tending to the plants that grow on the lower shelves. It's easier on the knees." He sat the mats down in front of the waterfall and motioned for her to sit beside him.

She sat down, and he handed her a fork. They both went to work on the cake. "I come here when I need to think. Something about the sound of the water helps me get my head on proper." He pointed at the waterfall with his fork. "They oxygenate the water this way and then it flows into the shelves that hold the plants."

She hadn't thought she was hungry, but as she ate one bite after another she wanted more. "This is incredible."

She looked at Jack and wondered about him. It seemed so strange to her that a man with access to such wealth would spend his time on Mars. For her, the lines between the people struggling in the colonies and the ones babysitting a dead ship were clearly drawn; but now, she had to reframe everything. It was confusing because it pulled the threads of her lifelong identity in such a way that they couldn't ever be woven back together in the same tapestry again. It was a little sad and refreshing all at once. She thought of a little girl with golden eyes and braids waiting for her to dish out candy and wondered if Piper would look at her with that sense of awe and respect ever again or would she just be a sellout to the young girl? The colonists only knew one way: us and them. She looked up at Jack and found it hard to see him as a "them," anymore. It was all so tangled. She turned her mind off for a moment as the sound of the water infiltrated her thoughts. Harlow felt her eyes get heavy and a jaw-cracking yawn overtook her. Her mind was still loose and hazy around the edges from the drug they had given her.

"Let me walk you back to your room. You're positively knackered." Jack said.

"No, please. Just a few more minutes."

He looked at her a moment too long.

Harlow almost laughed that he seemed busy trying to figure her out, too. He leaned back against a wall and stretched his long legs out in front of him. She was crashing from the crazy evening and could have fallen asleep sitting up. She leaned her head against his shoulder. The last thing she knew, Jack was gently stroking the hair from her face as she fell into sweet oblivion.

CHAPTER 9

FROZEN TEARS

Jack's nerves spiked as he felt the resistance of Enceladus's atmosphere pushing back against the ship. He looked out the window as the light outside changed to an ice blue glow. The place had an eerie feel to it. Far in the distance, he could see icy geysers exploding into the sky. They had placed artificial pressure points—a technology too late for Yellowstone—under the ice to direct them to erupt in a more controlled way. Some geysers were enormous. No one wanted to get knocked off their feet or split in half by them—which is exactly what had happened to the first explorers. Jack tried to keep his mind on the protocol of visiting the space station. He knew if he allowed his mind to drift too far into the past—his wife, his child, his ache for revenge—he would slip as a Marshal, and things could get real personal, real quick. One of the crew interrupted his thoughts.

"Marshal, I'm getting a ping coming from a personnel beacon on the surface, but obviously none of our people have had time to disembark yet."

Jack looked perplexed when he walked over to the ensign to check it out. "Does it say who it is?"

The ensign said nothing but pointed to the screen. Jack looked and read a name as a wave of shock and grief washed over him. He hadn't expected this...not at all. Why had it not occurred to him? He looked at the ensign and shook his head almost imperceptibly. The ensign nodded but said nothing more.

"Got it," Jack said casually before turning around to address the others. "All right everyone, remember what I told you: No one goes off on their own for any reason whatsoever. Aye?"

They all replied, "Aye, Marshal."

A little over half the crew disembarked after taking nearly an hour for everyone to add enough layers and suits with built in heating systems. Jack had asked Harlow to remain on board. He could tell she didn't like it, but he worried the Chinese would learn that there was technology in her head. And even though he hated to admit it, Aldric was right about thinking there might be unfinished projects or secrets buried there that could be exploited in the wrong hands.

The Chinese knew of their arrival and sent out a delegation. Jack didn't want to be the first to mention it, but they all knew his Martian crew wasn't used to the level of cold on Enceladus. Though Mars was terraformed, it could be very cold, but the cold here was far beyond that, even though they managed to heat the surface to a survivable degree by harnessing the hydrothermal energy—the same heat and pressure that caused the icy geysers. They funneled the heat from the active core of the moon through the lunar ocean to reach the frozen surface, a constant, inexhaustible supply of energy that powered the entire colony. Still, it would never be warm in the manner Earth dwellers or Martians considered warm.

They welcomed them and took them to the outpost. He was uncertain what kind of reception he would receive given that the general had to know about his history with the fugitive they were harboring.

The first to come out of the building was wearing a thick coat that boasted insignia showing his esteemed rank. "Greetings, Marshal. I am Superior General Second Class Cheung. This is our Middle Field Officer Zhang." The crew gave small obligatory bows as they were introduced. "This is Dr. Quan, our Chief Medical Officer. We are pleased to have you here. We have much to learn from each other. You are very skilled to have led your team to solve the mystery of your sleeping ship."

"You are kind, thank you. I'm looking forward to working with all of you."

"We should continue our greetings inside," the General said.

Jack was in great shape but having a hard time concealing his urge to gasp as he spoke. The cold burned his throat, his eyes, and ice weighted his eyebrows as he followed the general to the entrance. Once inside, the tour of the huge outpost began. It was warmer in the building, but still not warm enough for anyone to shed coats. Even the Chinese kept them on but unbuttoned them. Jack couldn't help but be impressed. They had transformed an icy moon halfway across the solar system with geysers spewing shards of ice, no less, and made it livable.

Dr. Quan and their own Doc Hagen were excitedly talking in English as if no one else existed. Jack knew Enceladus could go without visitors for years. Thus, despite political tensions, he detected a buzz of excitement over the visit. After most everyone had dispersed to speak with their scientific counterparts, the General invited Jack to join him in his study. Jack motioned for his personal guard, Evelyn, to remain just outside the office door. He noticed General Cheung's guard stood on the other side of the door and nodded at Evelyn before Jack walked in and General Cheung closed the door behind them.

Transporting supplies across a galaxy meant the office was sparsely furnished. To compensate, someone had painted the walls with warm tones. Jack settled into the only other chair in the room. He needed to ask a favor before any of the business with Mikhail came up and he knew it would, because he didn't plan to leave without arresting or killing the man who'd murdered his family.

After a few pleasantries, Jack got to his question. "Upon arrival, we began getting a ping from a type of device that all personnel carry in case they need to be tracked."

"Ah, yes. We are all required to wear such a thing as well. If you get stuck outside too long in a place like this, there are only minutes left to save you."

"Of course, the thing is, it came up as one of our own. It's old." Jack pulled out his personal device that was in contact with the ship and showed him the identifying info that kept coming in repeatedly.

"Ah, I see," the General said.

"I would very much like to know what is there, if anything. It may just be a tracker dropped in the snow long ago, but if it isn't...Do I have your permission to pursue it?" Jack didn't feel that he should have to ask permission, but he had learned the fine art of diplomacy; if you adhered to the local protocol, you could often get what you needed with very little hassle. If that failed, well, he also wasn't leaving without finding out about the personnel tracker.

"Yes, of course. However, I insist you take four of my men with you. The environment is unknown and harsh to you."

"That is very gracious. Thank you." Jack knew the general really wanted to make sure Jack and his men didn't venture anywhere they weren't supposed to. But it was just as well. What he planned was exactly what he told the general, though he might have other plans later.

Within two hours, Jack, Evelyn, Carlos, Daniel, and AVM Miller, rode in the electric buggy that heated the icy terrain beneath them and rode on a cushion of air. The ground itself was too littered with ice shards to keep a steady current of cold air. The buggy smoothed the ground as it passed over.

Half an hour later, they trudged along the snow and ice with the four-man team that General Cheung had sent. According to Jack's device, the beacon was just in front of them in a cave. He scanned the area to make sure it was stable, then entered. They had to chop and remove ice. He worried that they might not be able to get to it if it had been here as long as he feared. Then finally, there it was. He exhaled and fell to his knees. It wasn't simply a dropped personnel beacon—it was with its host. The ice had preserved the man almost perfectly. Of course, the coloring was off, but there was no mistaking the uniform, or the raven hair that he had seen fall about Harlow's shoulders. "Damn," he whispered, and crossed himself for the first time in a long while. He'd learned to pray as his aunt did. A quiet act of defiance against a king that had rejected his sister for her faith. The man in the ice was Colonel Michael Hanson. "Oh, Harlow," he said under his breath. It was startling to realize that this man appeared to be barely older than Harlow was now. He looked back at AVM Miller, who'd served with Michael Hanson and saw the stark difference of how time had continued for her and left him literally frozen in time.

Jack knew the Brotherhood had come to Enceladus to see if they could take the outpost from the Chinese, but the coalition had gotten intel about it and sent Colonel Hanson and several others to deal with it. There were only four survivors from the coalition and none from the Brotherhood. Now he had gotten wind that the Chinese had their eye on Mars—it angered him that many of the coalition had fought defending the Chinese outpost from the Brotherhood, and now they were coming to Mars to tear it from the hands of the people who'd saved their assess. But he realized in the game of politics the Chinese saw it as the coalition only defending them because they didn't want the Brotherhood having a place to hide among the stars. They weren't completely wrong. Politics sucked.

Carlos came to stand beside him. "It's him, isn't it?"

"Yeah," Jack said. He turned to the Chinese team. "May we excavate him for burial?"

The Middle Subaltern, the equivalent of a First Lieutenant, answered him. "Our team should have no trouble removing him. I will need to get the General's permission first."

"Of course," Jack said. He listened to the man speak in Mandarin on his radio for a few moments before he nodded at Jack.

"Is fine," he said in a somber tone. "We brought the necessary items."

Jack nodded, then turned to go get the cryo container they had brought.

An hour later, Jack watched as Miller stepped forward and saluted Colonel Hanson as they lifted the cryo container into the transport to make its way back to the ship. She was one of the four that had made it back from Enceladus twenty years ago. Jack could only imagine how haunted she'd been ever since. He could only hope this would bring her some form of closure, if not comfort. Jack had approached her more than once over the years to seek advice. Only when the body was loaded and ready to go did Miller release her salute, and Jack didn't miss the frozen tear that had stopped halfway down her cheek.

Harlow sat in the ship looking out the large observation windows, watching the snow blow across the ice field. In the distance, the geysers went off at regular intervals, blowing ice into the frigid air. For a moment, she felt no separation between herself and the ice. Her emotions were just as frozen since Jack had told her they'd found her father. The security and love of a father was something only others had. She was fine without them, but now she was forced to deal with the loss all over again. Out of her periphery, she saw Jack. He made his way over to where she sat and settled beside her.

"Harlow?" Jack spoke quietly.

"Yeah." Her voice sounded strange in her own ears.

"He's ready. You should know that he's well-preserved from the ice if you would like to see him. No one expects you to. I just thought you should have the option."

Harlow did not know what she wanted.

"We can do whatever you like, but if you have no specific opinion about it, I feel that we should take him back home and bury him with honors in the colony he fought so hard to make a reality."

Bitterness sprang up in her heart as she heard Jack speak of the colony. It had taken her father from her and turned her mom into an angry shell of herself. The memory of her mother made her cringe, especially the last time she had spoken to her before going to work on the *Ares*. Her mom had told her she'd rather see her in a Martian prison than on the ship. Whether Judith had meant it, it was a verbal dagger that still protruded from her chest. She took a deep breath and chose to leave the bitterness there to freeze on the planet, never to return home with her. As she exhaled and watched her breath trail out, a little peace found its way in. She spoke to Jack without turning to look at him. "Take me to him, please."

Jack led her to a lower deck on the ship. He pulled out a chair for her. A dreamlike state washed over her as she sat. She looked around and realized she was in the cryogenics department. It made sense to leave her father's body frozen the entire way home.

Jack, Carlos, Daniel, and two others she didn't know by name came in carrying the freezing rectangle containing her father. They sat him down a few feet from her and took the lid off his chamber. "We'll give you a few minutes. If this is still what you want?" Jack looked at her with questioning eyes.

She nodded. Just before Jack left the room, she almost called out to him. Something in her that she couldn't quite identify wanted him to stay. An ache settled in her chest as he shut the door behind him.

"It's all right. It's a weird day," she said into the silence of the room. She didn't stop to wonder why she needed to justify the vulnerability wrapping around her. Only that she was walking an emotional razor's edge and didn't care for it one damn bit.

Vapor poured from the icy cold rectangle to dissipate into the warm air of the ship. She got up and ran her hand through the fog, displacing it. Suddenly, life felt as fleeting, an attempt to say, "I'm here," changing, and if we we're lucky, lending meaning to what little we could as the vapor of our own lives dissipated into eternity.

She watched the vapor swirl and dance but didn't look down. It was him, but it wasn't. A determination to think of him as he'd been in the video when she first stood on the bridge of the ship washed over her. There was no desire to look into the cold emptiness of the container. Remembering the recording and how he believed in her when his eyes lit up as he spoke, everything became clear. She passed the icy coffin and left the room. Jack was waiting just outside the door like a sentinel. The others had already gone.

"You okay?" he asked.

"Yeah, I really am."

Jack put an arm around her and pulled her close to rest her head on his shoulder as they walked back to the upper decks.

They passed a port window without noticing that a man ran through the icy landscape, camouflaged in white.

CHAPTER 10

COMRADE ALDRIC

He ran across the frozen surface wearing several layers of stark white clothing. After getting only a few feet from the ship, the sameness of the ice and snow swallowed him up and disoriented him, but the steady beep in his ear let him know he was closing in on his destination. Should the tone go silent, he'd be a goner in the whiteout. It was unlikely someone would notice his absence until they needed his services. Besides, he didn't plan on being gone long. He understood how easy it was to freeze to death on Enceladus. The journey wouldn't take him far—a short walk past the main outpost to a small building camouflaged around back. Camouflage was easy in such a landscape: just paint it white.

By the time he made it to the building, ice crystals coated his goggles. He knocked on the door four times and a man with a Russian accent answered.

"Comrade, it's been too long," Mikhail said.

Aldric walked into the room and reveled in the warmth. A faux fire burned brightly in a small fireplace, bathing the living space in an amber glow. "Too damn long on that ship, brother. The hypocrisy sickens me." He realized his mistake as he watched his mentor's eyes darken dangerously. "Of course, it is nothing like what you have sacrificed for the greater good," he added quickly. "It cannot be easy here on this icy moon." Aldric took a narrow box from his coat and handed it to Mikhail, a peace offering. "As you requested."

Mikhail opened the box, pulled out a cigar, and ran the length of it under his nose as he inhaled deeply. "After so many years, I believe I've missed this most of all."

Aldric noted the passing of years on Mikhail. His thick beard had gone gray and deep lines formed between his brows as if he'd spent the years since their last meeting in a perpetual state of deep worry. Perhaps he had. In a place like this, he supposed there was nothing to do but think.

"More than this?" Aldric pulled a small bottle of vodka from his inner pocket.

"Only a little more." Mikhail took two tumblers from the cupboard and poured them each some vodka. He picked them up, handed one to Aldric, and retrieved a silver lighter from a side table drawer and went to sit in the chair opposite him.

As Mikhail took his first sip, Aldric watched his shoulders drop and the deep lines of his face soften before he spoke.

"It was clever to imbed your message in the flight plans sent to the outpost. When I first heard the *Ares* had woken from her sleep, I thought that arrogant buffoon they have the nerve to call a prince had pulled a miracle out of his ass, but what you mention is more than we could have possibly hoped for. The thief appears with the actual miracle, and she is one of them. The power of the people, my brother. That's what it's all about." He nodded in agreement with his own words.

Aldric followed Mikhail's gaze until it landed on a battered Soviet flag on display above the fireplace. It was clearly hundreds of years old. The whiskey made a pleasant burn as it tracked a path down his throat and warmed his insides, still shocked from the intense cold. "I marvel at the genius of the late Colonel Hanson. Too bad we couldn't get him to see reason. Luckily, he left his best ideas and biggest prize in the head of that ridiculous little thief."

"You've retrieved all the information from her?" Mikhail asked.

"Not everything. The prince blocked my access to the files I managed to retrieve, and it was only a quarter of it, but it contained an outline for the rest of the classified files. I think what we have been searching for is in there."

Mikhail raised his glass in a toast toward Aldric. "You've always been an asset to the Brotherhood."

"You are too kind, comrade. But taking the fall for the assassination of the prince's family so that I could avoid prison and stay on the *Ares*...that took a kind of devotion to the cause that is rare."

Aldric gazed into the fire as he remembered how close they'd come to ending Jack. The prince was the only one that was any threat to them—they all knew it. The rest of the family would roll over for the right motivation, but Jack was a whole other matter. At every turn, he would fight them. He had gone against popular opinion in order to hunt down members of their Brotherhood. He had voted in favor of military action that bombed the hell out of their strongholds when the rest of the family had sided with those who demanded what little gold they had be used to help in more practical ways. Jack had argued it didn't matter how comfortable the people were if they were constantly terrorized. In a strange way, choosing to assassinate him was a compliment. Had he been no threat, he would have been left alone. He and perhaps his offspring were the only ones worth killing, but trying to take him out had backfired and driven him straight to the one place they were looking to conquer.

Swirls of cigar smoke drifted lazily across the room as Aldric mused on his failure. "Had I done my job successfully, the prince would have fallen when his wife and child did, as it is...Well, he is smart, and I fear his alliance with the Colonel's daughter might endear him to the colonists. If he wins them over, it will set us back years. A revolution was brewing. We could have come to their aid and brought them vaccines, food, whatever they whine about these days, and we could have had them in complete devotion to the Brotherhood. We could have been saviors, but this thief gets closer to him every day. I suspect he may even be falling in love with her.

Can you believe I was even approached on behalf of the royal family to keep them apart by any means?" Aldric laughed.

Mikhail didn't seem share his mirth but lowered his glass and looked at him. "Is that so? Huh?" He reached up and rubbed his beard. Silver threads shone in the firelight. The alchemy was beginning. He could feel it. There had always been a brilliance that bade Aldric follow him anywhere.

"An idea, old friend?"

"Think about it. We cannot kill her; we need what's in her head and can't be sure her death won't deactivate the chip. It's too risky. And you are right in assuming a union between the two would likely cause the colonists to settle and accept this man because their heroine does, but suppose you do as his highness's parent's wish and separate them?"

"I can't. I see it happening a little more every day."

"What would make her fall from grace in the prince's eyes?"

"I can't imagine anything. She's already a thief and that was not enough to deter him."

"Everyone has a limit to which even the finest breasts and warmest bed cannot buy a pardon. It seems to me that your mission there on that ship, as valuable as it has been, may no longer be needed. Perhaps the prince learns that his love betrays him to the man that killed his family. Perhaps it is time to unburden your conscience, comrade."

"What?" Aldric realized he had become comfortable not being the assassin. Over the years, he had seen the looks that crossed people's faces when they spoke of Mikhail and the treachery of killing a young mother and child. He wasn't sure he was ready to take that on, but if his mentor asked him, he knew he would. Despite the assassinations, it had been easy to ignore the blame when the eyes looking back at him didn't reflect it.

"You still have some viruses hidden away, yes?" Mikhail asked.

"Yes."

"Half of the colonies have no immunity to the viruses still, correct?"

Aldric nodded.

"Demand the information in her head, then threaten those she loves if she doesn't comply. Make it known to his highness that you are the assassin. Let her betray him to the man that destroyed his entire world seven years ago."

"What makes you think she will do it?"

"Because I have lived on this icy hell for over seven years now in order to protect what I believe in. She will protect what *she* believes in. I almost hate to do it. She would have made a remarkable communist. Once the prince hears she aided the man who killed his family, he will turn on her with a vengeance. She won't see life outside a prison ever again. The colonists will turn on him for jailing their champion, and we get that uprising we want. We will come in and fight for their right to survive and get a fair wage for what they mine. Those people are descended from brilliant minds and giant balls. They will make excellent additions to our cause."

"I agree, but if Harlow is in prison, we can't finish getting what we need."

"Try to get it before you leave. If you can't, there are ways to get her out of prison. In fact, breaking her out of jail will only endear the colonists to our cause." He smiled as a cloud of smoke drifted from his lips. "You can take her somewhere long enough to extract what you need, erase what you don't want her to remember, and then you go into hiding somewhere nice and warm, and one of the brothers can come back with her to the colonies as a savior."

"I could use a change of scenery. I've been on that ship for over two decades. What about these people?" Aldric pointed in the outpost's direction. "Don't they want to get their hands on Mars?"

"They've agreed to leave it to us if we give them a better alternative. I believe that alternative is buried in Harlow's head. I tried to get it out of her father before I shot him, but that bastard wouldn't let go of it. I admired him. I did not relish having to kill him." Mikhail took another drag from his cigar. His face was bathed in a red-orange glow in the dim lighting. The man's easy genius mesmerized Aldric.

Mikhail blew a smoke ring and watched it race away from him before he continued speaking. "It would do you well to inform the royal family that you are going to help them separate those two. If you are caught executing your plans, they may help *you*. They need not know that Harlow's thievery is part of *our* plan. They will believe it is for their goals. You can be a double agent like in the days of the Cold War. You know your history, right?"

"I know it well." Aldric nodded. He took another sip of his vodka. He was finally getting off the damn ship that had taken two decades of his life.

CHAPTER 11

MURPHY'S LAW IN THE SNOW

Jack couldn't sleep. He was worried about Harlow. She was a strong woman but finding her father's body must have torn open an old wound. He gazed out into the darkness and watched the mesmerizing ice geysers in the distance. He thought he saw movement out on the surface, but no one was supposed to be off ship without permission, and they knew it. But if it wasn't his crew, then the Chinese were way too close to the *Ares* for comfort. He squinted and made out the form of a man. He put on his gear and paged Carlos.

Carlos scrambled security, and they traced the man's heat signature. They'd have to act fast. Freezing to death on Enceladus was an ever-present threat. They got into their gear much quicker than last time and out of the ship. It took only moments to spot the man, who was already making his way back to base.

They were only about ten feet away when the man appeared to realize he was being followed and ran. Carlos and Jack took off after him. Luckily, the area around the base had been cleared of the shards that lay everywhere else on Enceladus. Otherwise, there would have been no chasing anyone. Carlos and Jack had the advantage of not having been out in the cold as long as he had. They tackled him, pulled off his goggles—dislodging the icicles that had formed on the hood of his jacket, and lowered the woolen buff that covered his mouth. They didn't recognize the Asian man. He was clearly one of Cheung's men. Jack and Carlos yanked him to his feet and dragged him back to the outpost. They looked up into the security camera just outside the entrance of the Chinese base and held the man between them. After a few moments, the doors opened and the three men, along with ten others making up their security team, walked inside.

Field Officer Zhang came forward and immediately denied he knew anything about the man creeping around the ship. "I assure you he will be thoroughly dealt with, your Highness." The man stood silently between the two of them. Jack and Carlos exchanged glances. They knew they might well execute him after they left because he had gotten himself caught. The whole thing was complete shite but arguing wouldn't change anything. Of course, they were spying. But Jack had another idea in mind. "I'd like to speak to General Cheung in private, please."

"Please know that we will deal with this situation. I believe the general has retired for the night already. I do not wish to wake him," Officer Zhang said.

"Well, given that this is an espionage incident, I feel that it warrants attention now. We came here on a friendly exchange of scientific information and find that our security has been violated. Please wake your general," Jack said calmly.

Fifteen minutes later, Jack sat in the general's office, and they had taken the spy for what was sure to be either a serious beating or an execution. Jack knew he had no control over either but thought it possible that he could use the incident as leverage.

"I assure you I did not know of one of my men leaving our post," the general said.

"So, you are used to people defying your orders? That's common around here?" Jack goaded.

The general started to defend himself, then realized the game. There was no way to reply to Jack's questions that wouldn't cause him to lose face. The two sat in silence for several moments.

The general blinked first. "What is it you want, Highness?"

"Give me Mikhail, and I can keep this whole spy business to myself. There might be some negotiation room between our nations in the future."

Jack could tell the general wasn't surprised by the offer. He also didn't miss the mask of arrogance that fell into place. He knew he wasn't going to win this.

"I know nothing about this 'Mikhail' you speak of."

"Huh," Jack said, lifting one eyebrow as he stared down the general. *Yeah, he's here.* "All right then." Jack got up to leave, knowing his abrupt departure would surprise.

He walked out the door and into the hallway without another word and back to where his men waited. They readied themselves with goggles and snugged their hoods. The general nodded at the guard to open the door for them, and they walked out into the icy blast.

Once they were back inside the *Ares*, AVM Miller met them. "How did it go?"

Jack looked at Daniel, who had come with them despite the fact that he was a tech genius and no warrior. "Did you get it?"

Daniel's face broke into a smile as he pulled out the clear glass rectangle and moved his fingers across it in an elegant dance. "Yes, there is a building behind the outpost. From the heat signature, there is one man living in there, but that's not the most interesting thing about it. I could only retrieve security footage for the last twenty minutes. Someone left that building and boarded our ship."

"What? Who?" Jack demanded.

"Well, you can't tell from the footage, but it was someone with clearance. We would have detected a break in."

"Someone on board is conspiring with him?"

"Looks like it," Daniel said.

"Run a scan on everyone's whereabouts for the last twenty-four hours."

"Already on it."

Jack's mind swirled with questions and anger. He couldn't think of anyone on the ship who would have conspired with Mikhail.

Daniel completed the scan. "No one is unaccounted for, Highness."

"Then maybe we saw wrong." Jack didn't want to believe a member of his crew worked with the man who killed his wife and child.

"I don't think so. He could have made it look as if he had never left. At some point, who knows when, he could have duplicated his signal and had the one in his body turned off. You can find someone savvy enough to do that for the right price."

"I've certainly heard of this," Miller added.

Jack's mind raced. He wanted vengeance. He wouldn't deny that, but he was even more bothered by the idea of a mole.

Sleep eluded Jack once more. He knew that if anyone could figure out what was going on, it would be Daniel—his mind was wired for the technical. He probably dreamed in ones and zeros.

Jack finally drifted off at some point and woke to find the comm in his room was going off incessantly. He must have been ignoring it for a while because soon the pounding began on his door. He scrubbed a hand across his face and got up to find Carlos already talking the moment he opened the door.

"What?" Jack said, not sure he was hearing Carlos correctly.

"Field Officer Zhang is demanding to speak with you. He's brought a security team with him."

He walked back into his room and armed himself. He didn't have any idea what was about to happen, but something niggled at the back of his mind, telling him it was no damn good.

AVM Miller met him as soon as he exited his room.

"Sir, what are your orders?"

"Make sure the shields are up when we head out there. You remain on the ship no matter what. If he kills me, leave my body where it lies and head back to Mars."

Jack and Carlos walked outside the ship. The *Ares* security team had already assembled and stood facing Zhang and his soldiers. Zhang's stance was immediately offensive. Jack instinctively knew there was something very wrong with this exchange. Worse than that, he could see the faint fluctuation of a protective field around Zhang and his men, lending further credence to the uneasy feeling blooming inside Jack's chest. If things were going bad, Jack and his team wouldn't be able to take a shot, and it would take the *Ares* a while to catch up to the algorithm that would scramble the protective field and hold it firm.

"May I help you?" Jack asked, keeping his tone light.

Before another word was spoken a weight hit Jack squarely in the chest. He'd not put the layers of cold weather gear on as the *Ares* was programmed to warm the area within a ten-foot radius of the ship for just such icy missions.

"Bugger me!" Jack looked down at his chest and saw a metal clamp that looked like a large beetle. It had tentacles that were burrowing in. That's when he realized they'd disabled the *Ares'* shields. It shouldn't have made it through. *What else have they done?*

He heard the unmistakable gasp of a female. *Harlow, damn it!*

"Get her inside," he yelled to Evelyn.

"No!" Harlow said.

Jack felt the device digging in deeper. Despite the excruciating pain, he felt a sense of annoyance at Harlow. She'd promised him she would follow orders.

Zhang spoke. "I'm going to need you to evacuate that ship, or the bug punctures your heart in fifteen minutes. And don't get crafty with me. I pulled your weapons offline the moment you came into this atmosphere. Why weren't you notified by your precious machines? You wouldn't believe the genius inside that building over there. Now go!"

The three of them hesitated for a moment. Zhang shot one guard behind Jack, proving his seriousness. As shocking as it was for Zhang to shoot the guard, things got even more shocking as a man came running from behind the outpost, speaking Mandarin with a Russian accent.

Jack knew who it was immediately. He'd studied the man's face, burned it into his soul. Despite the gun pointed at him, despite the metal bug poised above his heart, he went for Mikhail. He only made it a few feet before Zhang shot at the ground in front of him, barely missing blowing his foot off. Jack froze and looked at Zhang with hatred for keeping him from his revenge.

"Easy, Highness," Evelyn whispered beside him.

Zhang shouted orders at his two guards to keep their weapons turned on Jack while he dealt with Mikhail. Jack got the distinct impression that Mikhail was not happy about Zhang attacking the ship, but it wasn't clear why. The man obviously didn't give a shite about Jack—so he couldn't have been defending the ship. There had to be another reason.

Mikhail yelled at Zhang until he drew his weapon on Mikhail and screamed at him. It worked.

"Inside!" Zhang ordered.

Mikhail smirked at Jack. "Sucks to be on the losing side, no? But this isn't the first time, is it?"

"What the fuck is your problem?" Harlow spat at Mikhail.

Jack rolled his eyes, feeling helpless at the power of her defiance. He knew commanding her to go inside again was useless. If he got out of this alive, he made plans to handcuff her to a chair somewhere.

"This one is interesting, isn't she?" Mikhail said. "I know who you are. You are the Colonel's daughter." He shook his head in mock disappointment. "You've got enough warrants to make your father roll over in his grave."

Harlow started running toward the man in a pure, blind rage. Carlos was faster. He grabbed her around the waist as she fought and kicked.

"I knew him. Loyal to the mission. To a disgusting degree."

Mikhail pointed at Jack, who was still trying to dislodge the metal beetle from his chest but only succeeded in making his shirt a bloody mess. "My problem is this pompous bastard right here and his family. Colony six was mine. It was my company that brought the first colonists here. I set up the first mines, and the Crown came in and confiscated everything for their glory. It's time I got it back."

"I know who you are! You're that asshole that put entire families under slave labor for defaulting on their loans. What else could they do? After the gray death, no one was getting paid!"

"It wasn't slave labor. I was helping them. Establishing loyalty and feeding them. It wasn't the Crown's job to interfere with my operation. It was your father who dragged me out into the street in front of the people by order of the Crown and their precious coalition. A man doesn't forget a thing like that."

Jack took a deep breath to calm the adrenaline and focus beyond the pain. He didn't know it was Harlow's father that had enforced Mikhail's removal. He realized he and Harlow were tied together in more ways than one. He was also wondering why Zhang didn't just shoot the man to shut him up, but he got the idea that Zhang didn't know the entire story as to why they were harboring the man and was actually a little curious. It wouldn't be the first time that only those at the highest level understood what was going on. They were concealing him because they were in on his assassination of Jack's family. If he were bold enough to kill them, he wouldn't hesitate to get revenge on Harlow's father for humiliating him.

"Oh, God! You killed him. The rest of the bodies were returned, except for his. He didn't die with the others."

She said it so quietly that Jack doubted Mikhail heard her. He realized she was piecing it together at the same time he was.

"That's enough!" Zhang shouted. "The ship is ours. Evacuate."

Jack contemplated his own stupidity while he gritted his teeth against the pain. Sweat ran down his face, despite the bitter cold. He had come there knowing the *Ares* had excellent firepower. It had never occurred to him that the Chinese could get the weapons offline. He knew why it hadn't, too. He struggled to get the ship online for seven years; that someone else could figure the thing out in a day felt preposterous. But getting it online was the only problem. After that, it behaved like any other ship. They were about to lose their only hope of getting off this damn snowball, and it was because of his oversight and lust for vengeance.

Zhang was playing his hand well—no one in the coalition had the funds to come after them and retake the *Ares*, and now the Chinese would have a formidable weapon in their hands. He had fucked up beyond repair. He hoped the metal doom beetle on his chest hurt like hell as it killed him.

CHAPTER 12

UNCIVIL DISOBEDIENCE

They all turned to go inside, knowing it would do no good to argue with a madman until another guard was shot. Two of the security team hefted their dead colleague.

As Harlow followed them in, she heard the sounds of at least a dozen *Ares* personnel moving across the top of the ship. She knew they were all armed and had looked through their sights to see that the Chinese, and by extension, Mikhail, had a protective field around them. It wouldn't do any good to take a shot. She glanced behind her and saw that the looks on Zhang and his men were as cold as Enceladus itself. They seemed content and confident in their win.

Once they were back onboard, Harlow watched Jack walk through the ship, giving orders as if he had no knife poised over his heart. Then Jack and AVM Miller spent a minute in quiet conversation. Blood soaked the left side of his shirt, and sweat ran down his face, yet his tone was calm and commanding. Harlow looked at him with awe and respect. She had no need to wonder why his crew was so loyal.

Lieutenant Faust, the engineer in charge of hydraulics, looked sick as he relayed the news. "It can't be done right now, Highness. They've neutralized the carbon atoms inside the fluid."

"It can't be replaced?"

"Without getting the hydraulics online? No, a job of that magnitude would need to be done manually. It would take an entire day, at least, and you only have fifteen minutes."

Jack raked a hand across his face. He stood with the engineer just outside the door to the main weapons station. Even the door leading in was controlled by hydraulics. They couldn't squeeze through to get in and look at what they were dealing with—though the same "malfunction" message scrolled across the screen on all the terminals.

Harlow watched in horror, afraid to breathe. The ship she hadn't given a damn about two weeks ago was about to be in the hands of a madman, and there was nothing they could do other than the unthinkable.

"Get around this. No matter how long it takes."

The engineer stood there, not appearing to know how to respond.

"No," Harlow whispered. She knew where Jack was going with it. He was going to call Zhang's bluff, let time run out, and sacrifice himself.

He met her eyes briefly, then turned his attention back to Faust. "You can batten down the hatches on this thing and find a way to get it online. You could hold out in here indefinitely while that bastard freezes trying to get inside. I'm his only insurance, and that makes him weak."

"No!" she said again.

Jack turned to her and spoke calmly. He took her hands in his before he spoke. "Harlow, listen to me. He's going to kill me no matter what we do. He has no intention of letting me live. It wouldn't make sense. He only sent me in here to clear everyone out, so he won't have a mutiny on his hands later. He knows he can't control this many people, and he doesn't want to bother with killing everyone himself. The second the last person is off this ship he will kill me anyway."

Harlow stood speechless as what he was saying sank in. He leaned over and kissed her forehead and whispered in her ear. "Don't waste your potential, Harlow." He held her eyes a second longer, then let go of her hands and turned to Faust. "I've written a letter to my family. It will be on my personal link. Be sure you let them know to look for it."

Faust nodded and spoke a few words to Jack, but they were lost to Harlow as all she could hear was the blood rushing through her ears. Nausea threatened to overcome her. Between finding her father's body and now this, she had reached her limit. She had never felt so helpless. She willed her legs to move and ran after Jack. "I can link with the ship again and try to get it going, then we can blast them off their asses."

"Harlow, that is not an option. Another hit to your brain could be fatal. The last scan showed scarring. I won't risk it, and neither should you."

"I'm a thief. You're a prince. You can help people on a level that I can't. If I die, it won't be that big a deal. If you die, who will be left to advocate for the colonists? You *know* you're the only one currently giving a damn."

"No. This is my responsibility, and I will deal with it. You also promised me you would follow orders, and I'm going to hold you to it."

He walked away as she waited long enough for him to disappear around the corner. Then she went to find Doc. Having her father's corpse on the ship was enough loss for one day.

She didn't have to go far. He'd been close by, keeping a helpless eye on Jack, she was sure. "Doc, it's time. I can be the reboot."

He gave an explosive sigh of relief. "I thought you would never ask." Without another word, they both ran to sick bay where he walked over to a cabinet and pulled out a syringe, then they turned down the hall together toward the hydraulics department.

"You could lose your career with this," she said.

"And piss off the Chinese for thwarting their plans. I know, but you are very likely to come out of this just fine, and there is little to no chance of him surviving. I'm willing to lose my job over it."

When they reached their destination, Doc said, "You have nothing to prove."

His last-minute statement made her nervous. Images of lying in a vegetative state flashed through her mind. Or, what if her brain were damaged in such a way that her speech disorder returned like it was when she was younger? What if it gave her a stroke? She wondered how much confidence he had in his serum, but she shoved it from her mind. She took the syringe from him. "I'll do it. Maybe it will mean fewer charges against you if you don't actually administer it."

She saw Jack come around the corner. Carlos was in tow, looking exactly as somber as a man about to lose his best friend.

Jack looked at Harlow and locked eyes before he looked down to see the syringe in her hand. "What's going on?"

Doc said nothing, and Harlow certainly wasn't about to respond.

"I'm not dead yet. Somebody better answer me!"

Harlow knew whatever she was going to do, she better do it quick. Jack was coming toward her with purpose. She squeezed through the small opening in the glass door where the frozen hydraulics held it stuck—where she knew a man of his size couldn't follow.

Once inside, she walked over to operating station, sat down in front of it, and emptied the syringe into her leg. She laid her arms and head on the console, having no idea if she would pass out, fall asleep, or start having seizures. Doc had tweaked the serum since last time. Moments later, she felt as if she were floating. Everything around her seemed to fade away: Jack screaming at Doc, the engineer frantically trying to fix the hydraulics on the door, so Jack could get to her. She felt as if she were in a dream state, aware enough to see images in her head but unable to move or talk. Ones and zeros raced behind her eyelids in an endless stream as she spoke to the ship about hydraulics and the weapons they desperately needed. The ship rocked beneath her, but she couldn't understand why. She had no idea how much time had passed. It could have been minutes, days, or years. She didn't know, and it didn't really matter. Soon even the ones and zeros stopped appearing behind her eyelids, and everything went black.

CHAPTER 13

SWIMMING TO THE SURFACE

The shaking woke her up. It was endless. Once the upper half of her body stopped shaking, the lower half would begin. A needle pierced her arm, and then came stillness. It didn't last long before the headaches and vomiting arrived. At some point, needles stuck her arms again. Then, eventually, after what felt like decades, there was quiet, interrupted only by distant sobbing. She felt as if she were swimming toward the surface, and then suddenly broke through to find herself staring up at *him*.

"Never do that again," Jack said as he pulled her to his chest.

She opened her eyes long enough to look around and discover that she was in his room. She lay in his arms, on his bed.

Confusion reigned. "Do what?" she asked.

A horrified look crossed his face. "How much do you remember?"

"Of what?"

She thought his eyes looked round and frightened. "Of anything."

"I love you," Harlow answered.

He looked at her with an emotion she couldn't quite discern. Joy? Confusion? Worry?

He pulled her back into his arms again and lay back against the wall. He kissed the top of her head. "Go back to sleep. I'll watch over you."

She knew there was something she was supposed to do in this situation. Some joke she was supposed to make. Some reason to get up and say she was okay. Whether it was the migraine meds or a breakdown of will, she couldn't think of a single thing to do but lie back in his arms, close her eyes, and surrender.

· · ·

The next time she woke, Jack was gone. The ever-present inky blackness outside the window was replaced by the Martian landscape—green to the north of the ship, more orange to the south. *They were back on Mars. It must have worked. What must have worked?*

She swung her legs around to dangle off the edge of the bed. Dark spots closed in on her field of vision as she breathed deeply, knowing better than to stand up just yet. On the nightstand were several bottles of pills. She briefly remembered waking up at one point, and Jack giving her two of them. An IV port was taped to the top of her hand. She removed the tape and pulled the needle out with a grimace. Jack had pretty much turned his room into an infirmary. Remembering how he'd lost it when he'd found her on the observation deck after the first experiment, she assumed that he no longer had any trust left in Doc and moved her to his room because of it. Older memories seemed easier to access than the more recent.

Shaky legs led her to the bathroom. Getting up had made her blood pressure drop too quickly, and she took a deep breath and braced an arm against the wall as she began seeing stars in her peripheral vision. She had no idea how long she had been lying there. It would've been at least two weeks.

After splashing cold water on her face, she became more coherent. A frayed gown from the infirmary draped her as she looked around the room for her clothes. She found them neatly folded on top of Jack's chest of drawers. Her face felt hot as she realized he might have been the one to remove them. She picked up her clothes and began getting dressed with trembling hands.

Once in the hallway, Doc was there as if he'd been waiting. He sported a huge black eye that had turned to shades of green and yellow. He looked surprised to see her up.

"What happened to *you*?" she said, gaping at his eye.

He didn't answer but began shooing Harlow back toward Jack's room. "Get back in bed. He's going to kill me if you pass out again."

"What?" She smacked at Doc's hands as he tried to steer her in the right direction. "I don't want to go back to bed. I'm not tired." She was exhausted but didn't like being told what to do.

"Harlow!" Jack's voice called from the other end of the hallway. "What in the hell is she doing up?" She didn't miss the accusatory glare leveled at Doc.

Harlow jumped in to defend him. "I got up on my own, and he's trying to get me to go back to bed. Which I have no intention of doing."

Jack rushed down the long hallway at a near run. When he reached Harlow, he scooped her up in his arms and brushed past Doc, practically knocking him against the wall.

"Put me down! I'm fine." She pushed Jack but didn't have enough energy to put her heart into it.

"You have a real problem taking orders, Harlow. We wouldn't be in this situation if you had listened to me in the first place."

"No, you would be dead!"

Jack said nothing in return.

He slammed his hand against the outside panel to open the door. Soon Harlow found herself back in Jack's bed. Her head was spinning from the effort of walking down the hallway and having Jack scoop her up so quick made it worse. "Ugh." She placed her palms against her eyes and groaned.

"It's been six hours already. You need more medication." He filled the glass with water from the bathroom sink, doled out two pills from one bottle on the nightstand, and watched her take them as if he didn't think she would follow those orders either.

His eyebrows knitted together. She had had no one watch over her that intently before. It was like hearing another language spoken. She wasn't sure how to interpret it. Trying to decide whether she should be angry at taking orders or touched by his concern was making her headache worse; she couldn't wrap her mind around such a thing. Even her mother hadn't cared for her to that degree. Her head pounded harder as she thought of her mother. She shoved the thoughts away and changed her train of thought. "What happened to Doc's eye?"

"I beat his ass," Jack said, without preamble or apology.

"What? Why?"

"Because I've already been through this with him and Aldric, by the way. You were there. You know that. He didn't consult with me first. I told him not to give you that brain-altering shite. He disobeyed a direct order and nearly got you killed."

"Well, he had my permission. We couldn't just let you die." Harlow was finally remembering what had happened. The details were still a little fuzzy, but she remembered going into the weapons chamber and agreeing to the shot.

"I'm glad to see your memory isn't damaged. I was afraid of that."

"There are still a few gaps. Did I wake up at all before we reached Mars?"

Jack hesitated. "Yes. Briefly."

"Hmm. I can't remember that. Anyway, Doc did the right thing."

"No. Doc didn't have *my* permission. Doc and Aldric both are getting transferred and are extremely lucky I'm not sending them to the Bastille." He picked up the water Harlow set aside and began drinking it. No one wasted water on Mars.

Harlow leaned back against the headboard and squeezed her eyes shut against the searing pain. "Look, I agree Aldric is a dick and helped make the serum after you said not to, but—"

She heard Jack cough on the water he was drinking and then laugh in succession before coughing again.

She was too tired to filter herself—of course, she didn't do that much filtering in her day to day either. "Anyway, I wish you would go easy on Doc. I don't believe he would have ever given me the serum as an experiment again. I think he only kept it for an emergency and that's exactly what it was. It was the best chance to save your life. At least think about it, for me."

"You saved my life. I will consider it, for you, but I still get to take the *Ares* back up and throw Aldric out the airlock, right?"

"Oh, of course." Harlow laughed but quickly stopped as every little movement made her headache worse.

She held the sides of her skull, hoping the pressure would ease the pain. "What happened to the Chinese base?"

"The weapons came back online a couple of minutes after you went under. Soon as they did, we lit them up."

"The entire base?" she asked.

"Just the twenty troops outside the ship trying to kill us. There were families inside the compound. It might come back to bite me in the ass, especially knowing General Cheung was hiding inside while he sent Zhang out to do his dirty work for him. But I went to Enceladus to make Mikhail answer for my wife and child, not kill someone else's."

She was afraid to ask her next question, but curiosity got the best of her.

"Did you get Mikhail?"

"I think so, but there was no way to say for sure without going out there and surveying the bodies. We had to go before we got fired on or they did something else to the ship."

She remembered his bloody chest and noticed he seemed fine now. She reached up and gently placed her palm over his heart—her boldness fueled by the strong medication just kicking in. "How?" she said, wondering about how he got the fatal bug off him before it pierced his heart. The very thought made her feel sick.

She watched Jack wince and look down where her hand rested against his chest.

"Sorry." She started to move her hand, but he covered it with his own.

"It's okay," he whispered. She observed his Adam's apple bob up and down as he swallowed before continuing to tell her the rest of the story. "Once the weapons were online, Daniel found a frequency to disable the lock on the bloody thing. It fell right off. Not something we could have done without the ship's tech being online though. You saved my life."

"I'm glad you're okay."

The pills were making her want to sleep. She felt her eyelids start to droop just as Jack got up and started unzipping her boots.

"Lie down. You're still tired."

She complied and started to drift off, but she wanted to ask more questions about their escape. Her body jerked as tendrils of sleep began pulling her deeper but opened her eyes one more time and saw Jack across the room at his desk and realized she must've dozed off without knowing it.

He looked up as if he felt her looking at him. "Go to sleep, sweetheart."

She knew there was something different about what he was saying, but his face began to blur before her; she couldn't follow her own line of thought and didn't really want to. For the first time in her life, she wondered if this was what safety felt like.

"It's weird but kind of nice, too," she said out loud without realizing it.

"What is?" he asked.

She smiled. "Nothing."

They were good meds.

After another couple of days Harlow felt well enough to be up and around. She'd also moved back into her own room, though she had to admit, if only to herself, that she missed sharing a room with Jack.

Waking up in the middle of the night and hearing his breathing and occasional snoring—while he lay on a couch that was way too small for him—was oddly comforting to her.

She knew, now that she was better, they would need to make plans for her father's memorial, but she wasn't ready to wrap her head around that yet. For now, she lay in her own room remembering what it felt like to be in Jack's arms and listening to the soothing sound of his heartbeat as he held her close.

CHAPTER 14

A Time for Tears

Harlow stood outside her mother's home and wrapped her arms around herself. Her father had been gone twenty years. Her mother would have accepted his death and moved on long ago. In fact, they had barely spoken about him since he'd died. After it happened, Harlow remembered crying for him, and her mother comforted her, but once the tears were gone, she knew it wasn't to be brought up. The few times she mentioned him were met with quick, clipped comments.

It was an ache in her heart, never addressed, never healed, never filled, just silent and bare. An unexpected sensation wash over her and she closed her eyes, trying to chase it to its core until it revealed itself: anger. It surprised her to find that she was angry at her mom for not allowing her to truly mourn her father. Rushing in behind the anger came fear. What if her mother didn't react well to the news of finding her father's body? She might blame her. Shoot the messenger was an easy reaction to news people could not accept. What if her mother dismissed it like she did when she was little? Harlow felt fragmented and, as much as she hated to admit it to herself, fragile.

Hesitating at the door, she wondered if she should knock. She lived on the ship now and during their last visit, her mother was none too pleased that Harlow wanted to join the prince on the *Ares*. Would she even be happy to see her? She knocked a few times, then tried the door. Finding it unlocked, she took a deep breath and stepped inside. "Mom?"

Judith came from Harlow's old room. A muscle twitched in her jaw when she looked at her daughter—the closest Harlow could hope to get to an emotion from the inscrutable woman. Her mother had never been one for hugging, but something in Harlow longed for it, for the first time in years, but knew it wouldn't be coming. A little ache formed in her heart at the knowledge.

She remembered it clearly—the day her mother told her Harlow's dad was gone forever. Try as she might, her six-year-old brain couldn't wrap around the thought that he wouldn't return. Years went by, expecting him to come through the door, day after day. After all, if there was no body, then there was always a chance that he could return. She held out hope for years as she watched other families together. Seeing fathers and daughters talk and play made the heaviness in her chest threaten to take the very breath from her. The one time she'd mentioned it to Judith, she'd gotten angry at her—she never spoke of it again. It became a secret hope, night after night, listening to every little sound, thinking he might be coming through the door at any moment. All that time, he had lain frozen on Saturn's cold and unforgiving moon—waiting in that cave day after day with his tracker pinging away.

Harlow felt a lump in her throat, but she would let it choke her before she would allow her mom to see her tears. It wasn't done in this house. *Where was it done?* His preserved body had rested in front of her in the cryo lab after Jack found him, and she hadn't cried and wouldn't now. There would be no crying at the funeral with so damn many eyes on her. *Was there ever a place for tears?*

She thought of Jack and then immediately scolded herself for it without understanding why.

"How are things on the ship?" her mother asked with an edge in her voice.

Harlow did not know how to answer that. If she said she hated it, her mother would say, "I told you so." If she told her she loved it, Judith would let her know she'd sold out the colonists. It made her wonder exactly how she felt about it. She had not allowed herself to address it. The lump in her throat suddenly disappeared and was replaced by a fire in her gut.

She stood up straight and refused to answer her mother's goading question but continued with the reason she had come.

"You need to know that Dad's body was located on Enceladus. It was well preserved in the ice. He's been brought home for burial here in the colonies. A service is being planned. It will be two days from now. The prince wants to know if you would like to come to the ship to help coordinate plans, or he could send an official to you if you would feel more comfortable." Harlow watched her mother. She held her breath and realized that she was looking for a certain reaction but braced herself that it might not be there.

Judith appeared to have stopped breathing. She leaned over and placed a hand on the worn red sofa.

"Are you okay?" Without thinking Harlow started to go to her but stopped when her mother held a flat palm up to her. She knew her mother didn't like being touched when she was emotional. Moments later, Judith stood up erect again, and her look was one of resolve, perhaps ready for battle.

"The usual protocol for informing a military family of their loved one's demise is sending an official to the house, but the prince sends you to do his dirty work?"

"Jack asked if he could send some men to tell you, officially. He even asked to deliver the news himself. I told him I would do it."

Judith raised her eyebrows at her. "You call him Jack?"

"The prince, yes."

"You are on a first name basis with him now? Don't become his whore, Harlow."

She felt the sting of her mother's words deeper than she would ever let her know. The urge to defend herself was almost overwhelming. Not only that, but she also wanted to defend Jack. Part of her wanted to swear to her mother that nothing had happened, but she knew it wouldn't matter. If she couldn't believe the best about her own daughter, there was no chance she could believe the best about Jack. "If you have any input about the service, please feel free to come to the ship."

"I'm not going in there, and you know it."

Harlow felt exhaustion wash over her but quickly held up her chin before answering. "Fine. I'll see you at the memorial. As you know, there was a space left empty beside the graves of the others who were brought back for burial. The service will be held there. The Mother will be presiding."

Harlow watched as her mother's features softened for a moment at mention of the nun.

"Okay," Judith said.

Harlow turned to go but paused with her hand on the door as a sense of emptiness permeated her. Shock washed over her as words tore from her throat, her heart, her soul: "I miss Dad." She never saw Judith's reaction. She didn't care or maybe just didn't want to be disappointed to learn that it didn't matter. She left without looking back.

• • •

The borrowed buggy sputtered and bumped its way across the broken road as she drove to the cemetery with little thought. Tears clouded her eyes as the cold, dusty air hit her face. She came to a stop, got out, and went straight to the five-foot memorial. The names of the fallen were etched in the Martian rock, her father's name at the bottom. She'd always been glad his name was last. That way, when he returned alive, they could remove it easily without leaving a space in the middle. She had believed they'd placed it last because they weren't sure he was dead. Looking at the graves of the other men and women from the ill-fated mission made her realize the group would finally be complete. She sat down on the space where her father would be buried in just a couple days and dropped her head into her hands as grief washed over her. He wasn't coming back. Tears overtook her. She was thankful she had gotten out of her mother's house before losing control.

A male voice cut through her grief. "Harlow?"

She looked up through blurry eyes and saw Sergeant Carlos Gonsalves standing there. "I can leave if you would like, or maybe I could sit with you a minute?"

"You can stay."

Carlos sat down beside her in the patchy grass and red soil.

"I was out here helping get things together for your father's memorial."

"That's kind of you," she said as she wiped her nose with the sleeve of her sweatshirt.

Carlos looked at the monument that stood in the middle of the group of graves and spoke softly. "Many of my ancestors were Marines. One of them even had a base in Japan named after him, Pfc. Harold Gonsalves. He and two others were laying telephone lines for communication with the artillery battalion when they came under fire: rifles, grenades, mortar. They had just reached the front lines when a Japanese grenade landed a foot from them. Pfc. Gonsalves threw himself on it. The fragments did not even touch the other two Marines. He was only nineteen. But as amazing as that was, it wasn't him that made me want to be a Marine; it was my dad. He was so tough and respected, you know? I wanted to be just like him."

"I didn't know that."

"Yeah, he died when I was ten years old. My sister was eight. I miss him every day. He died during the food riots. After that, we were raised by my mom—a strong Colombian woman."

She turned to look at him with red rimmed eyes and a blotchy face.

"I'm sorry, Carlos."

He gave her a sad smile. "Is your mother okay?"

"Yeah, she's always okay."

"Did it help to talk to her? I don't know what I would have done if my mother hadn't been there for us."

"No. We never talked about him. We never even...She wouldn't ever..." Harlow struggled for the words to place how the years of stubborn refusal to discuss his death had made her feel but came up as empty as Judith's silence. "It doesn't matter."

"Yes, Harlow. It matters. It's okay for it to matter."

"Carlos?"

"Yeah?"

"I lost my dad," she sobbed out.

"Yes, you did, mi hermana pequeña. You surely did." He gently placed his hand on her back.

She laid her head on his shoulder and cried under the Martian sky.

• • •

Harlow stood next to Carlos and Jack in the gray-pink dusk. Her father's casket was draped with an American flag and a coalition flag was placed at the lower quarter. Beside his casket there was a picture of him that looked like they had taken it from the message he had sent her. She loved it because he had recorded it just for her—even knowing that he probably wasn't coming back. He was thinking of her at the time.

AVM Miller and many of the others who had worked alongside her father were there. As she looked at Miller, the woman looked back and gave her a sad smile.

Jack kept looking around, and Harlow guessed that he was searching for Judith. He leaned over and asked Seraph and Evelyn a quiet question. They shook their heads while glancing at Harlow. It was time to start the service, and the widow still wasn't there. Jack leaned over to whisper into Harlow's ear, "Would you like to wait a little longer?"

"No. Let's get started." She knew waiting on her mother was an exercise in futility. She glanced to her left and spotted Mike O'Malley, who nodded at her. She returned it, feeling comforted to see another familiar face.

Jack looked at Mother, who began with prayers and blessed the ground according to Catholic tradition. That was right about when Judith appeared. Harlow hadn't heard her drive up in a buggy and realized that she must have been there the whole time, sitting behind the tree. She looked pale, the effect more pronounced by the black dress she wore, hair pulled into a severe bun. A soft breeze freed several strands of her bright red hair from the bun and blew them across her face, but she made no move to tuck them back. She stared straight ahead at her late husband's picture. Her expression was unchanging, yet to Harlow's complete shock, tears were flowing down her mother's face. She thought about going to her but knew it would be a mistake. She looked like an alabaster statue that might crack from the slightest touch.

Mother looked at Harlow's father's picture and spoke.

"I had the joy of spending time with the Colonel's daughter when she was a little girl. She looked so much like her father with the soulful blue eyes and shiny dark hair. One night, we had one of those mutated moths smacking against the window. Half the sisters were terrified of those things back then and started screaming. Harlow ran in front of us all and said, 'Don't worry. I'll protect you.' She was so tiny, but she spread her arms to shield us. Sometimes we only see the gifts they leave us through the lens of another, and I see her father in her, looking back at me."

Harlow glanced at her mother, but Judith only had eyes for the portrait of Michael Hanson. She tried but couldn't reconcile the widow that stared at the photo while tears flooded her face with the mother who refused to speak of him or allow her daughter to do so. Harlow couldn't help but feel robbed. There was an abyss of feelings she'd needed to express so badly they'd coiled inside her for years, giving her headaches and near crippling stomach pain. Yet there it was. The woman felt. She mourned.

A few others got up to speak about working with her father. Not once did Judith move from her spot. Finally, the color guard stepped forward and folded both flags. The American flag was taken to Harlow's mother, the coalition flag to Harlow. She held out some hope that Judith would come to her. She hated that she even wanted that, but maybe because Jack stood beside her, Judith never approached.

Harlow stood beside the grave as everyone began to disperse. Her mother didn't speak to anyone but simply turned and walked home. After watching her mother weep, she was certain that she had feelings...just not for her, not anymore.

Jack, Carlos, and Mother stood together after everyone had gone. For the first time since Harlow had known him, Jack seemed lost, as if wondering what he *should* do. Carlos appeared to know there was nothing he *could* do, but Mother had somehow figured out *exactly* what to do. She put her arms around Harlow, pulled her close, and said, "I'm proud of you."

CHAPTER 15

JUDITH

Judith walked into her flat and went straight to her pantry to find the bottle of red she had been saving for a rainy day; it was an emotional downpour. She reached for a glass and noticed her hand trembled. Deciding she didn't need the glass, she uncorked the bottle and went back to the couch. Sitting there alone with the bottle in one hand and the neatly folded flag in the other, she leaned forward to set the flag down on the table and found that she couldn't. It had been on *his* casket. They had found him. Now she had a place to visit when the world felt like it was caving in, which was every damn day since he'd left on the recon mission.

She held the flag to her chest, turned up the bottle again, and dissolved into tears, nearly choking on the wine. She remembered the day they had met.

. . .

Michael was at the Air Force Academy at its new home in North Florida. When Yellowstone had started spewing the caustic gray death, the academy couldn't stay at its location in Colorado Springs. No one could.

He stopped at the bar in Warrington near Pensacola where Judith worked. Just like she'd read about in history books, when water couldn't be trusted to be clean, beer could. There were more pubs than restaurants. She had been attending nursing school but had taken the summer off to make some money. Working long hours meant no time for dating or socializing. She had always been single-minded whenever she wanted something, and more than anything in the world, she wanted to be a nurse. The gray death had taken her mother when Judith was sixteen. It almost took her father from her as well, but he pulled through. Even though the nanobots constantly cleaned the air, Yellowstone continued to pump out the caustic ash. Miraculously, her lungs had suffered no ill effects.

She remembered visiting her mother in the hospital and being so impressed by the nurses who worked around the clock—they had to because half the staff had died, not just from lung conditions but from lack of supplies like antibiotics and vaccines for common illnesses. There were more than air problems. There were supply chain problems as well. It was obvious the staff was exhausted, but when they saw Judith crying, they would often stop what they were doing to give her a hug. They had put their own exhaustion aside to comfort her. They were the kind of hero Judith wanted to be. She was halfway done with her degree when Michael Hanson walked into her bar. He was with two other young men, but she only noticed him. The black hair and striking blue eyes had her mesmerized right from the start.

She chastised herself when she felt that punch in the gut—the one she hadn't even felt with her first boyfriend, Aiden. Aiden had come along on the heels of losing her mother. He had lost an older sister and their combined grief pulled them deeper into the relationship. It was a passionate, yet naïve match between the two, and they had soon learned that they had little in common other than their mutual grief and confusion from living in a world where death was a daily part of life that had robbed an entire generation of their childhood and filled it with suffering. The funerals that should have honored the dead became a routine hardship at best, an assembly line at worst.

But at twenty-three, she was older, wiser, and knew how to put the brakes on. Michael spent his evenings in the bar talking to her when things were slow. He told her he was about to graduate from the Air Force Academy and all about the family he had lost, including his dad and younger brother. Night after night, he came in to see her. She scolded herself to take a step back, but when he looked at her, her resolve melted. He made it impossible to maintain her stoic demeanor. It wasn't just sexual. It would have been much easier if it were. Instead, it was a feeling as if she had known him forever, as if their entire lives had been leading up to their meeting.

The grief and isolation that had become an integral part of her existence could not stand in the light he brought into her life. He was kind, gentle, but tough enough to call her on her bullshit. She had tried to send him away once, and he called her a coward and showed up at the bar the very next night as usual. She picked fights with him more than once just to push him away, but he wouldn't be bullied and wouldn't let her lie to herself, either.

After graduation, his duties kept him in Pensacola, and it was time for her to get back to Atlanta and her studies at Emory University. They still saw each other every chance they got and by the end of the fall semester, they both knew they were "it" for each other.

She remembered the day he came to her apartment to tell her he was going to Mars. His grandfather, a highly decorated general, had served there until his death just two years before ash blanketed the Earth. Judith felt as if he had kicked her in the teeth when he brought her the news of his move—pretty much a permanent one. It wasn't like being stationed across the country or even on the other side of the world. When you left for Mars, you could take family but not girlfriends.

"Speak to me, Judith."

She sat in stunned silence, reminding herself to breathe. *This is why you don't get attached to people. You knew better.*

"I'm wondering if you might come with me. I would wait for you to finish school if I could, but there are rumors that this convoy to

Mars will be the last one for a very long time because the funding simply isn't there since the economy tanked."

Judith swiped angrily at the tear running down her cheek, betraying her. As much as she loved Michael, she was uncomfortable with him seeing her like this. Since her mother's death, she despised the tears that had been her constant companion. Inside her mind, she shoved all her feelings into a closet and then stoically slammed it shut. "They won't let you bring your girlfriend. I suppose it's for the best. I'm only a few semesters from graduating. We knew it couldn't last. Who are we to think we can have it all, anyway? I mean, we knew better right—"

Michael grabbed her by the shoulders. "Stop. Stop running away."

"I'm not. I'm right here."

"The hell you are. You're in the same room, but that isn't the same as being with me." When she kept talking, he shoved her gently onto the couch, covered her with his body, and kissed her hungrily. She lay there, looking up at him in stunned silence. He wasn't playing fair, but it was effective. They were each other's only weakness. No amount of touching was ever enough. They had devoured each other more times than either could count since meeting the summer before.

He ran his fingers lightly across her collarbone, slowly tugged her shirt off her shoulder, and leaned over to kiss her neck, then gently raked his teeth across her skin. She shivered.

He leaned back and looked at her. "Marry me," he said. "I can't take a girlfriend to Mars, but I can take a wife. You're mine. I don't want this without you. Marry me."

A breathless "yes" escaped her throat before her brain had time to reason its way out of it or shove more feelings into storage.

⋅ • ⋅

Her dad was a wreck when she told him she was leaving. Judith was his only child. Leaving for nursing school had been emotional for them both, but Mars? They both dissolved into tears when she told him. He said he'd known from the moment he saw the way the two looked at each other that the man had stolen his baby's heart, and nothing was going to change it—not even the love of a father.

Neither she nor Michael spoke about Judith leaving her nursing dream behind. She knew he wasn't being cold about it. They were living in a world that knew the frivolity of crying over the inevitable. Staying together was their inevitability. They both knew nothing could be done about it, and you didn't just reschedule a convoy to Mars. It left when it left, and you were either on it or you waited years for the next one, which might never come to pass.

• • • •

Mars brought love, laughter, tears, and Harlow. But a short seven years after arriving on Mars, a recon mission drew Michael's life and Judith's dreams to an abrupt end. The ship's chaplain had come to tell them the news. The bodies were lined up in the bay but no Michael. When Judith suggested that without a body, they couldn't confirm whether he was dead, she had been told that even if he hadn't died in combat, the elements they were fighting in would have killed him anyway. They said there was no doubt about it. Judith felt her heart freeze right along with him. But in her mind, if there was no body, then he might turn up someday. He couldn't come back and find her with another man, not that there were a whole lot of choices in the sparsely populated colonies anyway.

But now he was here, buried, and she sat there with the flag from his casket. The grief that flooded her soul now told her exactly how long she had held out hope he was alive. The man she had lived with when Harlow was little had asked her to marry him and she wouldn't. It was true that she didn't love him, she had just been lonely; but the deeper truth was she needed to be able to get out of the relationship quickly in case Michael came home.

Judith looked at the wine bottle that was now half empty. She chided herself. "What were you thinking? Twenty years? Of course, he was dead, idiot."

She had never allowed herself to believe he was really gone for good, but she had made sure Harlow believed it. The false hope was the worst. She wanted Harlow to be able to move on, even if she couldn't. Now she had no choice.

"Michael," she cried into the empty room. "What the hell do I do, now that I'm not waiting for you anymore?"

Night had long since fallen, and Judith had passed out on the old red couch. A knock at the door roused her. She sat up and rubbed her eyes as she tried to process what was going on and just how much time had gone by. She looked toward her windows and noticed that the afternoon glow no longer drove the gloom from the room. Now the long, unforgiving night was here. She had been dreading it since the walk back from the cemetery.

"I'm coming," she called out to the incessant knock. As soon as she stood, her head began to pound mercilessly. She reached up to rub her temples. That's when she noticed her hair was matted about her head. She tried smoothing it as best she could before reaching the door.

"Who is it?" Her voice sounded strange in her own ears, somehow hoarse and hollow.

"It's Mother."

Of all the people who could have shown up at her door, she found Mother to be the least objectionable, and these days she found almost everyone objectionable. When she opened the door, the woman was standing there with a bag in hand.

"Dinner?" Mother asked.

"Maybe." Judith wasn't sure whether she was hungry, nauseated, or a little of both. "Come in."

"Thank you." Judith took the bag and motioned for her to take a seat on the couch.

"I wanted to make sure you were okay. It's a rough day for you."

Judith waved off her comment. "I'm fine."

"Hasn't anyone ever told you that you're not supposed to lie to a holy woman?" Mother winked at her before leaning over to pick up the bottle of wine. "What have you got here? Merlot?"

"Are you judging me, Mother?"

Mother gave a wry laugh. "I was going to ask if you had a glass for *me*."

Judith smiled, remembering her time at the abbey. "Yeah, I remember you, wino," she said playfully as some of the sorrow retreated. She went into the kitchen to retrieve a glass.

Mother took the glass from Judith, who filled it a quarter of the way with the red wine. She remembered late nights in the abbey's kitchen, having a little wine with Mother after Harlow had gone to sleep. After Judith and Harlow left the convent, the two women only had passing contact, but there had always been an affinity between them; a mutual toughness that didn't require explanation to be understood.

Judith was glad Mother was there, especially when she realized she had slept off most of her buzz, and if it weren't for Mother, she would be alone with her grief and a little too hung over to get started on another buzz. She opened the bag and nibbled at the sandwich Mother had brought.

"It's good. Thank you."

"You're welcome. I didn't know if anyone had been by."

"Nah, not unless I was out so hard, I couldn't hear the door."

"Now *that* I would believe. Was this bottle full when you got started?"

Judith didn't lie. "Yeah."

"I'm sorry. This is painful for you."

Judith nodded almost imperceptibly. "How's Harlow?"

"She's holding up. She's made a few friends on the ship, but she still needs her mother."

Judith wasn't so sure about that last part but immediately thought of the prince and wondered exactly what her daughter's relationship was with him. When Harlow spoke of him, her voice changed in ways that Judith knew she didn't recognize. If her daughter knew it, it would mortify her. In that way, at least, they were the same. Harlow hated having "a tell" every bit as much as her mother did. Not only that, the prince, or Jack, as Harlow called him, had stood beside her daughter at the burial service like a sentinel, guarding her, and from Judith's perspective—though Jack himself probably didn't even realize it—he was claiming her in that subliminal, primal way that men often used to let onlookers know whom they belonged to. For the first time, for the briefest of moments, she wondered if that might not be a bad thing. Besides, he was in the same line as Mother, and she was wonderful. Still, something about Harlow being on that damn ship niggled at the back of her mind.

"You don't have to stay. It's been a long day. You're probably tired," Judith said. Though she suddenly felt very fragile even as she attempted to send the woman away.

"I had actually come by to see if you might like someone to see you through the night. A couple of old single gals having some wine and doing a little complaining and gossiping might be fun. What do ya say?"

Judith chewed the last of the sandwich she hadn't realized she had wanted and nodded. "Yeah, I could do with that."

She was glad for the company, but still had an uneasy feeling in her chest when it came to Harlow. Unable to shake it or decide exactly what it was, she picked up the wine bottle and decided she wasn't through with it just yet. She held it up to the other woman in a silent toast and then turned it up.

CHAPTER 16

O'MALLEY'S

Harlow walked into O'Malley's, wondering if Mike or anyone else there had changed their opinion of her since she had started working on the *Ares*—working for the enemy. She enjoyed being on the *Ares*. She loved her new sense of purpose—all she was learning about the ship, her connection to her father, Carlos, and Jack. Yet deep down, she felt a small sense of betrayal toward the colonists. It had always been an "us and them" situation with the *Ares*, and as much as she defended her right to be on the ship and become who she wanted to be, the idea of losing her friends in the colonies, or God forbid, have them think she had abandoned them was a painful thought. If anyone had a finger on the pulse of the people, it would be Mike. He didn't just run the bar and serve the drinks; he was also a therapist and confessor and heard all the gossip. She knew she could count on him for the truth; the truth she both wanted and feared all at once.

She took a deep breath as she approached the bar. It was noon, and only a few people were inside. A couple sat by the window chatting softly and nursing beers. The female looked up as Harlow passed, and then glanced away. Harlow only knew the woman vaguely, so it wasn't a shock that she didn't say hello. It also wasn't a shock that, out of her peripheral vision, she caught the woman nudging her partner. So, the talk had begun. She knew she shouldn't be surprised, but it lent credence to her worst fears.

She slid behind the scarred, polished oak bar that had won a "weight lottery" before the gray death, when the colonists were still well-funded and receiving supplies, when a few luxury items— luxury for the precious space and weight they took up on transport vessels to the Red Planet—were allowed. The old oak had seen better days but still did the job.

Mike looked into the mirrored glass behind the bar and winked at her without turning around. She smiled at him and felt her shoulders begin to relax as he poured O'Malley's ale into a thick mug. He brewed his own, literally from the ground up: the hops and barley grew in a greenhouse behind the bar. No one was shipping in something as extravagant as beer. So, the industrious Irishman grew and fermented everything himself.

He turned around and set the mug in front of her. "How ya been, girl?"

"Hanging in there. I wanted to thank you for coming to the funeral."

"Of course, we're family, right?"

Harlow tried not to read too much into his words but couldn't help wondering if it was a true question. A doubt. "Always, Mike." She took a long drink and savored the pale brew. It was the first beer she'd had since before boarding the *Ares*.

Mike casually picked up a glass and turned it in the light as if looking for spots or cracks, then polished a blemish she couldn't see. She realized he was avoiding eye contact. "How long are you planning on staying on board the ship?"

She stepped carefully around his feelings. "I'm not sure how long I'll be there."

He walked over and placed the glass with the others. "Your mother's worried about you."

"She resents the ship. I know."

"Judith is tough as shoe leather. Sometimes you have to read between the lines with her." Although he was talking about her mother, he looked straight at her.

Harlow nodded and took another drink to avoid addressing the complicated relationship with her mother. Not to mention the complicated relationship in front of her. She had known Mike her whole life. He was ten years older, and he'd looked out for her like an older brother. She had come to him to find out if everyone else had cast her aside, only to find his feelings were just as fragile. She knew Mike was loyal to his friends, but that might change in an instant if he thought she was using him for information. Before she could ask him anything more, he had questions of his own.

"Look, I'm just going to come right out and ask. Is the prince threatening you or keeping you from leaving?"

She nearly choked on her beer as Mike pinned her in place with his eyes, acting as a lie detector. She thought Mike might have been hoping she would say "yes," hoping that she didn't truly want to be there, that she would give him a reason to believe that she still belonged to the colony, and by extension, to him. "Jack has never threatened me."

He looked at her just as strangely as her mother had when she spoke of the prince. She realized he was as uncomfortable as her mother was with her calling the prince "Jack." It felt strange to her that it bothered them so much. And the fact that it felt strange to her told her just how far removed from them she had become in a month. No wonder they were worried.

Mike tried again. "Telling someone they have to work with you to avoid prison *is* a threat, Harlow."

She wondered if she should level with him and tell him she had made friends on the ship, but she remembered seeing Mike leave the funeral the day before, all alone, as she stood with her new friends from the ship. She had briefly thought about running over to say hello to him, but between her own emotions, and her conflicting feelings about Judith, she hadn't had enough emotional reserves left to chase after Mike.

She appealed to his heart with the truth, a truth she hadn't shared with many people. "The whole prison thing aside, I never knew my father, but now I stay in a room that he slept in; his name plate is by the door. Mike, he even left me a message. I *saw* my father. Mom rarely spoke of him and when she did, the anger overshadowed any memory that could have meant something to me. When I'm on the ship, I feel like I'm finally getting to know my dad." She felt her grip on the mug tightening. "I suspect some colonists see me as a sellout?"

Mike's voice had softened by the time he spoke again. "Well, you know how people are. They like to gossip, stir shit up. I don't take any of it too seriously."

"That's what I thought. From what Mom said, I suspected it, but still hoped they had a little more faith in me than that."

"You were their hero," he said as he turned around and pushed back the handle on a leaking tap.

"*Were*? Mike, it's me. I haven't changed. These are still my people. Why must me being on the ship equal betrayal?"

"For what it's worth, I don't think you betrayed anyone. It's just that...you know, you're our girl, not theirs, and certainly not the Crown's."

"Of course. Always. Never doubt that. I'm there for all of you."

Mike looked her in the eye and gave her a brief, sad smile. "I got a stew going in the back. I'll go get you a bowl. I doubt they've been feeding you well on that metal monstrosity."

Harlow stared into the mirror as Mike walked into the kitchen. She caught sight of Darnell, the best mechanic in the village, looking at her. She knew he had to have been at least seventy by now. While growing up, she had slowly watched the curly gray hair creep up from his hairline and steadily march its way across his scalp until it now hovered above his dark skin like a cloud of gray smoke. He lifted his mug in salute at Harlow's reflection in the mirror. Deciding she couldn't afford to lose anyone wishing her well in this colony, she grabbed her own beer and walked over to him.

"Did His Highness let you off for good behavior?" Darnell laughed at his own joke.

"Yeah, he unlocks the cell for an hour per day."

He ran a hand across his mouth as if wiping away the smile so that he could move on to something more serious. "I always wondered what would happen if you ever boarded that ship. A beautiful piece of work like the *Ares* can get under your skin. Maybe you'll grow to love it like your dad did."

Harlow was taken aback at his comment. She fought the heat that was gathering at the backs of her eyes. She hadn't realized how good it would feel to have one of her people tell her they actually understood why she stayed on the ship. "Did you know my father?" Her own voice sounded fragile in her ears, and she hated he had heard it.

"Of course I knew him. He was a good man. We used to talk when he came into the shop." He looked down at his glass and ran a thumb across the condensation. "Listen, if you want to be a part of that ship, don't let any of these bitter people out here make you feel bad. It's your legacy."

"Thank you, Darnell. Truly."

He nodded and tipped his beer toward her as Mike came out of the kitchen. "Time to eat, babe!" Mike called.

"That's a nice batch. Better get over there before it gets cold," Darnell said.

She smiled at him, walked over to the bar, and took her perch in front of the steaming bowl. "Looks good. Thanks."

Mike nodded. "Anytime. It's always here." He turned to meticulously place another glass.

"And I won't forget it," she said softly.

CHAPTER 17

THREAT AND REGRET

Harlow walked down the hallway, marveling at how much her life had changed in the past month. She was startled to see someone she thought might have already been thrown out of an airlock. "Harlow, just the person I was looking for," Aldric said.

"Okay." She didn't like him since his attempt to remove the information from her brain and his lack of concern that followed the scan that caused seizures.

"I was wondering if we might talk for a moment. I'm leaving for good on the next cargo transport tomorrow, and I just wanted to speak with you."

"Sure. Go ahead."

"Could we talk in private?"

"Yeah," she said, not really wanting to go anywhere with the man. Still, he would be gone soon. She followed him into a storage closet.

"My career is over, Harlow."

He stood there as if he were waiting for her to say something or even apologize to him.

"Clearly, that doesn't matter to you," he continued.

"I don't like seeing someone lose their job, but it seems like you don't like being here anyway." She remembered what he'd said about the colony being an "orange shithole."

"True, but I think my work should be respected, and your lover clearly doesn't respect me or the years of service I've put into this vessel."

"If you're referring to the prince, we aren't lovers, and I don't know what—"

"You know 'what.' Everyone on this ship knows *what* you two are. But that won't matter anymore because you are going to do something for me."

"Nope, I don't care for where this is going." Harlow turned to go.

"As I understand it, your little friend Piper has never had any vaccines," Aldric said.

Harlow felt her blood run cold as she turned around slowly. "What?"

"You heard me. Only half of the colonists have been vaccinated. The rest of them have been exposed to very little in the way of polio, flu viruses, you name it." He rattled off exactly where Piper and her mother lived. "I've got vials. You know how many labs I've worked in. I knew one day they would come in handy."

Harlow spoke through clenched teeth. "What do you want?" The thought of the man threatening Piper made her want to rip his head off.

"I just want what I'm owed. Your father refused to acknowledge my work. The prince can't appreciate what I'm trying to do. I want what's in your head. I'm going to shut down this ship, take the prince's personal transport, which means you're going to get me the codes. Last time he went home for a visit, I overheard him telling Carlos that they would have to go get the codes from his room before leaving. I won't be going down for it either. When the prince finds out, you will tell him you were offered more money than you had ever seen in your life, and you will make him believe it. By then, I will have what I need and release the viruses anyway, if you betray me."

"Who injured you to make you such a bastard?"

"Who made you a filthy thief?"

She ignored the question and tried to think her way through this. It wouldn't be the first time she'd had to use her wits to get out of something. If he wanted access to her head that badly then he must have had reason to believe that there was something in there that was very important, but she had no idea what. "How do I know you're even telling the truth?" she asked.

"Go look it up."

"Okay, assuming for a minute this isn't all an elaborate bluff, what could you gain if I said no, and you let the viruses free?"

"You won't. I'm leaving tomorrow night. That will give you time to get what I need from the prince. And don't think of running off to tell your little boyfriend and have him arrest me. I'm not the only one capable of releasing them. The moment my partner hears I'm arrested, you'll start watching people die, and you will know it's your fault. More dead colonists mean less resistance if the Brotherhood shows up, and I can make sure they do. You'll need to get back to me before then. I'll be easy to find."

He walked off without another word, and her mind swirled with confusion and disbelief. She went straight to her room and began researching to see if there had been any theft of serious note from a lab anywhere in the world—and there it was. She'd heard rumors about the missing vials of viruses that were being kept for testing, but it had been so long that she felt it was just a legend for people to scare themselves. But more than one source noted that a research group Aldric had spearheaded just before coming to the *Ares* was rumored to have bought viruses off the black market in order to do unauthorized testing. The authorities cleared Aldric of having any direct participation.

"Shit," Harlow said as she buried her face in her hands.

She knew what had to be done. She had gained the trust of the one man she needed to steal from. Normally, this would have been ideal. Today, it ripped her heart out. He had given her his trust, his friendship, and lately—though she had been trying to deny it, he had been trying to give her his heart. She'd spent the last couple weeks telling herself he was just friendly or sympathetic to her, but after the way he'd held her when she woke up from the last episode of mind melding with the ship, she knew it was too late to call it something other than love. In any relationship she'd been in, there always lurked that feeling of something missing that neither wanted to talk about, that small abyss of lonely behind a carefully concealed and ignored door. When she looked at Jack, there was no empty abyss to fall into. She'd looked for the emptiness between them, hoped for it, so she could get hurt before she got hurt, call it nonsense, and move on, but it wasn't there. Every time she tried to look into the void, she found something real.

And she knew it was likely the first time he'd gotten that close to another woman since his wife died. After he found out she'd betrayed him, there would be no going back to the way things were before. *Fucking universe. Stand me on the edge of heaven before dragging me back to hell. Figures.*

She knew, right now, while she was still the light in his eyes, there was something she could give him. She wanted to give him what she really was, the best she had to offer.

Though it would be sex, it wasn't about sex. Though it would be her body doing the talking, it was really just her heart. For once, she was reaching out and holding nothing back. It was all the sweeter, because she knew it wouldn't last. Something more unsettling than Aldric's contagion threat niggled at the back of her mind. She stared at the door to his quarters and let the answer bubble up from her subconscious. *You're a coward.* It was the first time she'd had something to lose. Something real. As grieved as she was to hurt the man, some small part of her was relieved. Under the best of circumstances, she believed it wouldn't last, anyway. *Jesus! Fatalistic much?*

None of that mattered now. When she'd looked into Aldric's eyes, she saw the cold, the evil. She saw Piper's body and all the others in her generation that hadn't been vaccinated. Even worse, she wouldn't be able to die with them. She'd have to stand by and watch. Her father had her vaccinated before he died.

She knocked on Jack's door.

"Harlow." The smile that stretched across his rugged face was like the sun coming out on a cloudy day.

"Can I come in?"

"Always."

She walked in, and the door closed behind her.

He tilted his head to the side, and she saw concern on his face that made her guilt worse. "Are you okay?" He cupped her cheek gently.

She nodded and turned her face in his hand until her lips pressed against his palm. She closed her eyes and kissed his hand, trailing the tip of her tongue along his palm.

Looking up from heavily lidded eyes, she watched him take a deep breath and wrap his other hand around the back of her head and lean forward until his mouth claimed hers. He'd clearly understood her wordless invitation. He backed her to the wall and placed his arms on either side of her, caging her in.

He bent his knees and rolled his hips under hers until her feet barely touched the floor. Waves of warmth spread through her body before finding the center of her being and sending a welcome clenching as he grabbed her buttocks. She wrapped her legs around his waist, and he pressed himself against her. He wrenched his mouth away from hers just long enough to groan, "I need you."

His words cut through her. She knew he was caught in the same ocean of lust she was, but it was so much more than that. It was the longing to be truly known by another, an ache to give oneself in a type of communion that is rare to find but longed for from the moment anyone took their first breath. She felt in him that same need she felt in herself—a need to let down her guard and trust, if only for a moment, to be truly known and safe. She hadn't believed it was something she needed, just something she wanted to give him, because she felt he was capable of that kind of connection. She'd been sure *she* could live without it—until now.

Oh, God, no. She knew she was in trouble, as surely as the day he had caught her trying to steal the gold out of the core. But this was so much more serious. This time she had caught him stealing her heart, and there was no going back. She wanted him to know her, too. She wanted him to look into her eyes and see her soul. It would've been easier if it were only something she was giving to *him*. "I need you, too," she whispered, and tumbled into the abyss.

He walked them over to his bed and pulled her shirt off and ran his hands lightly over her body, looking at and feeling every inch of her. He held her eyes as he reached a hand into her bra and cupped her breast as he lightly stroked her nipple with his thumb. She didn't dare look away from him. Out of all the things she had done in her life, not looking away from him was the most challenging. He removed his hand and let her pull his shirt off. Her palms caressed his shoulders, feeling his muscles tense and relax beneath them.

The urge to take in his scent was overwhelming. Seizing the initiative, she pulled him down onto the bed. She straddled him and trailed kisses down his neck and chest as she inhaled him. He was intoxicating, masculine like the pine grove in district seven after a good rain. She knew that for the rest of her life she could identify him by scent alone.

He freed her of her bra and unbuckled her pants. His hands had begun to tremble, and she couldn't help but wonder if he had been with anyone since his wife had passed five years ago. She reached down to help him, taking her clothes the rest of the way off. He had no trouble quickly getting out of his own. They lay naked in each other's arms. She felt him take a shaky breath beside her.

"Are you all right?" she asked as she traced a few kisses across his collarbone.

"Just working to control the animal, love." He kissed her fast and hard. "I need to be inside you. But I'd love to hold you for a moment longer." The vulnerability of what he was doing wasn't lost on her. He held her close then reached up and brushed her cheek with the back of his hand. She was beyond mortified to discover that a tear had pooled there. She was thinking so intensely about him that she hadn't considered her own emotions. Perhaps it had been that way for a lifetime—moving forward and ignoring her need for connection. The long-ago mastery of her feelings had been an illusion.

"Damn it," she muttered and swiped angrily at her face.

"Stop," he said as he wrapped his large hands around her wrists and pulled them to either side of her head. He pinned her with his gaze as well. "Don't run from me." His voice was hoarse and heavy with longing.

"I'm not running. I'm right here," she said as she found herself looking at his shoulder instead of his eyes.

"You know what I mean. Belong somewhere. Belong with me."

Look at him. At least do that much for him.

She watched him swallow before speaking again. "I love you." He searched her face and he looked for all the universe like he was holding his breath. She knew the admission had taken something from him, something only she could return. Jack had revealed his heart in all its vulnerability and let her decide whether to bless it or crush it.

"I love you, too, Jack. Always and no matter what. Believe *that*." Her voice caught on the words, and she knew she meant every one of them, though Jack had no idea just how much "no matter what" was going to mean.

Jack kissed her deeply as his hand slid between her thighs. She arched her body and pushed against his hand.

"Take everything," she whispered into his ear.

He groaned and found his way inside her. Her breath caught as she felt him thrust deep.

"Oh, God," she moaned. He was right. In many ways, she still wanted to run from him. He represented all the emotions she wanted to hide from, but she couldn't push him away if she tried. It was too late. She knew she would never be the same—could never go back and pretend she didn't love him.

Wrapping an arm around her lower back and the other under her neck, he held her as he made love to her. She was determined to give him all of her, all that he deserved. She held nothing back.

He took her to a place where all thought, control, and reason left her, and she cried out, grabbed frantically at his back, and became lost in pure sensation. "Jack!" she called, hoping he could catch her as she fell through one unfamiliar emotion after another. A raw, guttural sound escaped his own throat as he emptied himself inside and clung to her.

They both lay in a state of blissful fulfillment.

He rolled off her when she struggled to breathe beneath his weight.

"Better?" he said, smiling as she inhaled deeply, enjoying the mingled scents of their lovemaking.

"Yes, and no. I do like being beneath you." She laughed softly.

"I like you there, too. Although I think I might be happy beneath you as well."

Harlow contemplated the image he was conjuring. "Hmm."

• • •

Before long, Jack was asleep, and she listened to his steady, rhythmic breath and lay there for a while, reveling in what she knew couldn't last. Not after she gave up the secrets in her head and stole from him again. She prayed her dad had put nothing in there that would enable Aldric to take the ship or hurt anyone. Tears poured down her face as she realized this would be the last time she would lie next to this remarkable man. It was the first time in her life she had been in love. It was beautiful, devastating, amazing, and she very much feared, over. Jack had blocked Aldric's access for a reason, and for her to turn around and give Aldric what he wanted...she didn't know if there was any coming back from that.

She crept slowly from his bed, inch by inch, and moved soundlessly as she dressed. The thief in her had learned to fade into a ghost. It wouldn't be the first time she had soundlessly gotten in or out of somewhere with people sleeping or passed out. She crept over to Jack's desk and slid the drawer open. The codes were under a small panel that no one would know to look for, except that Jack had showed her exactly where it was. He'd told her that if something ever happened to him and she needed to escape, she could take his personal transport. He'd *trusted* her. The lump in her throat was threatening to strangle her. She couldn't breathe. She knew she was going to wake him up once she lost control of her emotions. She knew she had to get out of there and fast. All she had to do was wake him up and tell him. Maybe he could help her. *Maybe you're being selfish, and you're going to get half the colony killed because you want to sleep with him again. Stop it.*

She tilted and twisted her hand in the pattern that would activate the chip inside her hand to take photographs. Something else Jack gave her that he would regret. Then she ran her hand across the codes, quietly closed the panel, and left the room without looking back at him. One more glance and she knew she'd sell out half the colony to be in his arms again.

CHAPTER 18

BETRAYAL

The waiting was the worst part. She just wanted to get it over with. Leaving straight from Jack's room, she found Aldric, and it didn't take long. He stood at the end of the hallway. She jumped and gave a soft yelp when she saw him.

"Your father isn't the only one capable of planting chips in your head. I've known where you were for the last two weeks."

"Let's get this over with," she ground out through clenched teeth. The sorrow she'd felt in Jack's room was slowly being replaced by rage. Every kindness Jack had shown her, every touch...not to mention the friendships she'd made with Carlos, Doc, Evelyn, and so many others, was about to be torn from her by this sadistic man.

He led them down to an empty storage room in the basement where there were only two chairs, a personal data storage device, and a man with a scar above his left eyebrow. He looked vaguely familiar and glanced at her when she entered, then turned his attention back to the device that would house all the secrets her father had entrusted her with. She wondered if they would erase what was in her head after they retrieved what they needed or if her dad had arranged it so that it couldn't be erased. She suddenly felt the urge to hold on to whatever was in her mind, as if doing so would help her hold on to her dad.

"How do you know I won't die before you finish?" she asked.

"I know what I'm after, and I think I've figured out how to access it. You shouldn't be online near as long as you were either time before. I've brought some migraine meds with me. I need you coherent enough to give your confession. Sorry, no Rescue Wave. Those things have to be checked out of medical."

Waves of rage washed over her. She'd just buried her father; now she felt as if she were losing him again by giving this bastard information. Before she could think it through, she drove the heel of her palm into his chin, causing his teeth to crack together audibly. As his brain struggled to process what was happening, she grabbed his arm, hooked a foot behind his ankle, and he tumbled to the floor. "You're taking everything from me!" she roared, as she remembered the feel of Jack's body entwined with hers. Now another body grabbed hold of her. Eyebrow Scar restrained her while Aldric scrambled to his feet, yanked her from him, and shoved her against the wall while placing a forearm against her throat.

Despite her formidable fighting skills, she was no match for the bulk of the man when he wasn't surprised. His breath was hot against her skin as he spoke. "Do you have any idea how long I've had to put up with the nauseating hypocrisy of this place? It's something you ought to understand. Something you *did* understand until you allowed yourself to be seduced by that pompous prick." He increased the pressure on her windpipe until she saw stars and the faint image of his teeth pulling the cap off a syringe containing blue liquid. The needle pierced her shoulder, and she slid to the floor.

The familiar ones and zeros flashed behind her eyelids. She lost track of time, and just as the shaking began, she became aware of her surroundings once more. She fought back nausea as she listened to the two men talk and found tears streaming down her face. Aldric didn't seem to notice any of it as he looked at the screen and nodded along with the other man, seeming satisfied with what he had retrieved.

The auxiliary lighting came on. He had taken the ship offline. Thanks to her.

"Are you going to tell him it was her?" Eyebrow Scar asked.

"No, she's going to tell him. We'll be long gone. Right now, he's waking up to find that the ship is offline again. He will look and see that I've gained access, but he won't know how because he locked me out several days ago. He'll eventually see that I've already transferred the credits to Harlow. We're clear, comrade."

"I'm still worried they'll chase us to London and arrest us there. We're the ones who hijacked the system and stole a transport," Eyebrow Scar offered.

"It won't matter what I did or what they think of it. We're not going back to London. I only need to get out of here. I don't need to leave with a clean slate, but I do need for her to look like the thief that she is. All ties between her and Jack need to be severed completely.

Harlow knew she was on the verge of vomiting and couldn't pretend to be unconscious any longer. "Why do you care who um wif?" Her words began slurring as relentless ice picks slammed into her skull. She leaned over and vomited on the floor.

"I don't. You can screw half the crew for all I care, but there are others with a vested interest in keeping you two far apart. Think, Harlow. His family wants him home, not bound to the colonies by a good lay and, for God's sake, not bound by love. The Brotherhood doesn't want you two together either. It ensures the man with balls, firepower, influence, and connections stays on Mars. He's in their way. It endears the colonists to Jack if their thieving savior loves him. I'll help make it easier for you to ditch him: let him know it was me that poisoned him and his family. It wasn't Mikhail."

"What?" As much as she'd disliked him, she had never guessed that. "I don't understand; why would I need to tell him that? Is it even true?" Her voice sounded weak and annoyingly small to her ears. The fight had abandoned her.

"Yeah," he said nonchalantly. "Take these for the headache." He placed two pills into her hand. "I'm getting the hell out of here. And you're telling him to ensure that he won't forgive you. Trust me,

Harlow; I'm doing you a favor. When the Brotherhood arrives, you will do better to be on the side of the people, not the coalition, and certainly not the monarchy. If he even believes there's a chance you're not responsible for this, he'll keep trying to believe in you and it will bind him to the colonies and they to him. The power belongs to the people, and if the people belong to him, the Brotherhood won't suffer him to live. You've become a linchpin. Do you know what happens when you remove a linchpin?"

"Why do you hate me so bad?" She knew it shouldn't matter, but curiosity got the better of her.

"Oh, I don't hate you. Hell, you stole from some pompous fools that walked around here like they were invincible until they found their wallet missing or parts stolen off their transports. You're a valuable tool in the hands of Karma. But someone else does hate you and wants you to hang."

Aldric said nothing more and didn't even glance at her before he and Eyebrow Scar grabbed their equipment and left. Harlow thought about running. She knew that there were many people in the colonies loyal to her who would be more than happy to hide her for however long was needed, but truth be told, she felt she had failed Jack and everyone else for not finding a way around Aldric. Part of her really wanted to suffer for letting them down, and if she ran, Aldric might just drop the viruses anyway. She put her face in her hands and wept for several minutes. She was afraid to face Jack, but every time she thought about squirming out of it, she saw Piper's face and knew she had to follow through.

Harlow wandered down the hallway toward her room, hoping she could lie down for just a moment. She wanted to get Jack's wrath over with, but she kept coming loose at the seams, hovering on the edge of blacking out, and had to hold on to the wall to stay upright. She had almost reached her room when Jack spotted her.

"Harlow? Are you okay?"

"I'm fine," she answered.

"You're not." He picked her up and brought her back to his room. "Where have you been?" he asked.

She stared at him for a long, painful moment before running into the bathroom and vomiting again. The bulk of her migraine meds had come up as well. She wondered if Jack would give her anything for it after he threw her in jail. He sat down on the bathroom floor and wiped her face with a cold cloth but couldn't stay as people were pounding on his door in a panic. They weren't sure what was happening, and some even seemed to think they were under attack.

"I've got to go. Go lie down. I'll be back as soon as I can."

Harlow dragged herself back to the bed.

Jack returned an hour later and sat on the bed next to her. "Aldric hacked the system. What I don't get is how that was even possible. I had him completely locked out. We're still waiting to see if we can even get it back online or if he just disabled it long enough to escape. I was planning on opening an official investigation on him." After a pause, he spoke again. "Have you seen anything strange?"

She thought she heard a slowly building suspicion in his voice but guessed he didn't want to say it. But saying it first was a gift that she could give him, right here, right now; she could let him off the hook in some small way. Her hands shook, and her voice cracked. This was it. There was no coming back from this and no one coming to save her.

"It was more Earth credits than I've ever seen in my life. Aldric just wanted to escape. I knew I could use the money to help the people I've watched suffer for so long. I gave him access to my head."

"No," Jack said. She watched his blurry image as he ran his hands over his face and took a deep breath before looking down at her where she lay curled up. "I don't believe this. He threatened you. Whatever he threatened you with, just tell me. I can help you."

"No, no one can help me now. I'm a thief. You knew that going in." An odd, bittersweet, relief washed over her. It was a familiar skin, but she almost gasped out loud when she realized it didn't fit anymore. Despair unfurled and wrapped its gray wings around her: she couldn't go back to where she was, and now, she couldn't move forward.

She watched Jack kneel beside the bed, take her face into his hands, and look into her eyes. "Please tell me...Please."

Her head spun and the urge to vomit returned. "Don't make this harder than it has to be, Jack." The hurt that painted his face had the power to make her tell the truth. She took a breath to speak, to remove the pain she'd caused him; redemption was a heartbeat away. She knew she had to act quickly before she doomed them all. "You should know he told me he was the one that poisoned you and your family." She saw the very moment he shut down. The very moment he allowed logic to take over and slam the door of his heart. He stood and began talking his way through it.

The anger gave his voice a dangerous edge and made her want to run away. "When I saw you in the hallway. the first thing I thought of was how you looked after those bastards messed with your head, and I actually felt *sorry* for you. Bloody hell, you don't even know if there were things in your head that could be used against your people to destroy the colony. You sold us out, sold me out. Did you mean anything that happened here tonight? Christ, Harlow, did you..." His voice cracked and Harlow felt her heart shattering into thousands of shards, each one stabbing her. "Did you *use* me?"

"No, Jack. I—" She wanted to tell him last night was the best night of her life, that she loved him, but would that get him killed? Aldric seemed to think so.

"Stop talking. You went straight from my bed to conspire with that man. Now he says he killed my wife and daughter. Did you sell me out before or after he told you that? On second thought, don't answer. I don't even want to know. How am I to believe anything else about you? You're behaving like the thief you've always been. How could I have been so fucking stupid?"

"Jack, you're not stupid."

"Shut up. I can't do this. I trusted you, and you made a fool out of me. Get up."

She stood on wobbly legs as he grabbed her arm, and the room spun around her.

With no more words, he marched her back down to the exact cell he'd sent her to the first time he caught her stealing. He left again without a glance back. She sat down on the same cot and felt a numbness wash over her. It had all happened so quickly. Just over an hour ago she had been lying beside the man she loved. Now...nothing, empty.

Half an hour later, Harlow looked up to see AVM Miller's face in her cell door window. She stared at Harlow, moved her mouth as if she were about to say something, then heaved a sigh, turned, and walked away.

Harlow laid back down and began tallying up the losses. The strong, smart, kind, pilot of the *Ares* was lost to her now as well.

Doc showed up not long after Miller had left. "Jack said you were here and needed meds for a headache." He handed her a bottle of water and took out the Rescue Wave, programmed it, and held it at the base of her skull. After the device softly beeped, he set it aside, checked her pulse, and looked into each eye.

She was beyond grateful, but not just for the headache relief. If Jack had sent Doc to take care of her headache, then there must have been something still left for her in his heart.

"He wouldn't tell me why you're in here. Is there any way I can help you, love? You've come to my rescue more than once when Jack was about to oust me. If I can defend you, I will. Just talk to me."

"I wish I could, Doc."

She placed her hands on either side of her head and squeezed to ease the last of the headache.

"Oh, no, Harlow. You gave Aldric access to your brain, didn't you?"

"It doesn't matter anymore. I'm going to die in a Martian prison, and I deserve it. The people in the village think I've betrayed them for coming to live on this ship. My mother has disowned me. Now everyone on the crew will hate me. I have nothing left. This is how it ends for me."

Doc's Irish accent got thicker as he spoke. "I wouldn't be so sure about that, love. You've got me." He placed a hand on her arm. "Call for me if you need me." He started to walk away then stopped and came back. "I almost forgot. I brought you something." He reached into his lab coat and pulled out a wooden rosary and handed it to her.

She took it. "Thanks, but I'm not sure I believe anymore."

"That's okay. He believes in *you*."

KIM CONREY | 143

CHAPTER 19

CRAZY EYES AND WHISKEY

Mother stood by the windowed door of Harlow's cell and watched the young woman sleep with a set of wooden rosary beads clutched in her hand. She could see that one of the staff had slid food under the door. But it had only been picked at, not eaten. She hesitated to wake her. Nearly every thief she'd known had sleeping problems. She guessed it made perfect sense—once you steal enough, you realize how easily it could happen to you. After standing there for another moment, she saw Harlow jerk in her sleep and then open her eyes.

Mother motioned to the guard, who stood a few feet away. He unlocked the door and let her in. The ship was operating on auxiliary power since it had gone offline. The door had to be unlocked manually. Harlow sat up and rubbed her eyes. Mother sat on the cot beside her and placed her hand on her arm. "How are you?"

"I've been better," she said miserably. "But I think Doc must have slipped a something extra in my meds. I finally got some sleep."

Mother laughed. She had known Doc for a long time. She was sure Harlow was right about the sedative.

"Jack isn't well either. He's a wreck." Mother let the comment hang in the air. She wanted Harlow to understand Jack wasn't going about his business as usual. After a moment, she continued, "Is it true?"

Harlow opened her mouth to speak but closed it again. Mother knew well the look of someone who was about to lie to her. She felt pride swelling in her heart when she realized Harlow wasn't going to.

Instead, Harlow asked her a question. "You hear confessions, right? I mean, you can't ever tell anyone what I tell you, correct?"

"I do, and no, I cannot repeat it. If I break the Seal of Confession, they could excommunicate me."

"Would you hear mine?" she asked.

"Of course."

Harlow crossed herself. "Forgive me, Mother. I've sinned. It's been ten years since my last confession. Anyway, I've lied to someone I love."

Mother listened intently. When Harlow finished confessing, she prayed her Act of Contrition. Mother absolved her. "It's okay. It wasn't your fault. It was an impossible choice. You did the best you could."

"It doesn't matter now. Jack thinks I betrayed him. He hates me."

"No, he doesn't. He's just scared. I got the feeling there was more between the two of you than just friendship." And after Harlow's confession, which included several revelations, she didn't have to guess about any of it.

"Yes, but it's over now," Harlow sniffed and swiped at her nose.

"The truth has a way of finding its way into the light."

"But I can never tell it; no one can, or these people might die," she argued.

"You know the world isn't always all on your shoulders," Mother said.

"No, just at the moment, right?"

"Well, maybe. Yes." Mother reached up and pulled Harlow's head onto her shoulder and she leaned her head onto Harlow's as they sat in silence for a moment. She took Harlow's hand in hers before speaking again, noting the cold fingers that trembled in her grasp. Her next words wouldn't help, and she knew it. "Jack had something he wanted me to tell you. In a few days, there's a huge shipment of raw materials headed to London—engineering thinks they can get the ship back online. Jack has decided you will be extradited for trial then. He doesn't want you in the Bastille. There's a female penitentiary in London where you should receive decent treatment. If you'd like, I can arrange to go to London with you."

"Yes, I would like that," Harlow said. Her voice cracked as she continued to speak. "So, I won't be on the same planet as Jack anymore."

"Well, he's going, too. He's, um, the one filing charges against you."

"Oh."

She felt a tremble go through Harlow's body, and it made her want to cry for her. "It's going to be okay, Harlow. I promise."

"No, it can't. It will never be okay again."

"You're not alone," Mother said as she sat up and drew the sign of the cross on Harlow's forehead.

Mother hesitated before she spoke again. She wasn't sure how Harlow would react to her next question. "Would you like for me to arrange passage for your mother to come with us?"

"No," Harlow said quickly.

"I understand." Mother stood and moved toward the door. "If you need me, please don't hesitate to ask for me."

"I will. Thank you."

"You're welcome. And Harlow, no matter what, I want you to know that I'm so proud of you."

The irony of the situation wasn't lost on Mother: a holy woman came to tell a lifelong thief she was proud of her. It was an unexpected beauty—the holiest of things usually were.

Mother went to find Jack. No one seemed to know where he was. Finally, she found Carlos. He looked around as if cornered and trying to plan an escape, but they were in a hallway with no doors on either side.

She narrowed her eyes before speaking. "Have you seen my nephew?"

Carlos exhaled in what she could only interpret as resignation. She knew at that moment Jack was hiding.

"Maybe you *should* talk to him. He's in that little space to the north of the ship, in the goat pen."

"Don't worry. I won't tell him you told me."

"I'd appreciate that, Mother. Thank you. By the way, is Harlow okay?"

"No. Is my nephew okay?" She had only seen Jack in passing when she had come on board that morning. He had quickly told her what happened and asked her to give Harlow the message about the trial and avoided further conversation with his aunt. He had practically run from her.

"Honestly, no," Carlos replied. "She really disappointed us all. I thought she was my friend, too."

"She still is, Carlos. Don't give up on her. There may be things about this you don't yet understand."

"With respect, Mother, I'm not sure what there is to understand. She admitted what she did. No one is guessing here."

"Dig deeper, Carlos." Mother turned to go without another word. This was the first time she had felt the full weight of her calling pressing down on her, hurting her. She was the only one who knew the truth, and there wasn't a damn thing she could do about it. She felt every bit as stuck as Harlow.

Jack was exactly where Carlos had said. She started to go to him but hesitated and stayed behind the old shed. He was normally very perceptive and knew when anyone approached, but she suspected he was a little inebriated. He was a sorry sight: a prince sitting on top of an old carbon fiber picnic table with a bottle of whiskey—talking to a goat. His vulnerable moments were so few, and she wanted to understand this strange new light she was seeing him in.

Jack looked at the goat. "Stop staring at me, asshole."

The goat kept staring with horizontal pupils and a sideways chew.

Jack took another swig straight from the bottle. "Your eyes are weird."

"Mehhhh," the goat said, as if it understood and didn't appreciate the remark.

A scratchy male voice came from just over the fence on the far opposite side from where Mother stood. She stepped back a little deeper into the shadows but didn't leave. Her curiosity was getting the best of her.

"Stop picking on the damn goat. What did he ever do to you?"

Jack turned around to see who the Irish accent belonged to.

The man jumped the gate without being invited.

"Private property, Irish," the prince said.

"Whatever, English wanker. You're talking to a damn goat," Mike O'Malley said.

Jack spoke with a touch of sarcasm. "O'Malley, the unofficial mayor of our little hamlet."

With no warning, Mike punched Jack in the face. His head snapped back, and blood trickled from his nose, but he didn't fight back. He just stared at Mike.

"Well, that was not nearly as satisfying as I'd thought it would be. I had pictured more sprawling and begging for your life and such. I should've gotten here earlier." Mike surveyed the bottle in Jack's hand, then leaned over to get a closer look at his face. Jack swayed slightly. "You're proper pissed. Aren't ya, mate?" He gave a wry laugh, reached over, took the bottle from Jack, and turned it up before sitting down next to him on top of the table.

Mike passed the bottle back to Jack, who took another deep pull. "I've run a bar long enough to know sad drinking, lonely drinking, angry drinking, or guilty drinking. You're doing it all."

Jack didn't disagree but lifted the bottle at Mike in salute.

"You know, I always hated your arse. Thought you had a lot of nerve to be screwing around in that giant fecking piece of shite, but, when I heard Harlow had gone to work for you...well, I hated you even more, but *then*," he held up a finger for emphasis, "I thought that if Harlow trusted you, there must be something worthy in you I wasn't seeing. And this morning I hear that you've locked her up and are going to send her to London for trial. Listen, I don't even have to know what she did. All I know is that whatever it was, she had a good reason and now you're throwing her to the wolves."

Jack said nothing.

Mike hopped down off the table and stood in front of Jack.

"She came to see me, you know. She never told me so directly, but I knew when she started defending you, telling me how I was wrong about you, I knew she had fallen in love with you. Do you have any idea what I would give to have her look at me that way? And you don't even care."

"Mike, I love her."

"Prove it." He took the bottle from Jack once more, turned it up one last time, then jumped back over the fence and headed toward his pub.

Mother dangled a tissue in Jack's line of sight. "Here," she said. "You're bleeding. Take it."

He took the tissue from his aunt and dabbed at his nose.

"Huh." His eyes fell on the bloom of red across the tissue. "I sure am." Jack touched his nose and grimaced. "That wiry little bastard is stronger than he looks. Got some stones, too. He doesn't give a shite who I am." Jack laughed.

"It's a good thing you're heading to London along with us. These people are devoted to Harlow. I'm seriously worried for you."

"Everyone seems to be ignoring the fact that she sold me out for money. She admitted it to my face. The credits are already deposited in her account."

"Things aren't always what they seem, Jack."

"Then how are they, Mother?"

"Show mercy. Have faith."

"I can't live my life worrying about the next time she betrays me. I loved her, and she broke my heart. I'm not guessing here. She looked me in the eye and told me exactly what she did and why she did it. She's a thief. I thought that I could change that. I was stupid to believe such a thing."

Frustration washed over her. She loved her vocation, but today, it just plain sucked. "Scoot over and hand me the bottle, nephew."

He handed it to her, and it made a burning trail down her throat as she drank.

They both sat there watching a goat chew grass and stare at them...accusingly.

CHAPTER 20

LONDON

It had been over a month since she'd seen Jack, since she'd betrayed him. They had all been in London for five days. Harlow sat on her cot and remembered the last time Jack had thrown her in jail. She had thought little about him except that he was just another asshole government official fulfilling his dream while standing on the shoulders of the people whose backs he was slowly breaking.

She couldn't say that now. She knew how much he cared, and she had broken his heart. Thoroughly. Completely. There would be no going back. She put her head in her hands and cried, not caring who heard, not caring if she embarrassed herself. For the first time in her life, she didn't care who saw her broken. That's exactly what she was, and nothing could change that. She didn't *want* anything to change that. The pain over breaking his heart deserved nothing less than the opportunity to wreck her. It didn't matter why she had stolen from him. She should have found a better way. She knew she couldn't feel any worse. There would never be a way to feel any worse. She had hurt the man she loved beyond repair.

She almost didn't hear the old metal door open over her sobbing. Looking up through up through blurry eyes, she saw Jack there with his arms crossed over his chest. He observed her without emotion.

If he bore the same pain she did, he carefully disguised it behind a chilling mix of nothingness and rage, playing just about the edges and coiling about her like oily ropes.

She wiped at her eyes with her shirtsleeve, knowing there was no way to pretend she hadn't been crying.

He spoke. "According to the physical exam you had upon entering this facility, you are pregnant. Your hormone levels suggest it happened while you and I were together. Therefore, I assume this is my child."

"I...I didn't know I was." Harlow quickly did the math in her head. "I'm late," she said as the hurricane of it all slammed into her. "Jesus Christ," she whispered.

"Hmm, yes," Jack said, wryly.

Harlow put her hands over her mouth and stared at Jack's chest, unable to drag her eyes up any farther.

"For your crimes, you will be spending a significant amount of your life in jail. Obviously, I won't have my child raised in prison, or by a criminal. I'll be notified when you go into labor, and I will come get him or her. We can arrange visits, if you wish."

Harlow wrapped her arms around her midsection. "Jack. Please."

"Don't," he said in a deadly tone. "Just don't." He turned to go but paused by the door. "Have you considered that you didn't just let me down, but you let your father down, too? Christ, Harlow. He had so much faith in you he put secrets in your head that might help millions of people and you just gave it all away."

"You don't understand."

"No, I don't." He abruptly left without waiting for more. The pit of despair she'd been lying in since betraying Jack now crumbled beneath her, and she began free falling through levels of pain previously unfathomable. She reached into her back pocket and took out the small, smooth paper encased in flexmat—one of the few things they'd allowed her to bring into the prison—and read it again: *The deeper that sorrow carves into your being, the more joy you can contain.* When Mother gave her the quote as a child, she'd told her one day she would understand it. Only part of it made sense. When life was done carving her, she couldn't imagine there would be anything left, much less a container for joy.

. . .

Later that afternoon, Harlow was allowed into the courtyard. The beige dust that swirled about her ankles felt foreign. She missed the rusty orange regolith of home and feared she'd never see it again. She sat down on one of the benches along the concrete wall and leaned her head against it as the sunlight washed over her. For a moment, she allowed herself the luxury of forgetting that anything had changed. Her mind went back to the one night she and Jack shared. Trying to push it from her thoughts was a battle that had left her mentally exhausted—a war she no longer cared to wage.

The way he had touched her was gentle and fierce all at once. Though fertility was lower on Mars, she'd known she might end up pregnant but pushed it from her mind. *Why?* Maybe after years of defending the gates to her heart, she'd thrown down her sword and surrendered absolutely everything and pregnancy was the result. *Or you're romanticizing your stupidity.* She considered for a moment whether she would take it back if she'd had it to do all over again. She smiled sadly as the answer came to her: no.

Jack would be a wonderful father. There was no doubt he would guard their child with his life, but she wouldn't be there. She had hoped she was done with the ridiculous sobbing, but now she realized she would never be done.

She was shaken from her thoughts when chanting or yelling came from outside the prison walls. Prison riot was her first thought, but it wasn't coming from inside. Listening closer, she picked out her name, chanted repeatedly. She held onto it like a lifeline. They could only be the dozen miners who had come from the village with the ship to unload. Her people hadn't forgotten about her. She'd assumed they were done with her when word got out that she worked for the prince, and by now she was sure many of them knew their relationship went much further than that, but here they were, hoping she could hear them through the walls.

"I hear you," she whispered. A small smile broke through the mask of grief she'd worn for the last month. It had been so long that it felt strange as it rearranged the angles of her face.

. . .

Harlow picked up the piece of bread from her tray and tried chewing a bite, but it had no taste. If it weren't for the baby, she wouldn't bother. She made it halfway through the bread before her gagging started again. The guard called into her cell that she had a visitor; she was grateful for the distraction.

A gasp escaped her throat as her mother walked in.

"Mom?" Harlow was shocked to see her. "How did you even get here?"

"Mike arranged it. He knows people."

Harlow nodded. "Have you come to tell me, 'I told you so'?" She was in no mood for her mother to spew more bitterness at her over Jack, the ship, or anything else.

"No. I've come to tell you I'm sorry."

Judith looked at her in a way she hadn't since she was a child; it softened the lines around her eyes. She looked younger, maybe even vulnerable. Harlow stared but said nothing.

"I know what it is to be in love," she said quietly. "I never told you, but when I met your father, I was very close to graduating from nursing school."

"You told me you always wanted to be a nurse, but I didn't know you pursued it."

"Yes. I was almost done." Judith walked over to Harlow's cot to sit beside her. Guests were allowed to enter the cell with her; she didn't know if this was because it was a minimum-security women's prison or if Jack had arranged it to protect his family from scandal, but Harlow didn't want to have to go to one of the bright rooms upstairs and feel exposed. The darkness had become an oddly comforting cloak she wrapped around her.

Judith continued. "I was working at a bar near the Air Force Academy when I met your dad. I took one look at that man, and I was...lost, I guess you'd say. For the first time in my life, I felt that when someone looked at me, they actually saw me. *Really* saw me. It's hard to explain, you know?"

"I do know," Harlow said in a small voice, thinking of Jack.

"I hate Jack for what he's doing to you, but I don't hate you. You fell in love with the wrong man. I get that."

Harlow felt sick at her mother's words. She'd never thought of Jack as *the wrong man,* but she was sitting in jail, so maybe Judith was right.

"Was...Dad the wrong man?" Harlow held her breath as she waited for her mother to answer. Judith had just told her she'd loved her father, but Harlow still couldn't handle her saying that her time with him had been a mistake.

"No, baby. He was the right man. I don't regret a minute I spent loving him. I didn't give up anything that he didn't give me back a thousand times over. He was the love of my life."

Harlow said, "It just felt like you...I mean you were never sad, just angry. I wondered if you missed him. If there was something wrong with me for missing him so much, when you just moved on."

"I didn't move on. I lay in bed listening for the door to open. I always hoped..."

"I did, too. Why wouldn't you tell me? Why couldn't you just talk to me?"

"I'm sorry. I thought I was helping you. I thought if you knew I was hurting, you would feel like you couldn't count on me to be strong for you."

Harlow knew it didn't matter now but felt that if she didn't say it now, she never would. "I was alone, Mom."

Judith turned to her and did something that shocked Harlow to her core. She wrapped her in a hug. "I'm sorry. I'm going to fix this, baby. I will find a way. I won't give up on you. You know I can be a real pain in the ass when I want to, right?"

"I've noticed."

"Someone else is about to notice, too," Judith said in a tone that almost made Harlow shiver.

"Mom?"

"Yeah, baby?"

"Jack isn't a horrible man. He's just hurt."

She felt her mom stiffen at her words, but to her credit, she said nothing.

Harlow pulled back from the hug and braced herself for the next revelation. "Besides, you're going to have to get along with him. He will raise your grandchild, and I would imagine you will want to see him or her."

Her mother pulled away from her and studied her face. "You're pregnant?"

Harlow couldn't answer past the lump in her throat. She simply nodded.

She took Harlow's face into both her hands and looked her in the eye. "I will fix this for you, somehow. I mean it."

Her mother's hands felt warm on her cold face. Harlow didn't know that she could "fix it," but she believed her when she said she would try.

And that was all that mattered.

· · ·

Harlow had been dry heaving all morning by the time she got in the transport to be taken to trial. Dark smudges ringed her bloodshot eyes. She'd waited through two weeks of agony for her trial date, but according to Jack and her lawyer, her fate was decided. She had given up secrets, knowingly, and it was treason pure and simple. So why did she need to wait two weeks to start living out the rest of her miserable life?

She couldn't eat due to the stress and hormonal nausea that was getting worse by the day. The doctor in the women's prison had chided her about eating, but almost everything came back up. After she'd lost several pounds, the doctor had eventually put in an IV with a constant drip of medication, but the one thing he didn't have was a cure for heartbreak. She couldn't taste anything that she managed to keep down. Life had taken on a meaninglessness that she couldn't contend with. Jack had been a stone wall the last time she had seen him—the day he had told her she was pregnant. He hadn't been back since. It was over. Everything was over.

CHAPTER 21

FATHER ILLUSION

Jack sat in his father's office and watched the tiny dust motes illuminated by rays of light slanting in through the heavy, velvet drapes open to the afternoon sun. He and his aunt were staying at the palace during the trial. His parents had been away, by design, until this morning. He hadn't bothered to eat breakfast after he had woken with what felt like a hangover, though he hadn't had a drop of liquor the night before. He had barely slept all night and nearly choked on lunch. This meeting would not make things any better.

His father faced him and leaned his backside against the huge walnut desk with his arms across his chest as he stared his son down—a power move. He'd done it himself, many times. Now he saw himself through the mirror of his father. *O'Malley was right. I am a wanker.*

"We considered not returning until the trial was over, but your mother wanted to see you. It's admirable of her. To be truthful, I didn't wish to return until all of this had passed. Had we known of the latest news, we would have stayed away," the king said, referring to the pregnancy.

"I'll get a hotel room," Jack said.

"Now you're just being spiteful."

He marveled that his father thought he was playing games. Jack felt stripped to the core. There was nothing left in him that might be capable of games or double speak. Playing games indicated someone who had something to lose—he had nothing left. Joy, sunlight, meaning...love had entered his life and been snatched from him almost immediately. What anyone saw of him right now was what they got. His father was just too blind to see it, to see *him*.

He was hurting, and it might have been nice to have the kind of father he could talk to. That wasn't to be. It made him feel sympathy for Harlow, as he thought of Judith and how cold she could be. No, he wouldn't go there. He had no sympathy for Harlow. If he'd had any, he never would have left her slumped over in tears in that dark cell. He should have been glad to know he hurt her. He wasn't. The whole thing was just one ache after another.

Jack said, "I simply mean that I will leave if you wish me to—if it makes things easier on the family."

"The time for making things easier on the family has passed, James. Besides, if you leave now, it looks as if we have kicked you out. That might reflect poorly on us. If we let you stay, it looks as if we are united, nevertheless, the stain remains either way."

"Good, Lord. I thought I couldn't possibly be more exhausted," Jack said.

If observing from another place and time, he knew the conversation might be comical. He wondered if his father knew his own mind. He only made decisions in terms of how others might react to them. At what point did he lose touch with his own thoughts all together?

"The life of a servant is not his own. I belong to the people and must view my decisions through their eyes. You may as well learn now, that is how it is to be king. 'Heavy hangs the head that wears the crown,' my son."

"You assume I wish to wear it."

"You're exhausted and don't know what you are saying. That woman deceived you. You were lonely and isolated. She took advantage of you. It happens. You've learned your lesson. Now you can move on. This unpleasantness will pass. Besides, there is no actual evidence that this child is even yours."

"It's mine," Jack said with certainty.

"You can't possibly know that for sure."

Jack thought of their night together, how he'd held her, touched her. He felt his throat go tight. If he really believed she had deceived him in other ways, then his father had a point. Yet, in his heart, he knew. "I know it for sure."

The king exhaled, loudly. "This is all still fresh for you. Later, when the trial is over and you've had some rest, you will see a little more reason, and then you can submit the child to a paternity test. As much as this all hurts, it is for the best. It's so much better for you that you found out exactly what she was before this thing went any further. This is what happens when you aren't discerning—when you don't act with your people in mind."

It shocked Jack that his first instinct was to defend Harlow. He knew the last thing he wanted to do was allow his father to judge her—guilty or not. "I don't want to discuss this any further with you," Jack said.

The large room began to feel stifling and small. He wanted to run, find fresh air—to look out across the Martian landscape and breathe in the sense of freedom he loved. Jack looked up at his father to find his lips pressed into a thin line and a vein protruding by his temple.

"*You* don't wish to discuss it any further! I don't wish to discuss it at all! James, we expected better from you. There are plenty of women that could satisfy your bodily needs and keep it completely confidential. Hell, I could provide you with their contact codes if you wish."

Jack's head swam with the implications of what he was hearing. Was his father telling him he had been seeing other women for sex? It sounded like it. Only time away from the façade had made him able to see it. He felt bile rise in his throat. "Father, have you been..." Jack didn't even want to complete the sentence.

"Oh, please. You've been sleeping with that common thief!"

He realized he had made the same assumptions that any young man made about their father—until they learned better. How did he miss it? The ugly truth stood front and center at a time when he wished, more than anything, to come home and find the illusion. The rose-colored glasses weren't just off; they were stepped on, ground into the carpet, and could never be repaired. But now wasn't the time to dig into any of that, if ever. So he did what most would do in such a situation: he changed the subject.

"Have you spoken with Aunt Mary?" He knew his father and sister had never been close. The king, Mary's brother, had not been baptized Catholic since he could not wear the crown if he were. The 1701 Act of Settlement stated that Catholics could never take the throne. The act had not been overturned. Aunt Mary had made it no secret that she felt her brother should work to overturn such a blatant religious prejudice. They had argued about it more than once. But Jack had come to see there was more than religion separating the two. They were as different as siblings could possibly be.

"Yes, I spoke with her on the way in. She seems to believe she is your personal guardian—that it's her job to tell me how I should respond to my own son. Just because the Pope has jurisdiction over her uterus doesn't mean she has a right to claim one of my children."

"She's a sweet woman. We've spent a lot of time together. She's just trying to help."

"And we haven't? We've begged you to come home, for years."

"I realize that."

"She is also defending the woman who betrayed you. She won't tolerate me saying anything negative about this—what's her name?"

"Harlow, it's Harlow." Even saying her name sent daggers into his chest.

"I think she may just be taking up for her because she's also a Catholic. They tend to stick together."

"She knew Harlow when she was a little girl," Jack said. His voice sounded hollow and distant, even to his own ears.

His father studied him.

"You look pale. Go get some sleep."

Jack started to argue that he was thirty-three years old; he didn't need his father telling him how to live his life or giving him a list of women who would discreetly shag him whenever he got horny, but the fight had left him.

"You're right, Father," Jack said.

He rose to leave without looking at the man.

• • • • • • •

Jack stepped into the hall and shut the door as a wave of fatigue washed over him.

"Jack?"

He turned to see his brother, Marcus, looking at him with sympathy.

"You spoke to Father then?"

"Is it that obvious?" Jack said with a broken laugh.

"It is. You look positively knackered. He has that effect on people." Marcus paused. "You had everything. What were you thinking?"

Jack hesitated as he tried to process what his brother was trying to say. His first thought was of Harlow and the freedom he had experienced in the colonies, but he realized his brother was likely talking about the throne and his parent's approval. He said nothing.

Marcus thrust his fists into his pockets and traced a pattern on the carpet with the tip of his shoe before speaking again. Jack suddenly thought his brother looked much younger than just four years his junior. "Is...was it worth it? I mean, *if* you loved her, that is."

Though his heart remained heavy with pain and betrayal, he didn't have to take any time to contemplate his answer. "Yes, it was worth it."

Marcus nodded. "That's what I thought you would say."

Jack was having one of those rare moments where he realized that someone seemed to know something about him that he hadn't yet figured out himself. "Why? What made you think I would say that? *I* wasn't even sure until just now."

Marcus gave his brother a sad smile. "I knew because you're not a coward. You never have been."

Jack didn't know how to answer that. His first thought was to sift through the words as he always had, find out what his little brother needed to hear, and say exactly that, but for once, he was too exhausted and beaten.

Jack scratched at his chin and the stubble he hadn't bothered to get rid of that morning. "Thank you, Marcus."

Marcus nodded. "You look like hell, Jack. Go get some sleep. I'll walk you down."

The two walked down the hallway together in silence.

CHAPTER 22

UNVEILING

Mother reached up with shaking hands to remove the veil from her head. She looked into the mirror. Long, wavy gray hair fell about her shoulders. She'd seen herself without the veil before, but this time, it wouldn't be back. Panic washed over her as a sob escaped her throat. "Who are you?" she whispered to the image, gazing back at her. A trembling hand rose to cover her mouth.

Had the seven decades of confidence she'd proudly cultivated been so fragile that they'd be stripped away the moment she became just Mary again? Had she been hiding behind the covering? She'd asked every woman wishing to join her order if she was attempting to hide—always telling them not to join if they were running away from something. "You run *to* your calling, not *away* from something else," she'd repeated to women for decades. Now she had the urge to cover her head and cling to the notion that keeping the Seal of Confession was her duty when her heart told her, at least in this instance, it was selfish.

Have your identity crisis later. This isn't about you. She had tried repeatedly to get Jack to speak with Harlow. He wouldn't budge. He stayed in his room by himself, or he spent hours in the centuries-old chapel just staring at the sunshine filtering through the stained glass. He'd lost weight *and* the light in his eyes.

A hologram appeared in front of her, snapping her out of her reverie.

She spoke to the image. "Yes?"

"His Highness will meet you in the transport below."

Shaky fingers opened the door as she took a deep breath and walked out to have a serious conversation with Jack before they reached the courthouse. She knew what had finally caused her to come to this decision between the church's law and her own judgment. At their last visit together in the women's prison, Harlow had told her she didn't mind going to trial because she would at least get to be in the same room as Jack—even if he despised her. That was true love—a kind of love she had never experienced herself, and didn't it deserve to be protected and defended at all costs? What did it mean to serve God? To uphold man-made dogma at the expense of her own conscience? She'd lived long enough to understand there were higher laws and deeper truths.

Ultimately, she wondered if her whole life had been leading up to this—choosing love, but not for herself. The irony was that she had to *sacrifice* her life of sacrifice. That sounded oddly correct to her.

As she walked through the house, the servants who usually went about their business without interference or comment stopped what they were doing and looked up at the gray hair they'd never seen before. Apparently remembering themselves a mere second later, they suddenly had work of the utmost importance to focus on. She felt the air on her neck and the slight friction of her hair against her skin. Foreign to her. Part of her wanted to run back to the room and cover it up, but this was an act of courage. It wasn't supposed to be comfortable or easy. She wondered how many times she'd given such council to the women new to the convent. The habit was an act of courage for them—now it flowed back to her in reverse. Finally, she stood in front of the sleek hovercraft and saw her image in the tinted glass. A wry smile crossed her face. *They both ran on shite. No, you run on courage. Just like Harlow did.* Giving up the head covering had been symbolic; breaking the Seal of Confession was the irrevocable step. It couldn't be undone. This was the true crossing of the Rubicon. She exhaled as the driver approached her.

He greeted her formally, glanced at her hair and quickly away, then leaned over to open the door for her, and she slid into the seat opposite Jack. Before he closed the door, she looked up at the driver and spoke: "Please give us a few minutes before leaving." The man nodded and stood just outside. No one else would be coming along. Jack's parents and brother had made it clear that it would be unseemly for them to do so. She was thankful they were alone for this.

Jack looked up at his aunt in shock. Even though he was family, he had never seen her head uncovered before, ever.

"Mother—" he began.

"No, it's just Aunt Mary now." Her heart pounded in her ears as she spoke. "After what I'm about to say...I will have broken my vow."

"I don't understand," he said.

"I heard Harlow's confession on Mars. She was thoroughly blackmailed into what she did. Aldric has several viruses in his possession for which the colonists have no protection. He threatened to kill the little girl from the village, Piper, and everyone else on Mars who hadn't been vaccinated—which is most of them. He demanded Harlow give up the secrets in her head and take blame for the theft. If she didn't, he swore he would release all manner of disease on these first-generation Mars children. They would all die. She had no choice and never received any money for it. She loves you. She didn't betray you."

Mary watched the color drain from his tanned face before he lowered his head into his hands. "Oh, God. I could've been a better man. I could have believed in her, regardless. You had to break your vow to tell me. Jesus. I sent her to jail."

Her nephew seemed at a loss for words as he looked away from her, out the window. She watched him take a deep, shuddering breath. "I was so cold the last time I saw her. She may not forgive me."

"Jack, I *know* she will, but we have another problem. You can't tell this truth. Aldric could still poison those people if she breaks her word. I don't see how she can avoid jail, but at least you can go to her and tell her you still love her. I kept this to myself for far too long, believing that there was no sense in breaking my vow over it since we couldn't tell anyone about it anyway, but...I was a coward. It did matter all this time. I think Harlow would be okay, even behind bars, if she only knew you didn't despise her. And that is something you *can* do for her. Even if you can't tell the world she's innocent."

"No, I've got to do better than that, and I will. But what I don't understand is why that minging piece of shite would need her to take the blame for selling me out? Why would it matter if she took the blame or not? He would have been long gone by the time she told me anyway; and if he gets caught, he already has enough charges against him to send him to jail. There seems to be no point in making Harlow suffer for it."

"I've been wondering that myself. The only thing I can figure is that he or someone else wanted you to turn on her. It could start a riot or even a revolution. Her people love her and are on the verge of rioting now. I've honestly been wondering how you can return there without her. I fear for you and your crew. Maybe Aldric and whoever he's in league with wanted the colonies torn apart so that they could just move in and take over. Crucifying their hero could do exactly that."

Jack suddenly looked up at her as a sickening and profound revelation hit him.

"Bloody hell! Aldric is working for the Brotherhood. They want to rip the colonies apart from the inside, and then move right in." Jack said.

"It's possible or maybe he wanted to keep it a secret that he has the viruses?"

"I'm thinking both, but he can't poison those people if he's dead," Jack said.

"You don't know where he went," she argued.

"People always leave a trail somewhere. I'll find him," he said with certainty. "I don't think I will be able to get to Harlow before the trial though; there's not enough time. My God, how do I face her?"

She shook her head. "I don't know, love, but if we don't get going, we're going to be late, and I need for her to see me there." She reached up and touched her hair and then leaned over to give his hand a quick squeeze. "When she sees me, she'll know."

CHAPTER 23

BORED BARRISTERS

When Jack and Mary arrived for the trial, they were taken to a side entrance for security, but it didn't matter. People were running around the building to get to them. Jack's personal guard had arrived moments before and stood between Jack and Mary. But one person in particular would not be denied—a red-haired, green-eyed woman, with fire in her eyes, screaming threats at Jack.

"Shite," Jack whispered. "Harlow's mother." He had hoped it would be too difficult for her to find transport off Mars.

"You can head on in," Jack said to his Aunt Mary. "This won't be pretty."

Mary put her hand on his arm. "No, I'll stay. I know her."

He started to tell her he was thirty-three and didn't need a caretaker, but given the way he was feeling right now, he certainly wouldn't turn her down.

Evelyn tried to stop Judith, but she jerked free. Carlos rushed forward to help Evelyn restrain her.

Jack exhaled in resignation. "Let her go."

They looked at him as if he had lost his mind and seemed a little afraid of Judith themselves, but after what he had just learned, Jack felt he deserved whatever she intended to throw at him.

The second the guards let her go, she rushed at Jack and slapped him across the face, hard.

"Judith!" Mary said as she took a step toward her, but Jack held out his arm.

"It's okay," he said to Mary.

"Mother?"

Jack saw Judith looking at Mary's long, gray hair with questions written in her eyes before turning her attention back to Jack. He knew the reprieve wouldn't last. "How could you do this to my baby? Did you even bother to ask her why she did it? Did you consider another possibility?"

Jack was silent. He didn't like Judith after what he had heard her saying to Harlow when they had gone to tell her she was coming to work on the ship, but this was her mother and what she was saying now actually *was* true.

"You're right," he said softly.

He watched as Judith's eyes grew wide. She opened her mouth as if to speak again, then closed it, straightened her clothing, and folded her arms across her chest. "Well, fine then. How are you going to fix this? You took her from me, then threw her into prison. You're responsible. That's my daughter in there *and* my grandchild. *Fix this!*" she commanded. Despite the hard slap, he sensed there was still a world of anger waiting to snap him in two.

Jack swallowed hard before answering, but still looked her in the eye. "I will. I promise."

He turned to go inside but felt Judith's eyes boring into his back as he entered the building.

Security ushered Jack and Mary through a side door and past Harlow and her barrister, looking formally grim in his robe and short wig. He paid no attention to his client. Jack knew his parents made sure Harlow's representation was a mere formality. In his anger, he'd not said a word to ensure she got a decent barrister. Harlow sat beside the man, looking resigned to her fate. She looked gaunt and pale in the stark contrast of limp, raven hair that fell about her face. Look at me, please, Jack thought. He paused, hoping to will her eyes his way, as they were too far for her to hear him if he spoke, but felt the guard's gentle push toward their seats as the judge entered the room.

Minutes later, Harlow answered the same damning questions over again. As he looked at her, his chest ached so much that he had to take a deep breath to keep his emotions in check. She looked down at her lap as she spoke. All the reports back from the prison had informed him that her health was getting worse by the day. Despite his demands that she be forced to eat, she still had gained no weight. His arms ached to be around her, to take away the grief and despair that this whole bloody situation had put her in.

Mary sat beside him, and he wondered if Harlow had noticed she wasn't wearing her habit. Would Harlow even know what that meant? He thought she might, if she would just look at them.

Though he hoped they would get Harlow off the stand quickly, it seemed to drag on, or perhaps it was only a reflection of his guilt. He knew he would be next to testify. His plan was to tell them he'd learned new information and would need time to consult with council. All he could do at this point was buy enough time to find Aldric and figure out where the viruses were stashed. Even if Aldric were dead, he knew the Brotherhood could disperse it anyway. He also knew anyone would crack under enough pressure, and he planned on "pressuring" Aldric until the bastard would do or say anything to make it stop. Aldric would tell him where the viruses were, or he would rip his nuts off. He felt his hands clench into fists as he thought of taking the man apart. Of course, Harlow would still be stuck in prison, but he knew he could go to her and explain what was happening. Best of all, he could tell her he loved her and beg her forgiveness.

His white-knuckle grip was threatening to break the bench he sat on as he listened to her tell the same lie all over again about how she sold him out. It made him sick that they forced her to lie. She was giving up her entire future to save the people she loved. He knew in his heart she wouldn't betray him, but he had been afraid of being hurt.

His thoughts were interrupted by the building shifting beneath them. Only a beat later, a giant blast tore into the east side of the courtroom.

Rubble rained down from the ceiling, and Jack's ears rang, blocking out all sounds. It took a second to process what was happening. After making sure Mary was unhurt, he had only one thought in mind. *Harlow,* his mind screamed as the nightmare of losing Maggie and his unborn child came rushing back to him. He shoved the debris and stepped over the unconscious and dead. Wind blew in through the massive hole in the wall, and men dressed in black with ski masks pulled down over their faces came pouring in. A quick glance back found Evelyn rising from the debris like an avenging wraith, a look of fierce determination visible beneath the coating of dust that cloaked her like war paint. She screamed without a sound to Jack's still ringing ears as she fired her pulse weapon at the intruders.

There were still chairs, people, and chunks of wall blocking Jack's way to Harlow. He felt as if everything were in slow motion as he tried to reach her. Nausea washed over him at the thought she might have been killed in the explosion. Horrific images assaulted his mind. What if he looked behind the witness stand to find her mangled body? Relief washed over him when she rose from behind the stand, remarkably intact—by design, he began to suspect.

They locked eyes as she left the safety of the stand and moved toward him. Harlow appeared unharmed, but blood kept seeping into Jack's eye from an open wound on his forehead. He noticed she was looking him over as if worried about him. He wiped the blood from his brow, shook it from his fingers, and gave her a half smile as he continued to plow forward.

She tilted her head to the side and tears streaked the dust that had settled onto her face as she tromped forward, one precariously placed step after another.

I'm on my way. He reached out an arm toward her as if it could somehow bridge the ocean of debris between them, but everywhere he turned, there were chairs, plaster, and bricks in his way. He was nearly there when he realized he would not get to her before they took her.

A soundless scream escaped Harlow's mouth as well as his own, as he watched her put up a fight through the swirling dust. But a black clad stranger carried her out through the collapsed wall. Jack stumbled, groped, and fell in a futile attempt to get to her. As the ringing in his ears finally subsided, he heard the worst sound possible: the hum of a ship taking off moments later.

CHAPTER 24

THE ENEMY OF MY ENEMY

Jack shoved, lifted, pushed, and pulled rubble from his path to get outside as quickly as possible to gain some clue about the ship. By the time he made it out, it was a tiny dot in the sky. Then it disappeared. He looked around frantically. Mike O'Malley stared into the sky where Jack had gazed. Suddenly, Jack had a thought that brought a surge of hope through the swirling dust and chaos. "Mike!" he called as he began running in his direction.

Mike looked absolutely stricken, and Jack began to think that the hope blossoming in his chest was unfounded. Surely if the colonists had arranged her escape, Mike knew about it. Nothing in the colonies got past him, but Mike seemed as surprised as he was.

"What did you do?" Mike said through gritted teeth. "You let them take her? For fuck's sake, man! You're royalty. Couldn't you get better guards for her than this?" Mike punched him in the gut.

Jack doubled over. "Bloody Christ, do you people ever just use your words?" Adrenaline overtook his sensibility. He slammed Mike in the jaw. Mike stumbled backwards but caught himself before he went sprawling. To Jack's surprise, he was coming at him again. The whole thing dissolved into a slugfest. Both fighting for the same reason, same frustration, and the same woman. Carlos came running over and grabbed Mike, knocked him to the ground, and was about to tear into him when Jack pulled Carlos off.

"It's all right, Carlos. Let him go. We're just..." He wiped blood from his face and looked around in despair before addressing Mike. "I was hoping this might be the colonists trying to rescue Harlow and not the bastards that—" Jack stopped, realizing there were people dying in the rubble behind him. There were screams coming from the courtroom. He reached out his hand to Mike. "Help me in there?" Jack said, pointing back to the chaos. Mike took his hand and Jack pulled him to his feet.

Jack turned to go back into the wreckage as he saw Evelyn clambering over the rubble with blood running down her arms and making her way toward him. "Highness, no. You have to leave now," Evelyn said as she pulled him toward their transport.

"You know I can't do that." He tilted his head toward the building.

Evelyn looked around with her pulse weapon at the ready, then followed him back in. She sighed. "I took out four. There could always be more coming from elsewhere in the building or the other side of the street."

Mike, Carlos, and the rest of the guards joined them. Jack heard them protesting his decision to stay as Evelyn cut them short. "Shut up and follow orders!"

They, along with what remained of the constabulary, dug through the rubble, searching for survivors and removing the dead. He caught sight of his aunt, who had gone back into "Mother mode" and was praying with people and giving last rites to the dead and dying. There didn't appear to be more than seven or eight, but he knew there was likely more under the debris. Once help arrived, his aunt, Mike, and Judith joined Jack and his security team as they took the transport to a hotel room across town. He didn't dare take them to the palace. What he had to say couldn't risk being overheard, and truthfully, he wasn't sure who was listening at the palace. Besides, it wasn't a good time to hear his family make any sort of remark about Harlow, not after what he now knew. He could barely tolerate it before.

Back at the hotel room, they struggled to dislodge the shock and work the problem. "The feed from outside the courtroom should be here any minute. We should be able to find something. If it was intact," Carlos said.

"Assuming they didn't disable it," Jack replied. He was having a hard time believing they wouldn't have thought of it. "Mike, are you sure there isn't some other group from the colonies that could have helped her escape?" He hoped it might still be a friendly jailbreak.

"I really think I would have known about it. Besides, why the sudden interest in setting her free if you're the one who filed charges against her?"

"I have new information about the whole thing."

"You couldn't just believe in her before all this?" Harlow's mother said between clenched teeth.

"I should have, but she came directly to me, saying she betrayed me. She was convincing." His heart still ached with the memory. "But I was wrong to not look into it more."

"She truly didn't do what she said then?" Judith asked.

Jack paused. "She did what she had to, but that is all I can say."

"If you know something about my daughter, you best damn well tell me!"

"I wish I could. I wish I could tell the world, but the same reason she had to lie to me is the same reason I can't tell you right now. You are just going to have to trust that if Harlow would have put herself through all this to keep it a secret, then it's a secret worth keeping, for now."

Mike narrowed his eyes at Jack. "We're talking blackmail then? Possibly government involvement?"

"Why do you say that?" Jack asked, wondering if Mike was figuring something out that he wasn't.

"I say that because we are discussing this in a hotel room on the other side of town as opposed to you being in the palace consulting with Scotland Yard, MI5, and MI6, like I would think you would be."

Jack marveled at the wiry, little, street-smart bastard. "I need you in my corner. Do you think we could stop beating the hell out of each other long enough to work together?"

"If it helps Harlow, then I would tolerate you, English."

Jack nodded. He heard a soft ping. The footage from the kidnapping had arrived. He held his breath as a completely corrupted image projected into the room. "Okay, so we knew that was likely." He consoled himself with the inevitability.

"What about that bastard who escaped your ship?" Mike asked. "He's the one that started all this. Could he have taken her?"

"Sure, but why not take her with him the night he left? That's the part that makes no sense."

"Maybe he needed a public show. Everyone knows that what goes on in the colonies doesn't make a shite to anyone unless they live there. Is this a show of power, maybe? A pathological need for attention?" Mike asked.

Jack pondered that then dismissed it. "If he wanted the attention then wouldn't he just show himself?"

Carlos spoke from the other side of the room. "Yeah, I think this whole thing points back to Aldric or whoever he was working for, but why Harlow?"

Mike looked at the floor. "I heard rumors that she's pregnant. I'm sorry to bring this up, English, but could someone be planning on holding her hostage and pulling your strings by keeping your child captive? What would you do to protect your child?"

Jack's heart slammed against the walls of his chest. A wave of nausea swept over him. He had been so busy worrying about Harlow that he hadn't thought of that angle. He felt his legs turn weak beneath him. He practically stumbled back into the chair and sank his head into his hands. "Damn near anything to protect them." He knew Mike made an excellent point. He had always been able to comfort himself with the idea that he could hunt someone down and beat their ass, but all the confidence and bravado in the world couldn't change the fact that threatening his wife and child put him in a position of weakness, again.

Jack looked up to find Carlos staring at him. The man had become adept at reading him. "The way I see it is if we find out where Aldric went, we might well find Harlow. I say we start with Aldric's research, which should lead us to his colleagues. Wherever he went, he would need supplies. There has to be someone here supporting him."

The group spent the next few hours researching Aldric and his associates. He covered his tracks fairly well, but they knew there had to be a slip-up somewhere. They were all exhausted and red-eyed as sunset arrived. Jack heard his communication device ping for the tenth time that day. He knew it was his family and had refused to answer it all afternoon. Across the room he heard his aunt finally answer her own device.

She quietly spoke with whomever it was before silencing her communicator. "Jack, I think we have something."

He sighed heavily, hoping she was right. He knew that every minute that went by, the chances of finding Harlow, and getting the upper hand on her captors, shrank.

"Apparently, there is a man named Dr. Jenkins who has worked with Aldric off and on for years. He applied for permission to do those controversial viral tests on fetuses in utero." Jack's aunt said. "Had some ethics charges filed against him as well."

Jack cringed at where this seemed to be going. "Oh, dear God. Judith, has Harlow been vaccinated?"

"Yeah, her dad made sure she was before he died."

Jack breathed a sigh of relief. "But the baby..."

"I don't think they would harm the baby if they were going to use it for ransom," Judith said.

"You're probably right, but there are a lot of people that would enjoy believing they are putting me in my place." Jack had a thought and turned to his aunt. "Wait, who told you about this guy?"

She looked at him as if he was asking the one question she didn't want to answer. "Later, okay?"

Judith jumped to her feet. "No! No secrets. You won't tell us why my daughter was forced to lie and go to prison. Now someone is feeding you information, and you want to keep that to yourself as well? Mike and I have known Harlow longer than any of you have. The secrets stop now!"

Part of Jack wanted to tell her to piss off after the way she acted toward Harlow when she needed her most. Yet he knew he had deserted her when she had needed him, too. "It's okay, Moth—" Jack stopped himself, realizing that she had told him she was just Aunt Mary now. "Aunt Mary, if you can, please tell us who it was."

"Jack, it was your brother who told me about Dr. Jenkins," she said.

"Why would he help you if the family is in on it?" Mike asked.

Jack shrugged. "I don't know. My family doesn't want me with Harlow. It makes no sense."

"Then it could be a trap to flush you out," Mike said. "Maybe we should leave it alone."

Aunt Mary spoke. "It confirms the family might well have put Aldric up to this, but I think the real reason he is helping you is because for the last seven years you've been gone—he wasn't a ghost anymore. For the first time, he is more than a second choice. If you find Harlow, he knows the family won't welcome you back. He matters now and doesn't want to lose that. This isn't just about the crown, either. He's always been in your shadow. I think the lead is absolutely for real. He wants you to find her."

It was news to Jack. He understood the first-born inheritance issue, but the rest of it seemed odd to him. However, when he looked around the room, it seemed to make perfect sense to everyone else, and Jack marveled at how easy it was to miss something right in front of his face. He just shook his head as a wall of fatigue slammed into him. "We've got work to do. We're going to need a lot of coffee, more firepower, and Dr. Jenkins tied to a chair."

CHAPTER 25

DR. JENKINS

Jack and Aunt Mary stood in the hallway on the fourth floor of the hotel, listening as Judith walked through an open door of a room where the maid was busy at work. Despite the seriousness of the situation, Jack smiled and watched his aunt stifle a laugh as they listened to Judith pay off a maid for the use of her uniform.

"Listen, my husband has a thing about a woman in uniform, especially sexy maids in a hotel. I've got a handful of Earth credits if you'll sell it to me."

There was complete silence as the maid contemplated the offer, enough credits to replace the uniform ten times over.

"Come on," Judith said. "From one sexy gal to another. Help me out here."

The tone in Judith's voice made Jack miss Harlow even more. They both had a little crazy in them.

Judith emerged a few minutes later wearing the uniform.

"Okay, you two keep watch out here. It shouldn't take long to beat the truth out of him," Jack said.

"Huh, you're not leaving me out here," Judith said. "I want a shot at this son of a bitch, too! Nobody brings the pain like a pissed off mom!"

Jack believed it. The woman made him nervous as hell. He didn't doubt her presence would unnerve Jenkins, which was one of the reasons he didn't want Judith in there with him. Before he could respond, Mary chimed in. "I'm not staying out here either. I've dealt with his kind before."

She wasn't wrong. She'd served as chaplain in prisons and though caring and compassionate, she didn't let the inmates intimidate her.

"Aunt Mary, you're the toughest old broad I know, but what I'm about to do in there will be a side of me I'm just not comfortable with you seeing. Please, I need all my wits about me. I don't want to be thinking about how you view what I'm doing in there. Please."

Mary nodded. Jack felt grateful that she was willing to relent in order to make him comfortable. For the first time, in the middle of the chaos swirling about him, he realized one of the big truths of his life: why he was closer to Mary than anyone else in his family—she let him be the captain of his own story. She put her opinion aside and believed he could decide what was best for him.

"Thank you," Jack said. He turned to Judith. "The uniform will keep anyone from disturbing us. Tell them you're waiting for the occupants to emerge so you can restock the towels." He expected a fight but found—to his absolute shock—that she just nodded and stepped back. Judith had the power to surprise him. Perhaps she realized her presence wouldn't make things any easier.

Judith and Mary kept watch in the hallway as Carlos and Mike stepped out of the room and shut the door behind him. "Mike and I've got this. Highness, if he survives and starts talking, he may not figure out who Mike and I are, but he will know your face right away. This could reflect very bad on you."

"That's all right, Carlos," Jack said. The notion that had been in his subconscious for years finally surfaced, "My place isn't in the monarchy anymore." Mike's expression was unreadable, but Jack took one look at Carlos and saw that he wasn't surprised. Jack realized Carlos had known it before he had. He'd been among the colonists so long that his identity had even morphed. He was relieved to no longer bear the burden of having a foot in each world.

He was ready to leave his ties to the crown, and what he was about to do would sever those ties for sure. The three stepped inside.

Jenkins' head lolled to one side as Carlos checked the gag one more time. Good, Jack thought. There will be screaming.

Jack stepped forward and slapped the man hard. "Wake up!"

Jenkins opened his eyes and looked around the hotel room as confusion and then panic marched across his face.

Jack crouched down in front of him and spoke in a deadly tone. "Look into my eyes. I am a man with nothing to lose. The woman I love, and my unborn child are gone. A lunatic has them. I will take you apart piece by piece if I have to, but you will tell me where they are." Jack nodded at Carlos, who cut the gag from the man's mouth.

"This kind of behavior is unbecoming of a prince. Is it not?" Jenkins asked.

"You can take my crown and shove it up your arse sideways for all I care. I'm here for one reason. Where is Harlow?"

"I don't know anything about her."

"The fuck you don't! Why did you purchase neonatal respiration systems—the kind that are used for Mars births due to the fluctuating gravity? You've never been to Mars and haven't so much as applied to be a physician there. There's no need for those systems. You're sending them to Aldric."

The man said nothing.

Mike O'Malley casually lit a cigarette and looked at Jack. "May I?" he asked.

Jack stood and backed up a couple of steps. "Be my guest."

Carlos knew what Mike had in mind and taped Dr. Jenkins' mouth closed. Mike took a drag of his cigarette, then leaned over the man. "Where's our girl?" Mike asked.

Jenkins shook his head.

"Fine," Mike said before burning Jenkins' arm with his cigarette. Jenkins screamed beneath the gag, but he couldn't move his arms; they were tied to the chair. Mike yanked the tape from his mouth. "Got anything to say?"

"You all are going to fry for this. I know people that can make that happen."

Mike laughed out loud. "You don't know shite. Besides, if you're dead, you can't do anything about it."

"Fuck off, Irish," Jenkins said.

Mike replaced the gag. Jack guessed Mike was about to beat him senseless, but he stepped in first.

"You've insulted my friend, here." Jack gave no indication to anyone about what was to happen. All three men looked at Jack in shock as he yanked a knife from his boot so fast nobody registered it before he drove it into the man's thigh. More screams came from behind the tape as Jenkins broke out in a cold sweat.

Mike nodded in approval at Jack, winked, and pointed with the fingers that held the cigarette between them. "Didn't know you had it in you, English."

Jack looked at Jenkins and twisted the knife just enough to inflict more pain but, hopefully, keep him conscious enough to speak. "Look at me!"

The man looked at him with wild eyes as Jack spoke. "I've recently learned that Aldric is the one responsible for killing my wife and my unborn child. I won't go through it again. I will end you right here if you don't give me something. Are you going to cooperate?"

Large beads of sweat rolled down the doctor's face as he nodded. He was shaking so hard that he was starting to jerk with the effort to control it. Jack had seen it before in combat; the man was going into shock. He knew he would have to be careful now, lest Jenkins mentally checked out on them.

Jack ripped the tape off again. Jenkins rattled off coordinates for a desolate part of Mars.

"I'm not stupid. There's nothing there," Jack said.

Jenkins spoke through the pain, slurring words. "Ya-Yes, there is. Cloaked. Most well-funded thing on that shit hole. Chinese sponsor it."

"What is it?" Jack asked.

"I've given the location. Now I'll be hunted, killed. May as well t-tell you. It's a place where they're using pregnant women." He sucked in a shaky breath. "Virus mutation studies."

"Fuck," Jack said. He felt the blood drain from his face.

"Don't worry about your b-baby. They won't use it for the study. It's just a place to hold Harlow because it's cloaked."

"How can you know they won't use her?"

"She's too valuable. They're going to ho-old her and the b-aby there. After it's born, they can make you do whatever they want. They know you are the only thing holding the colonies together. If you leave, the Brotherhood moves in. If they send you one of your baby's toes, what would you do?"

Jack felt lightheaded. He knew he would do whatever they said to keep Harlow and his child safe. "We've got to get over there."

Jenkins was getting pale and gasping. "She won't know you when you get there. You'll be lucky if she doesn't run from you."

"Why?"

"They know what a pain in the ass she is. She'll fight. Her memories of you will be taken. I'm sure they already have. She won't remember you're a good guy, and while they're in there messing around with her brain waves, they won't let her remain a firebrand either. She'll wake up docile as a kitten. I've t-told you what you want," he said, panting as sweat continued to run down his face. "Now get the knife out of my leg," he ground out.

"I can put it back just as quickly," Jack said as he ripped it free.

The man cried out and swayed as if he were about to lose consciousness.

"No passing out, you piece of shite. You're coming with us. If you're lying to me, I'll make sure you regret it." Jack sliced and ripped the corner of a bed sheet and roughly tied up the wound as the man jerked beneath his bindings.

Jack turned to Carlos. "Have Judith bring a maid's cart and come right back."

Carlos nodded and left quickly.

A few minutes later, Dr. Jenkins was bound, gagged, and unceremoniously dumped into the laundry cart, hauled out the alley entrance by Judith sporting her maid's uniform, and shoved into the vehicle that would take them back to the shuttle and off to the colonies to retrieve Harlow.

Jack only hoped that she could forgive him—that is, if she was ever able to remember him again, and if she did, he feared she could never put her faith in him again. He felt sick with uncertainty as they drove away.

CHAPTER 26

Forget Me Not

She stood on the edge of the tree line searching her mind for answers, hoping the cold wind would jar that memory, the one that niggled at her consciousness, just out of reach. Her soft red scarf blew out in front of her, and long black locks of hair trailed by her face in streams. The leaves on the trees were changing—gold, russet, and crimson inched their way up the leaves a little more every day. Fall was coming, her favorite time of year—seasons lasted twice as long on Mars compared to Earth. She remembered that much.

She wondered about her baby's father for the hundredth time. Aldric wouldn't tell her much about the man, only that she wasn't to trust anyone who might come for her because they were the same people who had falsely accused her and gotten her thrown in prison. She wondered if the baby's father had somehow deceived her, and Aldric just didn't have the heart to tell her. Whatever had happened, he said it was best for her to remember on her own. It didn't matter whether the father was a good guy. She loved her baby already, and she knew she was lucky to have the people here at the women's shelter looking out for her.

She placed a hand on her belly. "How are you doing in there?"

A familiar voice interrupted her thoughts.

"Harlow, there you are. It's chilly out here. Come inside. The others are worried about you."

"Hi, Aldric."

She turned to smile at the man who was always so kind to her. She tried to remember how long she had been there. Months? Weeks? The midwife had told her she was four months along. Whatever the people who were after her had done to erase her memory had made it hard for her to keep her timeline straight. As she pushed herself to remember, her head throbbed. She reached up and rubbed her temples briskly. The sudden onslaught of the headache—especially when she was this close to recovering a memory—was beyond annoying.

"Another headache?" Aldric asked. His voice was etched with sympathy as he placed a warm hand on her arm.

"Yeah."

"Well, come on in, and we will start the treatment again, if you would like."

"If you aren't too busy." She was trying to be respectful of his time, but the treatments really soothed her headaches. He never complained about helping her.

He walked up to her and put his arm around her shoulders. "Of course not," Aldric said.

The two walked back to the house together. She couldn't imagine what she would do without his help.

Inside, she saw the two other pregnant women who lived in the house: Tara and Safia. They smiled at her as she passed by. They didn't have the headaches like she did, but their babies apparently had some sort of virus—supposedly not contagious, and this was the only place that would be able to take care of them.

She walked into the treatment room, and Aldric slid out a chair for her. She smiled up at him as she sat.

"Thank you," she said.

He nodded.

Aldric's assistant, the man with the eyebrow scar that ran through his eyelid and down his cheek, nodded at her as he retrieved the cap that altered her brain waves. She didn't know his name. He never offered it, and she never asked. Something about him made her uneasy. But he'd never harmed her. Had he? She was sure it was just the scar that made him seem...ominous.

Harlow turned to Aldric. "I think I may have almost remembered something today. It feels like I'm just on the edge, and then it slips away again." The familiar rush of hope, followed by frustration, washed over her.

"Really? That's great news. Well, maybe this treatment will help you with that."

"That would be wonderful. Everyone here is so nice, but I would love to remember where I'm from, who my baby's father is, if I have any family." Grief washed over her as if her subconscious was telling her how she should feel about the lost memories but couldn't retrieve them for her.

"All right. Just lie back."

"You're sure this isn't harmful to my baby?" she asked.

"The old treatment that used drugs to simulate the theta state might have been somewhat harmful, but this device here only affects your brain. It doesn't go through the bloodstream. Not to worry."

"Okay."

Aldric gave her a reassuring smile as she relaxed into the overstuffed chair. She remembered when she had first arrived. When was it? She could never recall but remembered lying in bed crying. She felt that she had lost something of great importance. The sense of darkness and loss was almost unbearable. Perhaps someone had died? Was it her baby's father? She remembered having dreams about him, but what were they?

She felt herself floating. Next came the strange ones and zeros behind her eyelids. Then, just as always, came Aldric's voice. It had become a touchstone, grounding her back to reality.

"Wake up, sleepyhead. How's the headache?"

"Better now. Thank you."

"Before you go back to your room, I wanted to ask you, have you remembered anything? It doesn't have to be anything big. Do you ever feel as if you are just on the cusp of remembering, but you can't quite grasp it?"

"Nope. Should I?" she asked, not wanting to disappoint him if he was hoping the sessions would help her remember.

"It's okay if you don't. I'm sure with more treatment you will reach a point where you experience that sensation and just behind it should be your memories. Don't worry. It just takes a little time."

"Thanks, Aldric. I really appreciate all your help."

"No problem, love." He tilted his head and gave a sad smile. "I like to help whenever I can. I remember watching my people die because they couldn't afford simple vaccines or nanobots in their district to clear the air of the gray death." His voice lowered to a whisper. "They couldn't breathe..." His fingers whitened as they curled around the edge of the table he leaned against. "You've done so much to help your people. You were part of a larger community of those who cared and mattered to each other." His voice rose in intensity. "You would have never aligned yourself with that coalition, those who crawl into bed with the royal family and sell out their people." Eyebrow Scar looked up at Aldric from where he was putting away the cap.

"Of course not," she said feeling a little frightened of him for the first time since she'd arrived. The only memories she had were from her childhood and teen years but nothing from her twenties. Aldric had told her the sad news that she was one of only a few survivors of colony six, but she remembered how difficult life had been for her and her mother. Suffering could make a person angry like he was now. She watched Aldric loosen his grip on the table, take a shaky breath, and wipe his brow. "Are you feeling, okay?" she asked.

"Yes. I think we might both need a nap."

She nodded to Aldric and Eyebrow Scar. They both looked as if they had more to say. But before she could ponder it further, exhaustion took over and a jaw-popping, satisfying yawn escaped. "Thanks again," she said before heading toward her bedroom. She kicked her shoes off, drew the blanket up over her legs and drifted into sweet sleep, free from the grief, and the pull of memories that had almost broken through.

• • •

Safia went into labor around two in the morning. She moaned and squeezed her eyes shut against the pain, and now, ten hours in, she was getting very close to delivery.

Harlow had stayed with her the whole time. She and the younger woman had gotten close over their time together at the house. They had several things in common: they both remembered having to steal to get by—Harlow in the colonies and this woman on the streets of Spain. They both had nowhere else to go. When Safia had asked Harlow to stay with her during labor, she didn't hesitate.

Harlow wiped the woman's face with a cold cloth. The midwife had been in to check on her, but now it was just the two of them.

A contraction passed, and her face relaxed. She looked at Harlow as if she wanted to say something. Harlow had seen this look several times before. She leaned in, hoping the woman would finally unburden herself. She didn't want to push her.

"My baby is still moving," she said in a quiet voice that dared not believe too much. Harlow's heart broke as Safia spoke. Her mind raced to find the right words. She didn't want to give her false hope, but she didn't wish to make her any more miserable with negativity.

She knew Safia's baby had some sort of disorder caused by the mutation of a virus or something to do with a reaction to a vaccine—though she was told the child itself didn't have a virus but might not breathe once it was born.

Safia leaned in a little closer and looked around before speaking. "I'm sure I'm just tired and paranoid, but what if this is some kind of weird place where they are experimenting on our babies? We're out in the middle of nowhere; they have a lab here. I've seen it. They give us these special diets and vitamins. Does the vibe in this place just feel off to you? I just wish we were in a regular hospital."

Harlow squeezed her hand but didn't know what to say. She thought perhaps Safia was just scared because she had never been to

Mars before and, being that far away from home, took some getting used to, but Harlow had to admit that every once in a while, something felt off. The staff never had conversations in front of them. Harlow had always assumed that it was just because the babies might be sicker than anyone believed, and they didn't want to upset the mothers. She had been told that her own baby didn't have any issues, that she was solely here because she had been falsely accused of a crime, and the few remaining colonists were hiding her until they could clear her name, but sometimes she wondered what she didn't know. They told her the British government had erased her memories because she had knowledge of their plotting against the colonists. That sounded right to her.

Safia went into another contraction, and Harlow felt relieved because Safia couldn't speak during them. She wasn't sure how to address her concerns, but she also felt guilty that her friend's pain relieved her of the obligation to say something comforting. After all, the woman wanted to hear that her child would be okay, and she couldn't promise that and had no idea how to address the conspiracy theory. It was hard for her to entertain the thought of the staff lying to them, or worse, when they had been so kind. She also knew encouraging Safia's paranoia wouldn't be helpful in the middle of labor.

The midwife walked back in with her assistant, examined Safia, and informed her it was time to push. The next contraction hit her hard and fast. She turned her low moans into a full-out scream. She squeezed Harlow's hand until Harlow thought her fingers might break and then eased up again.

"I want to see her," Safia panted as sweat rolled down her face. "Regardless," she said to the midwife.

"We discussed this, honey. It's not a good idea to watch her pass away like that."

Safia looked at Harlow, silently pleading for her help.

Harlow knew that being there for her friend would be heartbreaking. Aldric and the midwife had tried to talk her out of it, but Harlow had dug her heels in and stubbornly refused to back down.

Safia spoke with effort. "I kn-know you're trying to look out for my feelings, but I want to see her anyway. I want to hold her... no matter what." Another contraction slammed into Safia, silencing her.

The midwife said nothing as she looked between her legs for progress.

Safia started crying and looked at Harlow again for answers. She knew what she was getting into when she chose to stay with her. Safia had no other advocate, and she shouldn't have to beg for her rights at a time like this.

Harlow addressed the midwife, already knowing it wouldn't be well received. "Vana, I think Safia needs closure. Maybe it would be a good idea for her to see her daughter. It might help her accept it quicker."

Harlow was totally unprepared for the look that Vana shot her: cold and unnerving.

"Harlow, we have her best interest at heart. If we didn't, she would still be on the street."

"I understand that, and I know she appreciates it. I just think it should be her decision." It angered Harlow that the woman was basically saying that since they had kept her from having her baby on the street, she should shut up and comply, as if her living situation took away her human rights.

"She's in labor, in pain, and she isn't thinking straight. She's just trying to go into denial," Vana countered.

Harlow took a deep breath. She was biting back her anger now for Safia's sake, but she was angry about the way the midwife said her name as if she were barely tolerating Harlow, and she was treating Safia as if she were a child who was incapable of deciding for herself. Harlow thought about going to get Aldric. He had always listened to her and hadn't treated her like a child, but she was afraid if she left, Vana wouldn't let her back in, and she couldn't leave the frightened woman alone.

Safia lay there pushing and crying, and Harlow couldn't help but think if it were her, she would want to see her baby. Having her child whisked away before she even got to wrap her arms around her just seemed wrong.

"It should be her decision," Harlow said.

"I'm not discussing this with you any further," Vana countered. "I've dealt with this before. You haven't." With that, Vana looked at her assistant and nodded almost imperceptibly, but the look wasn't lost on Harlow.

"The head's out," Vana announced.

At her words, the assistant walked over with a small syringe. Harlow met her eyes after she handed the syringe to the midwife. The young woman quickly looked away.

"One more push," Vana said.

Harlow watched as Safia's face turned almost purple with the effort of one more long push, and then her head fell back against the pillow as she took in a deep breath and tears poured down her face. The baby was out, and the fear and grief in the room settled in like a dense fog. Safia had been told from the beginning that being separated from the umbilical cord meant certain death for her daughter.

Safia looked at Vana and pleaded. "Please, I don't want to spend the rest of my life wondering what she looked like, what it would have felt like to hold her in my arms. Please."

Harlow became furious, thinking the woman shouldn't have to beg for something that should be her choice to begin with. Harlow felt her heart kick up a notch at what she was about to do. She walked down to the foot of the bed where Safia's legs were draped with the sheet, obscuring her view of the baby.

"Give Safia her baby. Now. This isn't your decision. You aren't the mother," Harlow said.

To Harlow's complete shock, the woman gave her a furious look but complied.

They wrapped the baby in a soft yellow blanket. She looked for the entire world like there was nothing wrong with her. She was bright pink like other newborns Harlow had seen, not the blue tones that she had expected—though she wasn't moving and truly didn't appear to be breathing.

Safia held the baby close and looked at her fingers and toes. She kissed a tiny red birthmark on the baby's neck. She ran her hand down the length of the little girl's body, memorizing her. She kissed her eyelids, her cheeks and rubbed the dark fuzz on her daughter's head. "I will always love you," she whispered softly into her ear.

Vana didn't allow her long with her child, but it seemed long enough for Safia. She did not cry as Vana took the baby from her and left the room. She looked straight ahead at the wall as the assistant cleaned her and began sewing up the tear. Only then did Safia cry, deep wailing sobs that tore at Harlow's heart, and in the distance, Harlow could have sworn she heard another cry, different and small, exactly how a newborn would sound, but she knew it was likely just her imagination, willing it to be so.

CHAPTER 27

MAN ON A MISSION

Jack secured the bullet- and pulse-proof vest across his chest, strapped two pulse weapons to his waist, and tucked his antique pistol into the holster built into the thigh of his pants. The solid weight of it was an old friend. Beside him, Carlos armored up as well.

"You got your cloak packed, Marshal?" Carlos asked Jack.

"Yeah, it's already on the buggy." Energy thrummed through Jack, every nerve ending tingling for battle. He looked up to find Carlos watching him.

"You okay, Marshal?"

Jack's first instinct was to say, "Yeah," and move on, but he wasn't okay, and Carlos, his faithful friend, deserved his honesty and wasn't asking just to be nice. "No, even if I find her... I fucked up, Carlos. And it's taken too damn long to get here."

They'd wanted to go back to Mars and find the coordinates they'd beaten out of Jenkins, but knowing the location was only half the picture. More recon was needed, and they had to track down a couple more people to find out how well-armed the outpost was and if there might be an underground component to the place where soldiers would pour out at the first sign of trouble.

Carlos nodded. "I understand, sir. I wrote her off, too. We were friends. I should have dug deeper."

Jack nodded. "No help for it now, mate."

"We get to beat, shoot, or kill the people who set her up, sir. That's something," Carlos said.

"That it is," Jack said as he grabbed the hilt of a dagger and shoved it into a sheath inside his boot.

. . .

After the craft flew them to the isolated area near the compound, they stopped short of the zone estimated to be scanned for intruders. Two buggies took them the rest of the way to the compound while wrapped in cloaking armor. Jack, Carlos, Evelyn, and Devante converged on the small building east of what looked like the main compound. Four others went ahead to the main building, while doc and one other remained in the buggy awaiting the injured. From all the intel they'd gathered, their numbers were good—Jack hoped. He was about to find out.

His heart raced as he stepped out of the buggy, not from battle nerves, but at the idea of seeing Harlow again. If she remembered him, could she forgive him? They all put the Chameleon cloaks on over their heads and faded into their surroundings. Once at the back door of the compound, Jack found a DNA scanner by the door with no idea whose DNA it required, but Evelyn had a reputation for being able to get past any lock. She stepped forward and busted the front off the device and looked around inside it for a few moments before giving Jack a smile and thumbs up. Seconds later, they were on their way through the door.

Once inside, they were shocked to find it wasn't guarded; that was the problem with placing too much faith in technology—the false sense of security it gave.

Carlos and Jack took the hallway to the left while Evelyn and Devante went right. They moved from one room to the other, finding them empty until finally entering a room with a sleeping nurse on a cot. Her eyes grew wide when she saw the disturbance in her room. The Chameleon cloaks worked better in a landscape. Up close, there was distortion. It would appear as if a heat wave were rising from the floor. Jack removed his cloak, believing it would scare her less to know who was there.

Recognition fluttered across her face when she saw Jack. "Highness?" she stammered in a British accent. By her head was a monitor showing the image of a sleeping baby.

"Yes. We aren't here to hurt you. We believe these women are in danger." For all he knew, the woman before him was part of the Brotherhood but thought it more likely they simply hired her to take care of the women and children.

"How many people are here other than the women and children?" Jack asked, as Carlos and Evelyn removed their cloaks as well. Devante stood guard in the hallway.

The nurse looked around the room as if she feared being observed.

"We'll take you with us," Jack said.

"I don't know exact numbers. Maybe twelve."

Her answer felt authentic to Jack. In fact, she seemed relieved to see him.

"Do you know of a woman here named Harlow? She has black hair and blue eyes."

The woman nodded. "I've seen Harlow. She's okay."

"Where is she?"

"Main building. First hallway on the left from the back entrance."

"Tie and gag her," Jack said to Carlos.

The woman gasped. "I thought you were taking me with you. You'll get me killed if they're watching me. Something's wrong with these people. I don't want to be here, but I can't leave. There is nothing between here and the colonies, I was told. I'm not even sure where here is."

"I'm good as my word, love. But I can't say for sure you won't sell us out. Someone will come for you before we bug out. Sorry."

The woman didn't look happy about it at all, but there was no alternative.

Carlos tied her wrists while Jack continued to the next room. When he walked in, he was shocked to find not one baby but three. The one he'd seen on the camera was a newborn. Two of the others were older. The newborn began to cry when it heard the noise they were making. The sound was like that of a kitten. It got louder, and Jack panicked when he thought about the fact that they had just tied up the nurse in the adjoining room. The other babies were stirring now, too.

"Oh, hell," Jack whispered. He hadn't anticipated soothing a room full of crying babies.

Jack looked up as Carlos walked in. "What the hell are they doing with them, sir? Could they really be experimenting on them? Where are the other two?"

Jack nodded. There were three babies and five cribs. "If he was evil enough to kill my wife and child, then I don't doubt he would hurt these in the name of science."

"Are they contagious, sir?" Carlos asked.

"I don't think so. They don't look sick. They aren't quarantined."

The newborn wailed. Jack worried about it waking up the others. He holstered his weapon and picked up the tiny baby wrapped in a yellow blanket. At first, he was concerned by the little red spot on the baby's neck, but quickly recognized it as a birthmark.

"Shh, shh, shh," Jack whispered. "We'll get you out of here."

He turned to Carlos. "We can't risk these babies getting hurt from us running out of here with them, but we can't leave them and have them disappearing while we clear the main house, either. I think we should call Doc and have him come wait with them. We can leave Evelyn and Devante here with Doc and the babies while we head over to the house to look for Harlow."

Carlos spoke what they were both thinking. "Using the comms will give us away."

"If you have a better solution, I'm listening," Jack said.

Carlos shook his head.

Jack tapped the plate on his shoulder, informing Doc of the new plan.

They both held their breath, knowing Doc might get caught on the way in. Jack said a silent prayer as he continued to pat the baby's back and whisper into its ear. "You look like a girl to me. Are you a girl?" The child looked at him with soulful eyes. Being with the tiny, warm bundle made him more determined than ever to find Harlow and get the hell out of there.

Not long after, Doc arrived looking winded. "Jesus, Mary, and Joseph," Doc said as he glanced around the room.

Jack knew Doc was more frightened by the viruses than most, but the man had no choice. He was the only one who had come with them who wasn't technically a warrior.

Jack handed the baby to Doc. "We've already taken too long. We have to get moving. If something happens, barricade yourself in here for as long as you can until we come for you."

On the way out, Jack nodded to Evelyn stationed in the hallway and Devante stationed just outside the main door.

Jack and Carlos threw their cloaks on and ran across to the compound. No sound was good news. The four men who had gone into the main building had yet to trip any alarms, or at least none that Jack could hear.

As soon as they entered the building, they removed their Chameleons and were met by one of their own with a small woman in tow. She seemed to know the good guys when she saw them.

"Give her your extra cloak and run her to the buggy," Jack ordered.

The woman hesitated.

The British soldier named Byrd gave a loud exhale. "Christ! I thought you wanted to get out of here?"

"I do. It's just that..."

Jack noticed the woman looked as if she were biting back a sob. "My baby died two days ago. At least they say she did, and I don't want to leave without her body. They wouldn't tell me where they buried her or if they did an autopsy or...she had some sort of disorder from a virus."

Carlos and Jack looked at each other.

"What's your name?" Jack asked.

"Safia," she said.

Jack wanted to tell the woman her baby might still be alive, but if it was the wrong baby...He was afraid to get her hopes up.

All of them snapped out of their standoff by the sounds of a pulse weapon being fired.

"Shite. They know we're here," Jack said.

Byrd threw the cloak over the woman and shoved her toward the door.

"No!" she cried. "I won't leave her here."

Jack walked over to the wavering spot where the woman stood. "I swear to you if she's here we'll find her, but for now, move your arse."

More gunfire from down the hallway caused her to comply.

CHAPTER 28

A PHASER SET TO REMEMBER

Harlow woke when her bed began shaking. She hadn't meant to fall asleep. Judging from the faint light outside, it was evening. She felt disoriented. *What's going on? Thunder?*

She heard other voices in the house. They sounded panicked. Harlow swung her feet over the side of the bed and slipped her shoes on just as another loud noise was followed by what sounded like the ground ripping not far from the house. She opened her bedroom door and ran through the house searching for Aldric; he would know what was happening.

She ran to the treatment room but couldn't find him. Next, she looked in his office, but he wasn't there either. The house shook once more. Whatever was happening was getting closer.

Dust rained down from above.

"Harlow!" Aldric called.

"I'm here," she answered.

He came into the room and locked the door behind him. She looked into his eyes and found panic, but his hands were steady as he switched on his weapon. He went straight past the stun setting and on to kill.

"We're friends. You trust me, right?"

Something strange stirred inside her at his words. If he'd stopped talking, if he hadn't asked her if she'd trusted him, the odd feeling might never have surfaced. Instead of answering, she nodded and felt suddenly alone.

"They've come. You must be brave now." Chaos sounded in the hallway: grunts, curses, and phase weapons being fired. "You mustn't let them take you. No matter what. Remember what I told you. If you let them take you, they will lock you away or maybe even execute you."

"I understand," she whispered. She had information about the British conspiring against the colonists, and they accused her of giving up government secrets and only he knew the truth—that she had been blackmailed. He had warned her that a day might come when they found her. He told her it wouldn't matter that she was pregnant—they would have no sympathy. She heard screams coming from outside. She screamed too when she heard the door to the study break from its hinges.

An enormous man with the fiercest eyes she had ever seen ducked as Aldric fired at him. The man tried to evade but wouldn't make it out of harm's way before Aldric took another shot. Fear for the man in the doorway flooded her, and she shoved Aldric, not understanding why.

Aldric hadn't expected it from her and tumbled to the ground.

For a second, the man in the doorway locked eyes with Harlow before closing the several foot gap between him and Aldric. He kicked the gun away and grabbed him by the collar, yanking him to his feet. "Where's the baby that you claim died two days ago?"

Harlow was frightened by what she had done and knew it was too late to run. She was certainly no match for his strength either. She stood to face him. And she was more than a little curious about Aldric's answer to the man's question. The question itself spoke to some of her own fears. But Aldric had been so kind to her...

Aldric fought to get away as Jack slammed his face against the desk, bloodying his nose.

"Harlow, grab my weapon," Aldric spat as blood reddened his teeth grotesquely. "This man will take you back to prison. They'll never let you go."

"He's lying to you," Jack said while looking at her as if he knew her. "It's okay. We've come to help you. Though you've never needed such a thing before." She looked at him in confusion as opposing emotions warred within her.

She found herself wanting to take a step back from the intimidating man but stood her ground.

Aldric continued his argument. "Shoot him, Harlow! He will take your child from you."

"Shut up, you minging piece of shite." Jack held him by the collar and pointed the phase weapon to Aldric's chest.

"See, Harlow! He's going to kill me."

"I'd love to, but unfortunately, I have questions for you."

Harlow retrieved Aldric's weapon from the floor and held it on both men.

The large man looked just about as confused as she felt. "Harlow?" He looked at her intently.

She felt naked beneath his gaze. "Am I supposed to know you?"

This man looked as if she had slapped him. "Yeah, you are. You do know me. I'm Jack."

"Thank you, Jack, but I'm fine. I don't require rescuing."

"Of course not. I take care of her," Aldric said as he looked at Jack with open disgust.

"You hold her prisoner here."

"She is no prisoner. She is well taken care of," Aldric argued.

Harlow couldn't deny that. They did take care of her. Except, she didn't believe Safia's baby had died, and they told her it had. She'd heard a baby crying after Safia gave birth. Every night since, she'd dreamed that hers would be taken, too. Though Aldric had assured her she had not heard crying.

Harlow looked between the two men. She fixed her eyes on Jack and couldn't look away. Then she realized where she knew him from; he was the British prince that had been trying to get that hunk of junk *Ares* going for the last seven years. Why would he be coming for her?

Shit, the warrants!

"Look, it's just petty theft," she said, having a hard time thinking he had gone through all of this for thievery.

Jack laughed. "Harlow, I don't give a shite about any of that."

That made sense to her. She hesitated, looking between the two men. Aldric had taken care of her, but this man had a sincerity about him that felt familiar. More than that, it felt genuine—something she hadn't really felt in a while. As nice as Aldric had been, it never quite seemed to reach below the surface. These people had an agenda, just as Safia had said.

It's okay," Jack whispered. "I know you don't remember me, but there must be something of me still in your mind."

Heat gathered at the backs of her eyes, though she didn't know why.

"I'm your baby's father. You don't have to be afraid of me."

Aldric spoke through a swollen mouth. "This man is your baby's father. It's true, but that is only because he raped you. We shouldn't have done it, but we wiped your memories so that you could find peace here."

"You are a fucking liar!" Jack roared.

Harlow took a step back from Jack as fear swept through her body. The man was terrifying when he was angry, and what did she really know about him anyway?

Aldric looked at the muscled man with what Harlow interpreted as a glare of smug triumph.

Jack pointed the weapon lower and shot Aldric in the leg.

Aldric went down on one knee and fought to catch his breath over the searing pain. "I told you! The man is violent." He ground the words out.

Jack turned to Harlow. "We've already rescued all the other women. Please, I don't want to have to grab you. Let it be your choice."

Harlow felt as if a great divide stood between her and the large man named Jack. *Jack*, she thought as she turned the name over in her mind, enjoying the simplicity of it. She glanced at Aldric shaking in the floor and holding his injured leg. He had ceased trying to convince her he was the good guy. He simply looked at Jack with pure hatred.

"It's over," Jack said to Aldric. "All your cronies have either been arrested or killed. The babies will be returned to their mothers."

"So, they are alive?" she asked, thinking of Safia.

"We found three," he said.

The grief that had vexed her since the death of Safia's baby began to lift. The sounds of chaos in the hallway subsided.

Aldric gripped his bleeding leg and gasped as he spoke to Jack. "This isn't over, you elitist prick. My comrades will rise to defend me." The voice he used now sounded like an entirely other person to Harlow. Aldric paid no more mind to her at all.

"Carlos!" Jack called to a man in the hallway.

The man came in wearing the uniform of the US Marine Corps and carrying a weapon. Harlow wondered if she knew him.

"Call Margaret and her team in to come get this piece of shite along with the others. Once we reach the *Ares*, we throw his ass in the brig. Bring the woman from the nursery on board with us."

"You got it," Carlos said. As the soldiers left the room with Aldric in shackles, Carlos looked at Harlow and smiled. "Nice to have you back, Harlow."

She wasn't sure who he was, but she had already decided she liked him.

"Let's get you out of here. Please do as I say and don't engage anyone on the way out?" He phrased it as a question like he wasn't sure he could trust her to comply.

"Why would I do that?" Harlow asked.

Jack smiled and Harlow thought that it looked like the sun coming out on a stormy day. "Let's just say you haven't always enjoyed being told what to do."

The man seemed to know her pretty well. She had felt fairly fragile since arriving at the center, but she remembered a lifetime of needing to go her own way. This man was giving her a sense of power back.

Whatever had been going on outside seemed to have died down, but Jack still pulled at her arm with a sense of urgency.

"Jack, wait. I won't leave without my friends. There were three other women here: Safia, Tara, and Tamar. We have to find them."

"Of course. We've already found Safia and Tamar. I would rather get you to the transport first though. I promise I will come back for Tara."

"Jack, you don't understand. I *cannot* leave without her. I think they did something to Safia's baby. If they get out of here with Tara, she may lose her child."

"I know," Jack said.

Harlow watched as a war raged inside Jack before he finally relented.

"Take me to her room," he said.

It was a short walk down the hallway, and they didn't encounter anymore fire, but when Jack tried the door, it was locked.

Harlow knocked. "Tara, it's me. I know the people who have come to get us out of here. Please open the door."

Tara opened the door just a crack, took one look at Jack, and slammed it again. It took Harlow a moment to realize that she was likely intimidated by his size. Harlow wasn't, which made her realize even more that what Aldric had told her about her baby's father couldn't be true. She instinctively trusted the man, even though she couldn't remember him.

Before Tara locked the door again, Harlow opened it.

Tara hunched down on the floor in fear. As they walked farther into the room, Tara crabbed backwards with her belly protruding in the air. "You can't trust anyone here. How do you know he isn't one of them?" Tara asked.

Harlow knew it was a valid question, and she didn't think she would have an answer to give Tara that wouldn't sound strange. She believed Jack on pure gut instinct.

"I—" Harlow began, but Jack apparently realized her distress and cut in to help her.

"Tara, you're right. You can't trust these people. We found babies in an outbuilding that we know are being experimented on." Jack pointed at Harlow. "I'm her baby's father and she won't leave here without *you*. So, please, I'm begging you, let's get the hell out of here."

Tara got up and grabbed a bag that she had already packed. Her distrust ran deeper than Harlow had realized. She still doubted Tara was convinced, but maybe saw Jack as the lesser of two evils.

On the way out of the compound, they ran into three guards that had been shot. All three looked dead. None seemed to be Jack's men.

Carlos met them on the way out and covered Tara with a Chameleon cloak even though night had fallen, and they had likely taken out anyone who was a threat by now. Jack ran beside them with a cloaked Harlow.

They reached the buggies where Safia waited for them and removed their camouflage.

Safia immediately reached for Harlow. "I can't leave without knowing where they buried her. She might even be...you know, in a freezer or something for their research."

Harlow glanced at Jack, and he quickly looked away. She knew he had heard what Safia had said. She somehow knew—even though she couldn't remember him—that he wasn't trying to ignore the woman but wasn't sure how to respond. Harlow thought to ask him if they were going to go through the lab and suggest what Safia had just mentioned, although the thoughts of those people turning Safia's child into an experiment made her feel sick. Before she could mention it to him, she heard men running through the night. Not only that, she heard the sounds of crying babies—more than one. She cringed, knowing that seeing these babies would only hurt Safia to know that her own baby didn't make it. But there was more than one baby and right now there were only three women at the shelter other than herself. Only one had given birth, Safia, and her baby had died. So, who did these children belong to? And what had happened to the mothers? The thought made her feel nauseous at all the possibilities—none of them good.

Two of the men that held babies were dressed like soldiers, but one looked like a civilian. Harlow heard one of the other men call him Doc. He seemed to have no problem holding the crying baby, but the other two men seemed preoccupied with security. They looked around under the dim glow of the stars as if they were waiting for an ambush at any moment. "We need to get these woman and children out of here," one of them said.

"You don't need to tell me twice," Jack said. "Give them the babies and let's go."

Harlow cringed as Carlos pointed at one of the babies and indicated that the soldier should give it to Safia. He nodded and handed the crying baby to Safia. Harlow opened her mouth to tell the guard "No," but everyone was scrambling to go. It was no place to deal with emotions.

Safia gently rocked the baby back and forth as the other two were given to Harlow and Tara to tend to so the soldiers could have their weapons ready to fire if the buggies were ambushed. Soon they were bumping along the deserted landscape and headed back toward the shuttle that would take them the rest of the way back to the *Ares.*

In the dim light of the two moons, Harlow watched Safia rock the smallest baby in the yellow bundle, but Safia wouldn't look closely at the little one.

• • •

Everyone made it back to the shuttle, along with a moaning Aldric strapped to a buggy and then not so gently secured in the shuttle. Jack and the other men were more relaxed now that everyone had boarded but still looked around to make sure they hadn't been followed. They looked into the sky as well but seemed satisfied. The women and babies boarded the shuttle, and the two buggies were driven into the back of the craft. Minutes later they were in the air.

Harlow couldn't help but notice that Carlos and Jack kept glancing at Safia and the baby, and she wondered how much they knew. She couldn't have had enough time to have told either of them the story. Carlos sat down on the other side of Safia while Harlow sat beside her.

"Will we be able to go back and look for my baby's grave?" Safia asked him.

Carlos didn't answer but held out his hands. "May I?"

Safia seemed upset about Carlos not answering but let him take the baby. It had settled down, though still remained awake. He sat the baby in his lap and unwrapped the little bundle so that the three of them could see its face. He put one finger beneath the little girl's chin and gently lifted, revealing a small red birthmark on her tiny neck.

Safia and Harlow both gasped.

"Bella?" Safia sobbed out as she moved a trembling hand toward the baby.

Fresh tears clouded Harlow's vision as she realized Safia had named her baby at some point, even though she believed her gone for good.

A gentle smile made its way across Carlos's face as Safia reached out for the baby. "How did you know?" she asked him.

"I thought maybe you had seen her when she was born, but I wasn't sure. I knew if you had, then you would surely remember a birthmark," he said.

"I remember it, too," Harlow said. Every moment of that sad day had been burned into her memory.

"Thank you," Safia said. She held the baby close to her and whispered into her ear.

Jack looked at the four of them from across the room and made his way over. "Doc downloaded a lot of the files from the lab before we left. I think maybe we will have some answers about what's going on with the babies and why you were lied to. Doc doesn't think they are contagious. We will go through everything and let you know whatever we find. Promise," Jack said.

"Thank you," Safia said.

Harlow looked at Jack and felt her faith in him rising by the minute. She hoped she remembered this man. He certainly held her curiosity, but she became worried about him as she watched his face turn from joy to concern as he looked at Carlos.

"You all right, mate?" Jack asked Carlos.

"Aye, Marshal," he said as he swayed in his seat and his eyes rolled back in his head.

"Doc!" Jack called as he got down on one knee and caught Carlos as he fell forward.

Harlow looked down when Jack did, and they both saw the same thing: the back of Carlos's jacket was soaked with blood.

CHAPTER 29

CARLOS

Carlos lay in the infirmary trying to swim his way to the surface. He heard voices that sounded as if they were traveling through a tunnel.

"Why didn't you tell me you were shot?" Doc said.

I wasn't shot. He tried to move his mouth to no avail. *Was I?*

Doc kept talking. "I can't believe you were just sitting there. Not telling a soul you'd been shot."

Carlos moaned.

"He'll be fine. You can get back to your baby. I'll take good care of him. I promise."

Who's he talking to?

"Just a few more minutes. I think he might be waking up," a woman's voice replied.

Carlos's eyes remained closed as he spoke. "I was worried about you," Carlos finally managed to mumble.

"Who?" the woman asked.

Carlos opened his eyes as confusion washed over him. "What am I doing here?" He turned to find a woman standing beside his bed. She had long brown hair and brown eyes that reminded him of the little chunks of amber he had seen at the museum when he was a kid. This amber didn't have insects trapped inside it but soulful eyes ringed by dark circles. They were no less beautiful for the exhaustion written in them. She reached over and adjusted the bed sheet at his chest. He felt his heart race and hoped his vitals weren't on display for her to see.

"You were shot, Sergeant Gonsalves."

Carlos had never been shot before—though he had prepared for it his whole life.

"Shot? What the hell? When?"

Carlos watched as worry settled into her eyes.

"Doc, is this normal?"

Carlos hadn't realized there was anyone else in the room, but he cut his eyes to see Doc standing beside his bed reviewing the vitals that flashed in the air before him. *Uh oh!*

"Yeah, he just needs a minute to orient himself. He lost a lot of blood and went under for surgery, but nothing happened that would have compromised his brain. He'll be fine."

"What surgery?"

Doc looked at him with a patient smile. "You had a bullet in your liver. I can't believe someone still uses those archaic projectiles. Jack said you were fine until you collapsed."

"Yeah, we all thought so," the woman said.

He liked the sound of her voice, melodic and soothing. It made him forget the ache in his side. "What is your name?" he asked.

She smiled at him, and he felt giddy but realized he was in the infirmary and there could be meds or at least a brain wave regulator used to control pain contributing to the euphoria. Maybe, but he could drown in the sound of her voice.

"Safia Asfour," she said.

He said it over again in his mind several times, hoping it would stick. The memories were starting to come back to him now: the raid on the compound, the babies...Safia's baby. She wouldn't have had a husband since the women there were chosen for the experiments because they had few ties; most were homeless. Perfect victims. It made him angry. But panic rushed in to take its place as he realized he was falling for the woman so quickly. He barely knew her, but damned if he wasn't happy just to be in the same room with her.

"How's your baby?" he asked.

"She's perfect. Thank you for helping me get her back. I can never repay you for what you've done for us."

He started to say, "It's my job," and it was, but that sounded too impersonal. The next choice was to look into those amber eyes and say, "Anything for you," but that sounded scary from someone she had just met, but whatever pain meds he was on made him want to blurt it all out. Somewhere logic called and waved its arms at him from the back of his mind and saved him from saying it in the nick of time. He settled for something somewhere in between the two. "Of course. My pleasure to help."

"Is there anything you need, Sergeant Gonsalves?" she asked him.

"Yes, start calling me Carlos."

"Carlos, got it. I'm going to let you get some rest now, Carlos."

As she turned and started to go, panic washed over him. "Safia?"

"Yes?"

"Will you be going back to family soon?"

She had an odd look on her face. "No, I won't. The prince has said I'm welcome to stay here on the *Ares* until I figure out what I want to do. You just get some rest and let me know if there is anything I can do for you."

"I will, Safia. Thank you."

"Thank me? No, thank you." She closed the door behind her, and he wanted to call her right back in. He marveled at his own emotions, but decided it was easiest to blame it all on pain medication.

Carlos dozed on and off for the next several hours. Another woman entering his room eventually awakened him. He turned to look at Harlow and smiled. She smiled back but still didn't have the level of familiarity in her eyes that would suggest she remembered him.

"I hope it's okay I came to see you. After Safia left, I tried to wait a bit. I didn't want to overwhelm you while you were trying to recover from your surgery."

"No, it's okay. I enjoy the company. How are you feeling? Have you remembered anything?"

Harlow laughed a little. "I'm feeling fine. I'm not the one with a hole in my liver. And no, I haven't remembered anything."

Carlos noticed the worry etched across her face. "It'll be okay," he said.

She sat down in the chair beside the bed.

"Worst-case scenario is you don't remember, right? But I think you could still be happy. Jack is a really good man."

"I believe that. I believe you are, too, and I wanted to tell you how much I appreciate what you did for me and the others, especially Safia."

Carlos watched as Harlow struggled for the right words. "She's been through a lot."

"She's..." Now it was Carlos's turn to struggle for the right word. He knew what he felt, but hesitated to tell her. "She's a sweet girl. How old is she?"

"She's about a year younger than me, twenty-five. Why?"

"Hmm." Carlos was thirty-one and wondered if Safia would think he was too old. He scolded himself for thinking of it at all. It had to be the meds. "Oh, just curious."

She laughed a little and looked at him strangely. He felt himself smiling and wondered what the hell he was doing grinning like an idiot.

Harlow smiled back at him. "Well, anyhow. Thank you for everything you've done for me and my friends. Jack won't tell me much about what I can't remember, but he told me why I was being held there, and I can't imagine what would have happened had I stayed longer."

"Of course," he said.

"Is there anything I can do for you?" Harlow asked.

"I'm okay."

She started to go and then paused before turning to leave. "I know what to do. I'll put in a good word for you with Safia." She winked and then left the room before he could argue.

. . .

As he watched her go, he knew he had seen his friend surface: she was that wonderful combination of mischievous and compassionate. He only wished he could say for sure that she would regain her memories. As much as they all pretended it didn't matter, he wanted his friend back. The one he had cried and laughed with. The harsh reality was the one nobody would tell her: her memory loss might well be permanent.

CHAPTER 30

THE WHISPER OF MEMORY

Jack and Harlow sat in the ship's mess hall eating lunch. "You're finally putting on a little weight. I was worried about you."

She shoved the last bite of potato into her mouth before speaking. "You want to fatten me up?" She smacked his arm playfully.

"A little, yeah," he said.

"Well, I can't remember if I was nauseous earlier. I'm not sure how I lost so much weight."

"You were..." he answered, but she couldn't help but notice the way he looked down and sorrow fluttered across his features. He looked back up at her and gave a sad smile. "You look beautiful, Harlow. Always have."

"You okay?" she asked.

"Yeah, I'm good," he said as he continued to look at her.

The spell was broken when another person came into the cafeteria.

They both looked up to find Safia standing there with her baby. Ever since Bella had been returned to her, they rarely saw her without her. The child even slept in her arms.

"Hope I'm not interrupting anything," Safia said.

"No, not at all," Jack said. "I have a lot I need to catch up on."

Harlow knew he wasn't kidding. He had been spending a lot of time with her, even though he was always bombarded with people needing his approval for a whole host of things.

Jack got up to go, but not before stopping by the sleeping baby. "May I?" he asked Safia.

"Of course," she said.

Jack leaned over and planted a gentle kiss on the baby's head. Safia looked at Harlow and smiled as Jack left the room.

She sat down beside Harlow. "So, how are things?"

"They're fine," she said. She had an inkling where this might be headed.

"Everyone dreams of falling in love with a prince, right? Lucky you!"

"Yes, but this lucky gal can't remember falling for him," she said.

"Oh, stop it. I've seen how he looks at you. All my life I've dreamed of finding a man to look at me like that."

Harlow knew what she meant, and while it made her feel warm all over and she counted the minutes until he came back to do it again, she wasn't ready to admit it to anyone just yet. She could barely admit it to herself.

"Will you try to find Bella's father?" Harlow asked.

"Well, that's a quick subject shift there, but no, I won't."

Harlow had never asked her about it before, and now she regretted doing it this time. A nervous and sorrowful look overtook Safia, that made Harlow drop the subject, but to her surprise, Safia continued. "Bella's father...he, uh, attacked me."

She gave no more details than that, and Harlow didn't push. Safia had told her that she would stay on Mars permanently. Now it certainly made sense. She couldn't blame her.

"I'm sorry. That's horrible."

"It doesn't change how I feel about her though." Safia smoothed her hand across Bella's soft downy hair. "She's amazing."

"She certainly is."

"Listen to me, Harlow. Give Jack a chance. You're crazy if you don't. Whether or not you get your memories back, promise me you will at least try."

"I promise, but what makes you think I wouldn't?"

"Take it from someone who has spent their life on the run. You're scared. I see it all over you. Don't let it keep you from happiness any longer."

The feeling of exposure made Harlow cringe, but it didn't mean Safia was wrong.

CHAPTER 31
WAFFLES AMONG THE STARS

Jack felt so familiar to her, but try as she might, the memories weren't coming back. The more she pushed, the more they seemed to elude her. He'd showed up every morning for the past week to walk her to breakfast. She felt calm around him. While she had been with Aldric, everything seemed fine, but panic had always bubbled just beneath the surface. Jack's smile set her at ease but also made her nervous in a way that she didn't entirely hate.

They sat on the observation deck looking out the windows as the stars sped by. The *Ares* was out on a short systems test, and Jack had brought their food with him so they could enjoy the view. She caught him looking at her again. The guilt of not being able to remember him was strong.

"I'm sorry, Jack," Harlow said.

"Remember what I told you the last twelve times you said that to me? It isn't your fault. You don't owe me an apology."

She nodded and took a bite of the fluffy waffle. She remembered her life before Jack. She remembered the colonies, the theft, her mother, but nothing more. There were some days where she felt that it was just beyond her reach: so close she could almost grasp it, but it wriggled away from her every time. She polished off the last of the waffle, leaned back against the wall, stretched her legs out on the window seat in front of her, and began rubbing a cramp from her calf.

"Tired already?"

"Yeah. Can't turn my brain off. You would think that would work to my advantage in a situation like this, and I would remember quicker."

Jack reached for her leg. "May I?"

"Of course," she said. He slid her skirt up to her knees and began rubbing her calves. She moaned with pleasure. She heard Jack give a breathy laugh, and she realized he was probably remembering something that she wished she could remember...or might be embarrassed to remember. She opened one eye to look at him. "Have I made that sound before?" she asked.

"You have," he said with a deep throaty tone that gave her a world of context. "This relaxes you?" he asked.

"Yeah, kind of like the room with the waterfall and all those plants. We've got to get back in there sometime." He stopped rubbing her leg. She opened her eyes. "What's wrong?"

"I never told you about that. Has someone taken you in there?" he asked.

"No, I don't know where such a place is."

Jack smiled. She knew he tried to hide his hope that she would remember him, but it was written on his face now. He stood and held out his hand.

"Where are we going?" she asked.

"To the waterfall."

• • •

As soon as he opened the door, the soothing sounds of cascading water filled her ears and soothed her senses.

"Good morning, Brigid," Jack said to a woman picking bean pods off a vine. "I hate to bother you, but we need the room for just a little while. We may remember something."

The young woman smiled at them both. Jack made no secret of Harlow's memory loss. He hoped the crew could help her remember. "That's great! Good luck," she said as she took off her gloves and set them aside before leaving the room.

Jack pulled out a couple of cushions for the two of them to sit on. He leaned back against the wall and patted the cushion beside him. Harlow complied. She closed her eyes and let the sounds of the water permeate her senses as Jack smoothed the hair back from her forehead. She was a moment from drifting off when she felt a thump come from inside her lower abdomen. Her eyes sprang open.

"Oh, wow!"

"Did you remember something?" he asked.

"No, sorry, but I just felt a little kick. First one."

Jack's hand drifted down to her swollen abdomen. "Is it okay if I—?"

"Of course it is. I doubt you'll feel anything yet. It was faint." She picked up his hand, lifted her shirt above her belly, and placed his hand on her. It was large and warm and shocked her as it sent waves of pleasure through her body. Even though he was attractive, the power of his touch stunned her. She recalled for the briefest of moments what it was like to be beneath him. She sucked in a quick breath.

"Is everything okay?" he asked.

She looked up at him and noticed a quizzical expression.

"Better than okay. I remember a little."

"What?"

She could feel her face turning crimson, giving away the nature of her memory. She said nothing.

Jack laughed. "One of those memories? Seriously? I like that. That's a good one to start with."

"Did it happen a lot?" she asked.

"Actually, no. Just once."

"Really?" she asked, incredulous.

"Yeah."

"Did I..." It was the first time since she'd returned that she felt frightened of what she might learn. "Did I disappoint you in some way?"

"What? Hell no. It was the best night of my life. I'm glad you remember at least some of it."

Harlow's mind raced. Jack had said little to her about what she couldn't remember. The doctors they'd consulted said that it was better for Harlow to remember on her own because they feared she would wonder if she was remembering someone else's version of the past and not be able to sort out her own feelings once it all returned. From what she knew of her own history, she assumed she had done something to hurt him. Maybe even stole from him.

"Jack, I may not remember much of us together, but I do recall my own past. I was a thief. Did I steal from you? Did I hurt you in some way?" She sat up and braced herself for what his answer might be.

"You know I'm not supposed to answer those questions."

"I can't stand to think that I hurt you. I may not remember our time together, but the feelings I have for you are...real and intense. Whether they are subconscious from before or brand new, I don't know. That's a little confusing. I just know that I don't want to believe that I ever hurt you." Tears welled up in her eyes.

Jack pulled her close. "Don't cry, Harlow. You have done nothing wrong. I promise." He ran his hand up and down her back. His touch soothed her frustration over not remembering, feeling lost in her own skin, and her fear that she might have done something during the lost time that she couldn't take back. She pulled away from him and looked into his eyes. She suddenly had an idea, an urge to return to something familiar. "Can you take me to my mother?"

"For...? Do you...? Are you wanting to stay with her?" he asked.

She heard something in his voice that sounded like fear. She rushed to reassure him.

"What? No! This is where I want to be."

She watched as his shoulders visibly relaxed.

"Sure. We can go see her."

The strain in his voice was clear, and she got the idea he didn't like her mother very much. She started to ask but realized that might just be one more thing she wasn't supposed to ask.

"Why don't we go right now?" He rose quickly, and she realized he had the look of a man trying to get something dreaded over with. It made her feel a little panicky, but that feeling made her want to get through it as well. There was something there. She was on to something and decided to follow it where it led—even if it wasn't something she was going to like.

CHAPTER 32

JUDITH AND JITTERS

Jack's breakfast had turned to stone inside his stomach. They were going to see Judith when Harlow was most vulnerable to suggestion. He knew that he and Judith had made some progress in their relationship, but he somehow didn't think she would be gracious with her opinion of him. He worried she might use this opportunity to take Harlow from the ship Judith had spent years resenting.

As he drove Harlow to her mother's flat, she kept turning to look at him. Harlow was perceptive. Even without her memories, she had keen intuition.

"Why are you so nervous about seeing my mother?" she asked.

"Well, I..."

Harlow exhaled. "I know. I know. I'm supposed to remember on my own."

Jack held his breath, terrified that he was taking Harlow to someone who might try to poison her against him. He knew he couldn't keep her from her mother. That would immediately put him in the position of bad guy. But he couldn't help but wonder— the same thing he'd been wondering since the day he rescued her— after her memories returned, would she be able to forgive him? He'd hurt her so badly there might not be any coming back from it. He had been faithless and cold when she needed him most. As the cool wind of a Martian autumn blew across Harlow's face through the open buggy, he wondered if he would ever hold her again. The wounds that had begun to heal in him would be fresh for her. He glanced her way as her raven hair blew across her face. She reached up with elegant hands to brush it back behind her ears. His urge to touch her tore at him every day. Now he might be taking her to the one woman that could put that dream even further away.

When they stopped in front of her mother's flat, he leaned over to take Harlow's face in his palms. Knowing things might be different when she emerged, he became bold enough to make these few moments count. He leaned over and kissed her forehead gently before making his way down to her mouth and brushing his lips lightly across hers. He held his breath in fear that it would be too much for the woman that didn't remember him, but to his surprise, she smiled and placed her palm on top of his. As she kissed his palm, he held his breath. She didn't remember, but she had done it on the night their child was conceived.

Judith walked out as if on cue. She waved at him.

He made eye contact with her and tried to get a read on her. "Good morning, Judith."

"Good morning." Her tone was pleasant, but damned if he could sense a thing.

"Harlow asked me to bring her over," he said.

Judith nodded as Harlow got out of the buggy. Judith walked around to embrace her. Harlow looked at her strangely but returned the hug. He supposed his guess was correct that Judith wasn't very generous with the affection. He wondered if she was different before she lost her husband and spent so many years struggling on Mars.

Jack nodded at the two guards he'd sent in advance to wait outside Judith's flat while Harlow visited. After what they'd all just been through, he wasn't taking any chances. Jack said, "I'm going to walk down to O'Malley's and get a beer. I'll be back in a couple hours."

"Sounds good," Harlow said. "Jack watched as the two of them walked inside with Judith's arm wrapped around her daughter's shoulder possessively.

•   •   •

Jack walked into O'Malley's and wondered if he had made a mistake. Though he had worked with Mike in London after Harlow's kidnapping, he knew the man was still in love with her. And though rescuing her had made the people happy, many still held a grudge against him for sending her to prison in the first place.

Jack looked around and noted three other people in the bar besides him: two were at a table engaged in conversation, another sat at the bar deep in thought while nursing a half-full beer. Jack pulled out a barstool and nodded at Mike.

"Your Highness. What brings you by?" Mike said.

Not a good start. He was already goading him by being formal. "It's just Jack." Well, the man hasn't come across the bar for my throat yet, Jack thought.

"I drove Harlow over to Judith's to visit with her mom."

Mike laughed and then whistled through his teeth. "No damn wonder you need a beer. That was a bold step taking her over there. Judith might not let you have her back. You know that, right?"

"That's what I'm afraid of. She still has very little of her memory about recent months," Jack said.

"Ah, she still doesn't remember you throwing her in prison then?"

Jack debated getting up and leaving right then, but he knew, at some point, he had to put up with a little harassment if he were to ever be accepted. He couldn't just get brassed off and march back to the ship every time someone gave him shite.

"She'll remember soon enough, mate." Mike sat the beer down in front of him.

He drank half of it right off.

Mike smiled at him.

"You're enjoying this a little too much right now," Jack said.

"Yeah, I am. I've loved her for as long as I can remember. I hated you for what you did. But for what it's worth, I believe you love her. You fecked up, but you love her. I can see it."

"Oh yeah?"

"Yeah, it's the same damn look I've been seeing on my face for years now." He pointed to the mirror lining the wall behind him, looked at Jack thoughtfully, then continued, "You didn't grow up here where you have to do whatever it takes to survive. You didn't grow up understanding thievery. Of course, that doesn't mean you didn't grow up among thieves."

Jack knew exactly what he meant. Politics could be just as dirty and grasping as anything on the streets. Jack raised his glass in salute to Mike. "You said it, brother."

"So, do we need to worry about your family and their intentions toward Harlow and her baby?"

It wasn't lost on Jack that he said do "we" need to worry. One thing was for certain: the colony took care of those they considered their own.

"They will never lay eyes on her or our child." Jack looked at Mike to see if his answer satisfied him.

Mike held his eye for a moment before nodding. "I need a favor, Prince."

Jack's impulse was to correct him again about the name, but it was feeling like a term of endearment, and he had to choose his battles anyway. "Name it," Jack said.

"You know that smart little blonde from engineering, right? Her name is Janet."

Jack laughed out loud. "Yeah, I know her. Harlow stole her boots before we met."

"Sounds about right," Mike nodded. "Anyway, she comes in here sometimes. I need you to put in a good word for me."

"Well, I could if I had one, mate." Jack laughed.

"Arse!" Mike said.

"All right. All right. I got it. Don't worry. I'm on it," Jack said.

Mike smiled. "Can I get you some stew, or are you too worried about what that red-headed devil is saying to your woman over there?"

Jack nearly choked on his beer, but whether it was the beer or the company, he quickly became introspective about Judith. "I think Harlow's mother carries a lot of pain. Maybe becoming a grandmother will help with that. Having said that, yeah, that 'red-headed devil' scares the hell out of me."

The two men talked for the next hour. As Jack looked at his watch, he felt a wave of nausea. It was time to go get Harlow, and he feared what he might be walking into.

"Wish me luck," Jack said as he rose to go.

"Yeah, you might need it."

Jack agreed.

CHAPTER 33

HERMANA PEQUEÑA

Harlow heard Jack knock on the door, and it sent a thrill through her. It startled her that she was so excited, and aroused, God help her, to know that he was about to take her back home to the ship with him. She started to rise to get the door, but her mother placed a hand on her shoulder and went to get it herself. She might not have remembered a lot about Jack, but she definitely remembered everything about her mother. Right now, her mother was making a power play. Despite her questions, Judith hadn't revealed much to her daughter. She'd told her the same thing Jack did: that she was to remember on her own. But she sensed her mother was begrudgingly accepting Jack. She knew her mother wouldn't even give him that much if she didn't trust him. But Judith acted as if there was a real future for her and Jack, and it was reassuring.

"Come on in. Have a seat," Judith said to Jack.

"Thank you," he said.

Harlow almost laughed out loud. Her mother liked very few people enough to invite them in. Even the ones she liked wouldn't always get in, depending on her mood. Harlow was sure Judith knew he wanted to get Harlow and leave, and she was calling him on it just to get the upper hand.

To his credit, Jack smiled and came in to sit beside Harlow. He placed a gentle hand on her knee. "Did you have a good visit?" Jack asked her.

"Yeah, we did." She smiled at him. Though her mother clearly wanted to make him uncomfortable. Harlow felt sorry for him.

"Harlow and I had a wonderful talk. Thanks for bringing her over."

"Sure. You can come see us anytime you want as well."

Though she didn't think he did it on purpose, rattling Judith was easy. All he had to do was mention visiting the ship. It hadn't been intentional, but it was effective.

Harlow laughed softly and rose to leave. "C'mon, Jack let's get going."

. . .

It was a quiet ride back to the ship. Harlow watched the muscles on Jack's arms flex as he drove. She wished she could remember more of the night they had spent together. At the same time, she was afraid to remember, but she knew if something horrific had happened between them, her mother would have never let her go without giving Jack complete hell. It eased any reservations she might have had. Judith had let them walk out together. She might not have been able to rely on her mother for the kind of affection she saw in other moms, but she could rely on her to be truthful when it was needed, and today had been oddly comforting.

After they reached the ship, Jack had duties to attend to. She knew he had been putting things off on her account. So, she told him she wanted a nap in order to free him up to go take care of things. After lunch, she had been tired anyway and ended up drifting off.

When she woke, they had dinner together. Sometimes she caught Jack looking at her in a way that let her know he was remembering their night together because he would quickly look down again the second she caught his eye. The hungry, intent look on his face made her heart flutter, and her legs turn to noodles, but she kept that to herself.

On the way out of the mess hall, they ran into Carlos. She was glad to see him up and about. It had been three days since his surgery. She didn't expect to see him so soon. Something about him made her stop and stare. She had a strange feeling that fluttered in the back of her mind like a moth against a windowpane trying to get in. She read the nametag on his camouflage uniform—for the first time or not, she didn't know: "Sgt. Carlos Gonsalves."

"Hi," he said, sweetly.

"Hi, I'm sorry. I don't mean to..." She suddenly felt very embarrassed. She felt for sure that she knew him before, but the memory remained just out of reach. "I'm sorry," she said in fear that she was making him uncomfortable.

"It's okay, mi hermana pequeña," he said as he lay a gentle hand on her shoulder.

She turned to walk away, then stood still and gasped as a memory slammed into her with an emotional punch that made her eyes water. She remembered tears under the warm Martian sun.

Jack quickly leaned over to look at her with worry painting his face. "You okay?"

She turned to face the sergeant. "Carlos?" she breathed.

He gave her a big, bright smile.

"I never told you *thank you* for sitting with me at the cemetery that day," she said.

Carlos opened his arms and laughed softly as Harlow fell into them. "You remember," he said with joy.

"Yes. Maybe the rest of them are on their way too," she said, unable to hide the hope that crept into her voice before her logic could protect her.

"I'm sure of it," Carlos said.

Jack chucked Carlos on the shoulder. She could see that he was feeling grateful that his friend had triggered her memory. Though she wondered if he felt a sense of jealousy that he and Harlow had shared sweet memories, too. There was nothing she could do about it either.

She wondered, not for the first time, if perhaps the memories of her and Jack contained something that she didn't *want* to remember.

CHAPTER 34

TINY SUPER SOLDIERS

Jack and Doc stared at the glass screen in the infirmary and read the reports that had been taken from the lab at the compound.

"Holy hell," Jack whispered. He tried to absorb the magnitude of what he was reading. "This is crazy."

Doc spoke. "Yeah, it is. I mean, it would be brilliant if it weren't so damn unethical, especially the way they got ahold of the babies in the first place. Taking advantage of homeless women like that is low. It wouldn't be the first time it's been done in the name of science, but still..."

"You're sure this isn't anything that will cause them long-term damage?" Jack said.

"It's a legitimate question, but no, I don't think so. What do you want to do with this information?"

"Bury it! This is playing God. It's dangerous. I don't doubt that they were reporting their findings to the Chinese regularly, so keeping it to ourselves probably won't help. But maybe they will keep it to themselves for a while, too. Perhaps it will buy some time for us to learn more."

"Meanwhile, they will use this information to build a superhuman army," Doc said.

"Yeah, probably, but I'm not about to start a crazy Franken-Mars lab here in the colonies just so we can keep up with them."

A knock at the door broke their speculation.

"Come in," Doc said as he waved a hand to close the file on screen.

Harlow and Carlos walked in. She said, "I hope I'm not disturbing you."

Jack smiled at her, and that familiar warmth spread through her veins once more.

"Not at all. In fact, you should hear this. Please know that it's strictly classified for now."

"Aye, Marshal," Carlos said immediately.

Harlow nodded. "Of course."

"The good news is that the babies really are going to be just fine. The strange news is that they have superpowers."

Harlow gave him an incredulous look. "They what now?"

"Aldric and his crew tinkered with a flu vaccine and mutated it until it morphed into a virus that actually transforms the lungs so that they can breathe in several different kinds of environments. Their bodies use less oxygen, right?" Jack looked at Doc to make sure he was getting it straight.

"Close, but it's more like their bodies use the oxygen that they *do* have in a much more efficient way. This means that these children will be able to run great distances without getting winded; they will survive in environments that have little oxygen and will be able to stay underwater for very long periods of time without coming up for air. We think they were creating super soldiers. The implications of this are staggering. This means they could go to planets that a human couldn't survive on and take over—provided the environment isn't toxic in other ways. They aren't immortal, but they could fight for days without tiring. An entire army of them could storm a beach after waiting underwater for hours...just so many possibilities."

"That explains something weird I saw the day Bella was born," Harlow said.

Carlos's head snapped up at the mention of Bella's birth. "What happened?" he asked before anyone else had the chance.

"They didn't want Safia to see the baby. They told her Bella was going to die as soon as she was born—that she wouldn't be able to breathe once she was no longer attached to the cord. Safia demanded to hold her, though. I saw the nurse hand a syringe to the midwife. I think they did something to keep Bella from breathing for a couple of minutes. When Safia held the baby, she looked healthy. She was pink. I thought she would turn blue and look sick, but she didn't. They only allowed her to hold her for a couple of minutes before they took her away."

Carlos looked angry. "Heartless fucking bastards."

"Yeah, they were," she said.

Doc chimed in. "Yeah, they probably gave the baby a shot of something to suppress her breathing for a minute. It would likely kill a child without the mutation, but Bella could go a couple minutes without breathing, even newly born. I'm sure it was a way to keep up the illusion of her dying at birth."

Jack took over as Doc became lost in his own thoughts. "It also doesn't look like it will be harmful to the children long-term either."

"Wow! I guess we should tell Safia, Tamar, and Tara then."

Jack agreed. "Yeah, they really should know. They might be a target now. We should guard them at all times. I think the colony is the best place for them because it's smaller, harder for someone up to no good to hide here and easier for us to see them coming."

"Yeah, they should stay on the ship," Carlos said quickly.

Jack smiled. "Yes, that would be best."

Jack noticed Harlow looked stricken. "I'm terrified to ask, but how many babies did they do this to?"

Doc and Jack both stopped cold; neither wanted to answer the question. Harlow got the impression that if she hadn't asked, the information would never have been volunteered.

The two men looked at each other. Doc wouldn't answer without Jack's consent. Jack knew it so he delivered the news.

"Sixteen babies. Before they moved on to human studies, they killed ten primates trying to find the correct balance. Then three human babies died before they got it right. They realized they needed gestating mothers in the laboratory setting. It looks like the mothers needed to be fed a certain balance of proteins during their pregnancy." Jack looked at Doc.

"We've already been through all you can remember about your stay there, medications, and treatments, but were you able to get your own food?" Doc asked.

"All our meals were served to us," Harlow said. "If they were spiking my food, nothing can be done now. Is there any way we can let the mothers know what happened to their children? If thirteen are still alive, and we have three of them, where are the other ten?" Harlow asked.

Jack looked at her with understanding but not much hope. "Looks like they were sent to another facility once they reached six months. The address isn't on here. It says three of the mothers of the living children died during childbirth. We have one of them here, Safia. Six mothers are unaccounted for. But I assume that if they made notations about the ones who died, then the others must have lived, but there is no record saying where the women were from or went to. I truly don't know how we would reach them. There's also a possibility that they were part of the study."

"You mean they consented to it?" Harlow asked.

"Maybe, I don't know." Jack shook his head.

"Why would they do such a thing?"

"Perhaps it depends on how it was presented to them," Doc said. "If you needed money and were promised your child would have superpowers, maybe you'd consent. Maybe you'd consent multiple times."

They all stood there in somber silence as they contemplated this. Finally, Carlos spoke. "I would like to be the one to speak with Safia. If that's okay with you, Marshal."

"Of course," Jack said.

Carlos left, and Jack nodded at Doc.

"You'll speak to Tara and Tamar let them know everything?"

"Right away, yes," Doc said.

Jack placed his arm on Harlow's back and steered her toward the door. Once they were in the hallway, she looked at Jack with a smile on her face, happy to move the subject to something more hopeful.

"Carlos has feelings for Safia, doesn't he?"

"I think so," he said. "Don't women tell each other these things?"

"From what I hear, yes, but I never had a lot of female friends. I think Safia is so in love with Bella right now that she might not notice someone falling in love with *her*. You know?"

"Yeah, well, put in a good word for Carlos if you get a chance."

"Already on it," she said. "It might be good for them to have each other."

He looked at her with a sense of grief, knowing that it would be good for them to have each other, too, but she felt as far away as the Earth, even though she stood right in front of him.

CHAPTER 35

A MEMORY TO TOUCH

Harlow lay in bed that night, trying to get to sleep. She moved from one side to the other. Blanket on, blanket off. Jack was across the hallway. It would be so easy to just walk over there. He wouldn't turn her away, would he? But what if he decided to be a gentleman and not sleep with her until she regained her memories? She plotted and planned for that answer. A simple explanation that sleeping with him would trigger her memories might work.

She laughed out loud into the silence of her room. He might buy it—if he really wanted to. It was more than that though. She wanted to touch him and ease the worry in his soulful brown eyes. More than once, she witnessed vulnerability ripple across his face and transfer an ache into her chest that she longed to ease. She knew he was worried and wanted to tell him it didn't matter what had happened between them. If she still loved him, then —

"I *love* him," she whispered into the darkness of her room. The revelation hit her like a stone. She had been feeling it all along, too afraid to call it what it was without her memories. With no more thought, she found she was walking out the door in her pajamas. She knew exactly where she was headed.

Nerves assaulted her as she waved a palm across the ID portal outside his door. Her logic started hounding her, begging her to consider that she didn't really know this man. Her heart told her she did.

He opened the door in a thin pair of lounge pants and no shirt. Never mind losing her memory, the sight of him shirtless almost made her forget her name. He gave her a broad smile that was quickly replaced by a touch of worry. "Is everything okay?"

"Yeah, can I come in?"

"You never have to ask. You're always welcome in here." He put his hand on the small of her back, led her inside, and shut the door behind them.

"Is there something you need to talk about? You were kind of quiet on the way home," he said.

She didn't know how much time they had spent together before—except that it was at least enough time for her to get pregnant—but he had looked nervous about the meeting with her mother.

"Yeah, it was a lot to think about."

She sat down on the bed, and he sat beside her.

"If there's anything I could shed some light on..." he began, seeming to have no idea how to continue without knowing what she had heard from her mom.

She got the idea there had been tension between them that extended beyond the colonists not really liking him before, but she had little idea how they felt now. She hadn't left the ship except to speak to her mom—fearful to deal with questions she couldn't answer.

"Oh, there's plenty you could shed some light on, but I know you can't or shouldn't. My mother says that I can trust you," she blurted out. She had the impression he needed to know that.

"She does?"

"Yeah, she wouldn't elaborate though. She told me the same thing you did—that Doc had said I needed to remember on my own. But the thing is, I don't think I needed her to tell me that." Harlow rolled her shoulders to release some of the tension she had carried into the room with her. She knew what she was coming in there to do and though she wanted it, meant it, and intended to follow through with it, it still made her nervous.

"Turn that way," Jack said, pointing toward the headboard. "I'll rub your shoulders for you."

"Okay." Harlow pulled her feet up onto the bed and turned as he asked.

His touch was wonderful. As another type of tension began to build much lower, she felt the tension release from her shoulders. She moaned in response to what he was making her feel. She heard his breathing increase behind her. He slid one finger underneath the collar of her shirt and pulled it down her shoulder enough to expose a soft length of skin. He leaned over and kissed her shoulder, working his way up to her neck.

"Is this, okay?" he asked breathlessly.

She nodded, sure of what she wanted, but almost paralyzed with nerves.

"I would never hurt you," he whispered.

"I know. It's all just a little scary."

He spoke softly into her ear. "What is?"

"The vulnerability. Falling like this. What if I can't catch myself?" she asked.

"There's my Harlow," he said. "Always worried about that."

She was touched and a little exposed to find that he was recognizing one of her weaknesses coming to the surface.

"Let go. I'll catch you," he said.

She still faced the headboard while he wrapped one hand around her abdomen—now swollen at a full four months along—and another arm came around so that he could cup her opposite cheek and bring her face to his. His kiss was slow at first, sweet and warm.

She melted into his touch and returned his kiss, giving him permission to deepen it. His tongue was insistent and dominant, mirroring what he wanted to do elsewhere. She wanted it, too. Desire had woken her up during the night so many times over the past week, wanting to come to his bed but afraid it was too soon for herself and him, but it was slowly eating away at her. She watched him work, move, laugh, smile, and carry out his duties with an intoxication slowly enveloping her. He rose on his knees, pulling her up to her knees with him behind. Instinctively, she leaned over and grabbed the headboard. She bent her head back, and he took her mouth hungrily. His erection pressed against her backside, hard and persistent. A groan escaped his throat. She felt herself arching into him, pressing herself against him, practically begging him to take her, but fear built up inside her once more. "If we do this, I'll get attached. I just know it."

"Is that so bad?" he asked in a husky voice, raspy with longing.

"No, it's just..." she couldn't say why it was bad, only that it would make it hard to let go, and she needed to be able to let go, didn't she? She wondered what had made her feel that way? What the hell had happened between them? But she remembered being that way before. It wasn't new. She wondered if she had ever truly been attached to anything or anyone.

"You aren't afraid of anything but vulnerability." He laughed softly against her shoulder. One hand slid wickedly down her thigh, pulling her loose-fitting pajama bottoms down with it. He seemed to know what she wanted and what she was having trouble asking for. She wanted him to move forward, push past her fears, and didn't need him to be a gentleman right now. She needed him to take over. She longed for it. Her body knew what she wanted; her mind was resisting, and he was the only one who could help her.

There were only two layers of fabric between them now. He rolled his hips against her. She didn't move as he reached between her legs and slid the fabric of her panties aside and rubbed the side of his right index finger across her. She inhaled sharply with surprise and squeezed the headboard, trying to anchor herself, but she was already losing control. She dropped her head so that her neck was bare to him. He bit her softly as a little cry escaped her throat. He whispered into her ear. "Let go, Harlow."

His fingers sped up only slightly, and she cried out, shocked over how quickly he had brought her to climax. She felt as if she couldn't move as her orgasm continued to break over her in waves. He pushed his fingers against her, intensifying what was left. She held onto the headboard, panting as his body remained wrapped around her, over her, covering her, making her feel infinitely safe. Finally, she lowered herself to the bed and lay on her back beneath him, feeling satiated. He placed both of his hands on the headboard above her and looked down at her with a lazy smile.

"Can you handle more?" he asked.

Harlow laughed softly. "I may never get enough." She reached up and felt his bare chest as he closed his eyes in pleasure at her touch. She ran her hands over his shoulders and down his arms, exploring every muscle, valley, and peak of him.

He sat up, straddling her, and unbuttoned her shirt. He placed a warm hand on her breast, and she sighed at his touch as he leaned down and took her nipple into his mouth. She curled her fingers through his hair.

He grasped her shoulder. Knowing he longed for release, she wanted to give it to him. She arched her body against him, knowing it would make him think of nothing more than getting inside her as quickly as possible. He released her breast, and her hand found its way to his erection, pressing against his thin pants. He groaned, and the sound was shaky with need.

She helped him pull his pants off as he lowered himself on top of her. He held his position just above her, looking into her eyes. Was she doing things differently than she had last time? She didn't know, but what was happening now felt right. He leaned over and whispered into her ear, "I won't hurt you, Harlow. Never again."

She wondered what it meant but surrendered to him anyway, to go with raw feeling, and gut-level trust. It had never come easy to her, and she knew it. But as he slowly, gently, entered her, she let go in so many more ways than one. He paused. "I know you can't remember us. That's okay, but I love you. Don't say it back tonight. Just let me love *you* this time. Let me carry the memories for both of us. If you remember or if you never do, that's okay. Just let me love you."

Even though she had already reached climax, she could feel another one building. He wouldn't put all his weight on her; instead, he remained propped on his elbows.

She felt him begin to throb, and he stopped to catch his breath. He stared deep into her eyes. There was something primal, hungry, and raw there that made her inner walls clench even though he had stopped moving inside her.

He moaned as his eyes rolled back into his head, and he began his rhythm from before with a more frantic urgency. She grasped at his shoulders, feeling wild and out of control.

"Jack!" she called to him as she slipped under the waves of ecstasy and what she knew to be utterly, completely, lost in love.

He didn't linger on top of her as her breath began to slow, but lay down next to her and pulled her into his arms. He kissed her again, deeply. She couldn't help but notice that even though his body was spent, he kept contact with her. Though satiated, he touched her intimately, her breasts, her swollen abdomen, her thighs. As she drifted off in his arms, only minutes later, she smiled to herself, knowing that she had been right—if they made love, she would get attached.

She sat in darkness as wave after wave of nausea rolled over her. She had lost him forever. Life had no more meaning. He had loved her, and she had broken his heart. But it wasn't her fault; was it? She wanted to die. If she didn't know his child was growing inside her, she would simply give up. It would be so easy to just simply...stop. Why not? People gave up all the time, didn't they?

"You have to eat something," the man in the medical scrubs said to her.

Mother had come to see her again. She brought light and love with her, but she couldn't change anything. But she was his aunt. She was part of him just as the baby was part of him, but when the baby was born, he would take that from her and leave her as an empty shell. Sobs wracked her body. At least there was one saving grace there; after the delivery, she could just give up. But he would be at the trial. She would get to be in the same room with the man she loved. Even if he didn't love her anymore, she would get to see him. She kept the faces of the people she was saving in front of her. If she didn't, she would just tell him. It would be so easy, but she couldn't. Piper with all the braids, Mike O'Malley, all the people that were counting on her; they always had. They stood on her shoulders. Beneath their weight, she was collapsing. She sobbed. She couldn't hold them anymore.

"Harlow? Harlow? Wake up." Choking sobs caused her body to shake as Jack held onto her, tight.

Jack had turned the light out while she slept, and the darkness she woke in mirrored her sorrow. "Don't leave me," she sobbed. "Please."

"I'm not going to leave you," Jack said.

She suddenly felt ridiculous and a little embarrassed. "I'm sorry. I was having nightmares," she said. She took a deep breath to calm herself as she felt Jack's body go rigid.

The sudden change in him alarmed her.

"What is it?" she asked.

"Tell me your dream," he said like a man who was forcing himself to ask something that he would rather not.

"Nah, it's silly. It's just a nightmare."

"Harlow, tell me. It's important."

His voice was sobering, and she complied because she trusted him. She relayed what she had dreamed, and the memory of it was almost as real and painful as the dream itself. "It felt so real," she said as she concluded telling him her dream.

He said nothing for several moments, then finally, "It was real."

"No, you wouldn't leave me like that," she said. The idea felt completely preposterous after what they had just shared.

Jack held on to her tightly as he spoke, as if he feared she would bolt at any moment. "You're remembering correctly. Aldric forced you to tell me you took a bribe from him. You informed me it was him—not the man who originally claimed responsibility for it—that killed my wife and child. After I heard you did it knowing what the man had done to me…I just couldn't…I just shut down on you. You gave him the codes to my personal shuttle so he could steal it and escape. You gave him access to your head and let him take information, secrets. It was treason, but you had no choice. Aldric told you he would release several different viruses on Mars and kill all those first and second-generation Martians that had no immunity. There was no choice. You couldn't tell me he threatened you, either. You were brave and faithful to all these people, giving up everything to keep them safe. They all know it, too, but we have asked them to keep it to themselves until you remember on your own. I suppose, when we were together tonight, it triggered your memories."

He ran a hand across his mouth as if he didn't want to keep talking but continued anyway. "I was faithless. When you said you sold me out for money, I believed you. I should have known. It is to my everlasting shame I didn't try harder to get to the truth. I will always have a hole in my heart where I've hurt you. I can only spend the rest of my life trying to make it up to you. You don't have to forgive me tonight...or ever. Just don't go. Please." His voice cracked on his words until he could no longer speak.

Harlow struggled to take in what he was telling her. It was too much. She felt numb. Quickly, behind the numb feeling, came a rush of anger. "When he held me captive, I believed he was the good guy. You said he's in the prison downstairs while you try to figure out what to do with him?"

"Yes," Jack said.

Harlow flung the covers off her body and stood in the darkened room with only a dim light coming from the tiny glow of emergency exit light around the floor in front of the door to illuminate her naked body. "Take me to him."

"What?" He appeared to be struggling to process what she was getting at.

"I deserve a shot at him, don't I?"

"What?" he said again.

Harlow felt him staring at her. She knew how she must look: a small, pregnant, and naked woman standing in the faint light in front of him with her hands on her hips, ready to go into battle. She knew he might have even found it downright funny if the situation wasn't so serious and heartbreaking for them both.

"I won't kill him if you have other plans for him, but I would like, very much, to hurt him. Do you have a problem with that?" she said.

"Are you seriously daring me to challenge you on this, Harlow?"

"Yes. I deserve this!"

"Can't argue with you there. You deserve the privilege of sticking hot pokers through his eyeballs and rip his nuts off, but I can't let you, and my unborn baby, go into the cell with a fucking lunatic. He killed my wife and child. What makes you think he wouldn't hurt you? Absolutely not. I promise that no matter what we do with him, I will beat his ass again on your behalf and make sure he knows which punches are from you. Deal?"

She said nothing but went to the bathroom. When she came back to bed a couple of minutes later, she was pouting and glad he couldn't see her face very well. She let out an annoyed sigh and punched the pillow before flopping her head onto it.

Jack spoke into the silence. "In one way, I'm angry that our night has been interrupted by these horrible memories, but in another way, I'm happy to see you get your fire back. The strong fiery part of your personality was part of why I fell in love with you."

She said nothing. Confusion swirled in her mind as she tried to piece it all together, but one thing she knew for sure: she never wanted to feel the way she did in that dream ever again. She never wanted to be apart from him. Despite her frustration, she scooted her backside toward him until it was flush with his body. He sighed as he wrapped his arms around her.

They lay there in a silence that spoke of a thousand mute emotions and hurts, but sometimes there was so much to say that it was better to say nothing at all, to wait until the mud settled and what needed to find clarity did and what needed to drift away into unspoken understanding simply bowed its head... and surrendered.

CHAPTER 36

JUST MARY

"Harlow!" Mary called as she watched her climb out of the buggy before Jack could come around and get the door for her. Harlow ran to Mary, kicking up the regolith on the way to her outstretched arms.

"I'm glad you've gotten your memories back. I've missed you."

Harlow reached up and touched one of the thick silver curls. "Your head is uncovered. They let you do that now?"

Jack and Mary exchanged a look.

"What's going on?" Harlow asked.

"From now on, just call me Aunt Mary."

Before she could explain, Jack interrupted. "The archbishop isn't here yet. You can still let this go. You don't have to tell him."

Mary sighed. "I've already told the sisters what I've done. It's too late to hide it, and I don't want to. It would haunt me."

"But it's *Harlow's* confession. She would have given you her permission anyway. Just ask her. You don't have to throw away your life's work over this," he pleaded.

Mary gave him a gentle smile. "First of all, you can't ask for permission after you've already broken the Seal of Confession. It doesn't work that way, and I don't think she would have given me permission. She would have been too worried about the viruses. I didn't ask her *on purpose*, and that's not okay. Furthermore, I'm not throwing away my life's work. Everything we do ripples out into eternity. I couldn't throw it away if I tried." As she spoke, she felt her own words coming back to comfort her—as if they had been given to her, unbidden.

"Is anyone going to tell me what's going on here?" Harlow asked.

"I broke the Seal of Confession. I told Jack about your being blackmailed and why you lied to him. That was all information you gave me in your confession. The penalty is excommunication. I knew that Jack still couldn't go tell the world you were innocent, but I couldn't watch you suffer anymore. You couldn't eat, couldn't sleep. It was wrong of me to go as long as I did without telling Jack. I was afraid for my life to change. I've dearly loved my vocation, but it's time. That part of my life is over."

"Mother, no—"

"It's Aunt Mary now."

"Okay, Aunt Mary. This convent is your life. You're good at it. It *is* you."

"God is my life, not this place. It's going to be okay. I've accepted it. I think at this point it is bothering you two more than it is me."

"This is my fault. You were just trying to help me," Harlow argued.

"No, it is not your fault. You were doing the best you could in a terrible situation. I wouldn't change what I did. My calling is to love, to serve. That's what I did. I don't regret it."

Mary walked over to the statue of her namesake. She ran her hand across the statue's hand. One was elegant, smooth, and cool, the other changed by time, bony and calloused. "Reality," she whispered.

"Are you going to be okay, Aunt Mary?"

She smiled. "Yeah, I'm going to be just fine."

"Can I take anything back to the ship with me now?" he asked.

"No, I have nothing that I can't throw in the buggy after I speak with the archbishop. Thank you for offering me a place on the *Ares*. I won't let you down."

He smiled at her. "I know you won't."

Harlow gasped. "You're coming to live on the *Ares*?"

"Yes, I'm glad to hear you won't mind," Mary said.

"Mind? Of course not. Do you have plans once you get there?"

"Yes, Jack has made me the liaison between the ship and the colonists. I think it's a terrific idea. I can still help people just like I always wanted. I can still organize, lead, and set up programs to help others lead a better, perhaps more spiritual life, but I won't have to wait for the church's approval. It's wonderful and strange, but it feels right, and I'm excited about it."

Mary straightened her shoulders, took a deep breath, and looked around the place she'd called home for over two decades. She looked directly at Harlow, knowing that she felt responsible for what was happening. "It's going to be okay, truly."

She watched Harlow wipe the corners of her eyes. "Come here." She embraced her and looked over her shoulder at Jack, who was somber but gave her a smile. He was the only one in her family that she felt a connection to. She had a feeling they were going to be all the family each other would have. They had evolved separately from the rest of their clan, and she knew in her heart there was no going back. In some ways she had been excommunicated from her family as surely as she would be from the Church as soon as the archbishop arrived.

Harlow and Jack kept her company until they saw the transport carrying the archbishop, kicking up dust as it neared the convent.

"I'll see you this evening. Call me when you are on your way. Deal?" Jack kissed his aunt on her cheek.

"Will do, baby."

Harlow squeezed her hand, and then the two of them were on their way.

· · · · ·

Archbishop Harding and his driver got out of the buggy. The driver retrieved the archbishop's bag and asked Mary where he should leave it. Mary pointed toward her office; just beyond it lay her personal quarters. But no more. "How was the transport from London?" Mary asked him.

"Just fine, thank you," he replied.

She motioned to a bench in the middle of the small garden. Most church business was done remotely. The coward in her had hoped this could be done that way also, but he'd found space on a mining transport to officially relieve her of her duties and ordain the new Mother, Theresa, who was to take over for her.

"Theresa will do a fine job," she said after she exhaled a deep breath. As much as she had accepted her fate on one level, another part of her found it to be incredibly surreal.

"I'm sure she will," he said. "I'm sorry for what is happening to you, but you don't need the Church in order to serve, Mary."

In one sense, hearing him refer to her as just Mary felt like the reverberations of a door slamming shut behind her, making her jump. In another sense, she wondered if he was using her name in a nostalgic sense. This wasn't their first encounter. They were roughly the same age and had discerned their calling at the same time. They'd become friends and felt the unmistakable pull of attraction for each other. Had he just said the word so many decades ago, she wouldn't be here now. It had been a good life, one she was proud of, but sometimes she couldn't help but wonder what life would have been like with him. Her mind wandered back in time to the last days before they took their vows to the church.

"It was nice of your father to invite all the candidates over," Mary said.

She watched William Harding look out across the lake as a gentle breeze blew and created ripples on the water.

Mary took a deep breath and spread her arms wide. "It's beautiful out here."

"It is," he replied.

It shocked Mary when she felt his eyes on her. Her heart picked up an erratic rhythm. This is trouble, she thought. Despite all the warning bells in her head, she turned to look at him. His dark hair and mossy green eyes intoxicated her. She wondered if she would be a coward to tell him how she felt or if not telling him was the cowardice. She had no idea.

They had been close friends for years now. Their two families knew each other. They had worked side by side, relieving the suffering of the impoverished. The gray death had practically destroyed those who could not live off the land with the temperature drop and short growing seasons. Those in cities had no employment and were subject to constant theft and violence. She knew the moment by the lake wasn't the first time they had looked at each other with innocent, albeit hungry, eyes. This time was different though: they had both finished seminary and would take vows soon. They each felt the finality of it pressing down on them. When they were away from each other Mary felt at peace, certain of her calling, but when they were together, something dangerous lurked in her—she could see it in him too—begging to find expression.

She knew it was unfair, but she left it all on his doorstep. If he took just one action, if he simply held out his hand...

She watched as he scrubbed his hands across his face and exhaled what Mary could only label as grief. Then he turned and practically ran from the lakeside, leaving Mary there to mourn the loss of him. She exhaled as relief and loss went to war with each other. Somehow, she knew that was it. The decision was made. There was a finality to it that made warm tears run down her face.

Mary felt the sun on her face as she shared her plans with him. When she looked at him, his expression was calm, but his hands gripped the bench he sat on as if he were holding himself in place. "I intend to serve on the *Ares*, to help people see my nephew is no mindless bureaucrat. This place is vulnerable, and division is dangerous."

"You always were the politically shrewd one."

She noticed the lines around his eyes were just a little deeper than last time. He was the shrewd one—always seeing her in a way that her family couldn't.

"My family would beg to differ, I'm sure."

"That's because they assume your calling is the limit of your sight. They don't see us as multifaceted individuals." He laughed sarcastically. "We are but mindless slaves to our calling."

She smiled and dared another look at him before his eyes met hers again and saw more than they should.

He cleared his throat. "Mary, it's my charge to let you know that you have been officially relieved of your orders."

Though she knew what was coming, his words still ripped through her heart like a bullet. She gasped, and a sob escaped her throat before she could rein it back in. She had never been a crier—the action shocked her.

His voice was as soft as a caress as he continued. "The loss of identity must be staggering to you. I'm sorry, but speaking as your friend, you have nothing but opportunity in front of you. You could even..." he swallowed hard, and she had an inkling of what he was about to say and even though years, decades, of ignoring their attraction had gone between them, she still didn't want to hear him say the words. She still wanted to believe that they were "it" for each other or nothing. She didn't want to believe that it would be easy for him to let her go, but he said it.

"You could even...find a companion."

At least it was hard for him to say.

"I'm an old woman, William."

"You are *everything*, Mary."

He got up quickly and walked away without another word. Just as he had the day at the lake.

She went to gather her things and be gone as fast as possible.

• • •

The sun was setting as Mary boarded the *Ares*. When she'd come on board before, she knew she would head back to the convent, but as she placed her bags in the room Jack had always given her for overnight stays, now to be permanent, she felt a surprising sense of possibility and something else unexpected wash over her...joy. She smiled at the unexpected gift. She unzipped her bags and began placing her belongings into drawers. When she reached the bottom of her duffel, she found the gift she'd brought for Harlow and headed out the door to find her.

"Harlow?" Aunt Mary called as she walked into the mess hall.

She turned, and Mary knew Harlow was immediately searching her face to make sure she was okay, and she loved her for it.

Harlow ran to her and wrapped her arms around her. As the two embraced, Mary felt an emotion she hadn't expected so soon. It was surprising and welcome. She felt as if she were *home*.

"I brought you something." Aunt Mary reached into her satchel and pulled out two small candlesticks.

Harlow laughed when she realized their significance. "These are the ones I tried to steal when I was a girl. We're coming around full circle today, aren't we?"

You have no idea, Mary thought.

"They looked bigger when I tried to steal them," Harlow said.

Jack walked up and put his arms around the two women.

Aunt Mary experienced something she hadn't thought she would ever feel in this life. She was home with her family, with no one to relocate her, with no sense that her life didn't belong to her. She knew it was hers to choose to give all over again, and she knew she would—Church or not.

CHAPTER 37

DON'T TREAD ON ME

Aldric sat in the prison beneath the *Ares,* wondering when Jack would be back to finish the job. It had occurred to him, followed by a bout of nervous vomiting, that Jack might have only shot him in the leg because he didn't want to kill him in front of Harlow and have her see him as a monster. So, when he heard the bay doors slide open, he broke out in a sweat. In the eight-by-eight square, there was nowhere to run. It wasn't a possibility with his leg shattered in three different places where Jack had shot him. Though the *Ares* possessed the technology to speed his healing along, Jack refused him access to it. He got minimal care for his leg and was left to heal the rest of the way naturally. He had been confined for nearly a week and still had not been told his fate. The irony wasn't lost on him. Jack probably wanted him to know how Harlow felt.

Jack stood in front of his cell and stared at him until he squirmed.

"You're going to the Bastille. You will be tried for treason, and then you will be executed."

"I hear that's what you said to your pregnant girlfriend before you abandoned her, too," Aldric said, with venom dripping from his voice.

"I deserve that. But no, despite what I thought she did, I would have given my own life before I would let anyone kill her. You, on the other hand…Tell me what you know. If the information is good enough, I may consider sparing your life."

Aldric laughed. "You make the mistake of believing you have the power to spare me. All your life, you have been royalty. You live within an illusion that you pull the strings. But I'm going to tell you what I know because I believe that you are the lesser of two evils. I was on a black op. They will deny all that I tell you. The press will say I'm lying to spare my life. Your family will call me mentally disturbed. I'll die anyway. If I make it through the trial with a life sentence, you will wake up one day to the news that another inmate shanked me in some arbitrary argument. But you and I," he said, pointing between the two of them, "will know the truth. I was hired by your family to separate you from Harlow and then dig around in her head. After I had retrieved everything, I was to kill her and your child as well. They wanted you home, and they damn well didn't want a petty thief giving birth to your heir. They aren't any better than me. They just don't get their hands dirty."

Aldric watched Jack squeeze his eyes shut. *The man's a realist, but he won't want to believe his clan capable of it. Somewhere inside, he knows. They always do.*

"You do nothing but play games. Why would I believe anything you say now?" Jack said.

"They're your family," Aldric said with a flip of his hand in Jack's direction. "You tell me what they're capable of," he said, locking eyes with Jack. He knew he had gotten under the prince's royal skin, and the sense of power, even behind bars, was a balm to his predicament. He watched Jack square his shoulders as if he'd read his mind and sensed his satisfaction.

"First of all, Harlow is no petty thief. She's damn good at what she does. Second, the fact that my family hired you doesn't change how I feel about you one bit."

He said "fact." Aldric knew the chasm between Jack and his family would never close now.

"You know what we do with trash on our ship, right? We burn it to ash and throw it out the airlock."

"Pft!" Aldric knew there was nothing he could do or say to redeem himself anymore. He shrugged. "Do whatever you must. I'm a dead man. But know this. You will either spend the rest of your life being plotted against or you will become their puppet. There is no other choice for you, prince."

• • • •

Jack had exchanged his utilitarian clothing he always wore on the *Ares* for a suit and tie—it was more becoming for someone of his station, or so he'd been told. That morning, he had stood in front of the mirror and barely recognized the man staring back at him.

Two weeks ago, he watched Harlow sleeping in his bed the morning he left. Curled up on her side like a cat—her black hair fanned out across her pillow. She barely budged when he rolled out of their warm cocoon. He didn't tell her he was leaving, didn't even want to speak of it. He leaned over and kissed her forehead, as if it were the last time. Then he walked out to the small transport that would take him back to his old life, to London.

The palace felt strange now, like shoes that were just a little too tight. Jack had enjoyed a peaceful lunch with his mother, father, and younger brother. Political business was *never* to be discussed over meals—it led to unpleasantness and was bad for the digestion, as his mother often said. Jack was by far the most direct of his family, but even he was glad for the rule. He needed a minute to size everyone up. Being raised in this world had taught him the art of subtlety, reading body language, and faces. Most information could be gathered in that way.

What he gathered from dining with them today was that he was on the outside looking in. It wasn't anything they said but the way they looked at him, the way they glanced at each other, and the way their smiles never extended to their eyes when they spoke to his brother, Marcus. The subject of Harlow hadn't come up once—even though she was carrying their first grandchild. His brother was four years younger and not yet married.

After lunch he had some time to spend with Marcus. They had been friends as children, but their personalities were so different that they often didn't see eye to eye. Still, Jack was grateful to have a little time with him, and he had been appreciative of Marcus's kindness before Harlow's trial. As they walked down the hallway together, Jack felt haunted by memories belonging to a person he no longer saw in the mirror. He'd been on Mars too long—he'd certainly been told that often enough. He was merely a visitor now.

"I'm glad you've returned to us, brother," Marcus said. He placed his arm around him and gave a small squeeze.

"It's good to see you, too."

"Dare I ask if you've returned for good?"

Jack looked at him with a world of unspoken questions in his mind. Questions he didn't care to know the answer to. He'd seen what happened when Harlow spoke to her mom about the colonies, the ship. Harlow had been hurt during that short conversation in a way that could never truly be repaired. He knew his brother was much better suited to life at court than he would ever be. He knew what Marcus's question was. He even wondered, for the first time, if Marcus knew about his parents hiring Aldric to kill Harlow.

Before he could answer, his parents rounded the corner. His father spoke first. "Marcus, we need to have a moment with your brother."

"Of course," Marcus said, then turned as if he were about to go, but Jack stopped him.

"Marcus," he said.

"Yes?" Marcus looked at Jack, perplexed.

Jack wrapped his arms around his brother and whispered into his ear. "Rule well, brother."

Jack took a step back and looked at Marcus for a moment. He gazed back with an unreadable expression. The two brothers went in different directions down the hallway. Jack and his parents went into their personal library. His father shut the door behind him. Jack and his mother sat down in the soft brown leather chairs circling the large mahogany desk.

Jack's father, James, stood in front of the desk, took a deep breath, and began. "We care a great deal for the colonies, son. That is why we've planned to put ten percent of all the money earned from the ore shipments toward improving infrastructures, schools, and vaccines for the children. Since you've spent so much time there, we would very much like for you to oversee these projects from the palace. We see no reason you can't fulfill your duties here while building a stronger colony there. We also have no problem if you wish to visit Harlow and her child. Maybe you could even build her a pleasant home on Mars. You know, make her feel special."

"Well, it sounds like you've thought all this through," Jack said, keeping his tone neutral.

"We have," Jack's mother chimed in. "We really want you to be happy. Everyone makes mistakes. We still think you are the one to lead this country and overseeing business in the colonies would give you an excuse to get back to see Harlow and her baby as often as possible."

Jack had to struggle to keep calm. He knew the moment he lost control, they would own the room, but that was the case in all things: the one who remained calm held the power. Those who yelled revealed a lack of it. "Harlow is not a mistake, neither is *my* child." It wasn't lost on him that they had referred to his baby as Harlow's child, effectively excluding kinship for all of them.

"Of course not," his mother said, though his dad's white-knuckled grip told him he didn't agree.

"Son, this is your mistake. You are thirty-three now and should know better than to share your family's heritage with a thief. It is a danger to us all."

Jack knew when his dad used the word "heritage" what he really meant to say was 'Why in hell didn't you use birth control?' but the truth was, he wasn't just caught up in passion when he slept with Harlow; part of him knew exactly what he was doing. He just didn't want there to be *anything* between them that day. He wasn't stupid or forgetful. When they looked at each other, they'd seen a twin need in each other's eyes. After years of protecting himself from the searing pain of losing his wife and child, shutting down so he wouldn't have to feel. He had been as powered down as that ship, and he knew it, but one look in Harlow's eyes...

"Marcus will make a fine successor. I'm not leaving Harlow, and I won't treat her like a mistress to be kept but never acknowledged."

His father took a deep breath, as if he were reaching the limits of his patience. "Marcus is a wonderful son. He listens to me. He knows to follow good advice, but he doesn't lead."

"You aren't asking me to lead, either. You're asking me to be your puppet. Isn't it ironic that the one thing that makes you want me to lead is the one reason I won't? If following my convictions means I have to go my own way, I will. As spokesman for the colonists, we feel that giving us ten percent back of the minerals mined by our blood, sweat, and tears is an insult. You're going to have to do better than that or we will take our product elsewhere."

"So, this is where we are at? You go back to that whore and start a revolution on Mars?" his dad said.

"I hadn't planned on a revolution but simply fair treatment," Jack said calmly. Now that he felt the bonds between him and his family ripping along the seams, it surprised him that he didn't find the grief of separation but the lightness of freedom. He stood up, knowing there would be no turning back—that was clear the moment Aldric had told him that his parents had hired him to do away with Harlow. "I know what you hired Aldric for. There's no coming back from that, for either of you. I'm going home to Mars, and I won't return."

He heard his mom gasp, and a sob escaped her throat, but neither denied their actions. He realized he'd been hoping that one of them might convince him it was all just a misunderstanding, and that they hadn't conspired to take the life of Harlow and his unborn child. They knew he had his soul ripped out the first time it had happened, and they had so little regard for him personally that they would do it again in the name of politics.

His father spoke in a deadly tone. "Once you walk out that door, the lines will be clearly drawn. We will strip you of you title in the RAF."

Jack couldn't deny how badly it hurt to hear that. It wasn't just a job; it was a calling. He'd loved the men he worked with. They were his brothers. His aunt suddenly flashed into his mind. He remembered the courage that she'd had when she gave up her own calling to tell him the truth about Harlow. It had gutted her, but she was never more "Mother" than when she sacrificed her identity and possibly her standing in the community, to do the right thing, the courageous thing, for Harlow. He knew he could do no less.

"Do what you have to," he replied.

His father continued to drive the point home. "We will deal with you as we would any leader starting a revolution against their sovereign. If you have anything to say to us, say it now. For the next time we meet, it may be with an army by my side."

Jack smiled, "Yeah, I've got something to say: 'Don't tread on me.'" With that, he turned and walked out the door without looking back.

CHAPTER 38

TRANSFORMATION

When Jack reached the cargo bay, he found his ship had been tampered with. He couldn't get it online.

"Damn it!" he yelled as he punched the console. He knew what had to be done. He changed out of his dress clothing, shedding the suit and tie, slowly transforming into his new life with every piece of finery traded in for the cargo pants and t-shirt of his revolution on Mars, his home. When he walked past the mechanics—kept on staff to tend to the various vehicles and transport craft—they wouldn't make eye contact. He wanted to smack the hell out of them or, at the very least, cuss in frustration, but he knew they were only following orders. He gathered his essentials off the transport, erased any information that would give them an insight into the colonies, if they hadn't already found it, and went to find transport for hire.

As he walked the streets of London, it struck him how things there almost seemed to have a blue cast to them. They were washed out for him now. Even the greener parts of Mars had a softer kind of glow that he had grown used to and was shocked and somehow pleased to find that he missed. He ducked into shadows whenever he could. He knew getting noticed would make it harder for anyone to agree to help him. No one would want it traced back to them.

Though his clothes no longer let the people know of his station, he was still recognizable. He took a ball cap out of his bag and pulled it down low before slipping into the back entrance of a bar that had its twin in Harlow's village back on Mars.

O'Malley's tavern was a proud hole in the wall, with only a few locals chatting quietly over beers at four in the afternoon. Jack walked up to the bar and ordered the same. The bartender glanced at him before going to pour his beer, then slid it over to him as he looked over Jack's shoulder.

"You Mike O'Malley's brother?" Jack asked softly as he took a long gulp of his beer. It had been a shitty day and ordering the beer wasn't just an excuse to talk to the owner, only part of it. After what he'd just done, he knew a keg would prove more useful to him.

"Who's asking?" the bartender said.

Jack knew good and damn well that the man knew who he was. He was just trying to feel the situation out, and he couldn't blame him.

"A man stranded on Earth when he has a revolution back on Mars that needs tending. Besides, I got a black-haired, blue-eyed hellcat in my bed that my parents hate. Can you get me transport?"

The man's cautious demeanor cracked as a smile tore across his face. "If I help you, my big brother will have my ass! He's in love with Harlow."

Jack laughed. "Everyone in that village is."

"Not like Mike. If you end up using her, he will hunt you down," the man said.

"I believe it. He has a mean left hook," Jack said as he ran his hand across his right cheek.

"Yeah, he hasn't stopped bragging about that one. By the way, I'm Eoghan."

Jack nodded.

"Meet me at 1 a.m. in that old whisky brewery with the caved-in ceiling."

"What the hell could even be in there?" Jack asked.

"Oh, you'd be surprised," Eoghan said with a wink.

Jack had some time to kill. It was only six in the evening, long before his meeting with Eoghan. He couldn't go back home; he couldn't stay out on the street. Knowing it might be a very long time before he came back to London again, if ever, he had one last goodbye that had to be said. Even though he knew he was taking a big chance, his heart led the way.

He walked into the cemetery in the back of St. Anne's Cathedral. He heard the soft wind rustling through the dry fall leaves and watched the sun filter through the trees, making dappled patterns across the headstones.

His heart sped up as he got closer. He guessed if it still hurt to visit their graves even after he had fallen in love again, then maybe it always would. For once, he was okay with it, peaceful even. For the first time, he was thankful for the ache. He would always be angry that their lives were cut short, but the pain had made him human, cracked him open—had him looking in the eyes of other souls and seeing his pain mirrored back to him. He wondered; would he have been able to recognize it before? Would he have had any sympathy for the colonists? Would he have been able to look at Harlow and see more than just a thief? He didn't think so. He had not given the colonists much thought before, but when he had shown up to tackle the *Ares,* he saw in the colonists' isolation, struggle, grief, and a fighting desire just to get through another day—though his struggle might have been for another reason—he was right there with them.

He looked around cautiously and didn't see or sense anyone nearby. He walked over and knelt by their graves. Tears ran down his face as he wondered what kind of man his son could have grown up to be. What he would have looked like? Now he would never know, and it hurt, but he had been given a chance to try again, at the beginning of a revolution, no less. It couldn't be easy, could it?

The sun went down, and darkness wrapped itself around him as he sat there in front of the headstones. He savored the way the earth smelled and the distant sounds of London traffic. He had a feeling this was it—the last time. That's when footsteps shuffled behind him at the old wrought-iron gate. It was only one man. Didn't sound like an exceptionally heavy man, but if he were armed...

"It's only me," his brother said from the shadows.

"Have you come to take me back?"

"God no," he said with a soft laugh. "For once, they acknowledge I might be able to lead. I know if you had stayed, they would have never come to it on their own."

"They just feel that way because of the old first-born nonsense," Jack said as he got to his feet.

"They see in you the will to fight for your convictions. That makes a great leader." Marcus said.

"Then anyone could be. Fight for yours."

"I'm not even sure I know what they are. It only occurred to me on this very day that I've spent my whole life trying to live up to what my parents saw in you, though I was never even sure what that was."

"Maybe now's the time to find out," Jack said.

"I think so. Though I worry that what has begun here today could take a bloody turn."

"Then let us not do that, brother. Let that be the first conviction you commit to," Jack said. Jack had the feeling he was standing on a great precipice and whatever he said now would echo far into the future. He knew it had to count. "Marcus, you have it in you to be a great ruler and a remarkable man. Let no one discount you—not even your own parents. I see greatness in you."

Silence held in the space between them before Marcus spoke again. "I didn't know about Aldric."

Jack nodded and almost asked what he would have done had he known. Would he have warned him? But he decided he didn't want to know the answer. He got the feeling even Marcus wouldn't know for sure. Time would tell what kind of man Marcus would be. What kind of ruler.

The two embraced. "Be well, brother," Marcus said.

As Jack walked away, part of him expected men to come running from the shadows to subdue him at any moment. It never happened.

CHAPTER 39

TURNCOAT

Jack sat under the stars, looking across the River Thames with Westminster Bridge to his left. He felt peace wash over him when he thought of his new life. It was a bittersweet moment, but as he gazed at the broken Big Ben that was still being repaired from an RPG attack during the looting and rioting of the past years of famine and unrest, he knew nothing was certain and the best anyone could do is move forward with their integrity intact.

A breeze blew across the water, bringing with it the smell of leaf mold from the bank and asphalt from the city streets on the other side of the river. As he let the wind cool his face, he breathed deeply and said farewell. He looked up at what stars he could see that weren't consumed by the light pollution of the city and longed for the quiet Martian night and the sky full of stars that punctured the blackness like a handful of glitter thrown into the heavens. He remembered night after night spent under those stars, talking to Maggie, long gone, and the little one he would never meet as he dealt with their passing. The stars witnessed his tears, anguish, and finally, his acceptance. Night by night, bit by bit, that Martian sky had become his own.

He took a deep breath, stood, looked around him again for any signs that he might be followed, and then made his way to the old whiskey warehouse.

As he approached, a small red flame flared to life and soon glowed on the end of a cigarette. It seemed to float through the air as the man waited for him to come closer.

"Eoghan," Jack said into the smoky darkness.

"The same. Follow me."

Jack said nothing as he went down a flight of stairs that led to a basement door. Eoghan leaned over and picked up a lantern just inside, and to Jack's surprise, they started down a tunnel that had to be heading well under the ground to God knew where.

After five or ten minutes of walking, Eoghan placed his index finger over a small blue light next to a large metal door. The light turned green, and the two walked in to find a large hangar with a small transport ship.

Jack looked up at the ship and nodded. "Not bad. How did you come by this beauty?"

"They scrapped her after the riots. Naturally, we weren't supposed to be going through the royal scrap yards," he said wryly, "but it was a shame to let it go to waste when I knew some folks who could fix her up. There was an RAF insignia we scraped off the hull."

"Well, I wasn't going to mention that," Jack said with a laugh. "How the hell did you get it here? Kind of hard to move a thing like that across town."

"Not if you pay off the right people," Eoghan said with a wink. "So, you're really doing this?"

"I am," Jack said with conviction.

Eoghan motioned for Jack to follow him on board. "I'll get everything set up for you and then leave you to it. I've got to get back to the pub before the drunks tear the place down."

Jack handed him a bag of gold coins—the only currency worth a damn anymore. Eoghan took it, then began tapping instructions into the console while speaking a combination of numbers and letters for the voice recognition, and the ship hummed to life as expected. Next, the ceiling high above them slowly began to part.

From the outside, the roof looked caved in. Jack couldn't help but think whatever genius arranged that illusion should come to Mars and work for the colony.

"Damn ballsy to set yourself at odds with your family," Eoghan said.

Jack walked around the bridge refamiliarizing himself with the ship. He had flown just this type of ship—possibly this exact ship—several times. "My course was set a long time ago. I wouldn't change it if I could. I believe in what I'm doing. The fact that it's difficult is just a confirmation."

"Well, like they say, anything worth having..."

"Isn't going to be easy," Jack said as he pointed to about a dozen chameleon cloaks being thrown into the air to reveal armed men intent on keeping the ship from leaving.

"Bugger me," Eoghan said.

"How the bloody hell did they know?" Jack asked. "I don't think I was followed."

"I don't know, man, but it's time to roll out. They could have nabbed us when we entered the hangar. They waited until we boarded to ensure theft and treason."

Jack looked at Eoghan knowing that he would have been identified by now. If he tried to get off the ship, he might very well be shot on sight. If he wasn't, he would spend years in jail, not only for helping Jack but for being in possession of the stolen RAF vessel. "Damn, I'm sorry, Eoghan."

They both knew exactly what he meant. Eoghan was headed to Mars to join his brother whether he wanted to or not.

"I threw a bag on board earlier today. I knew this was a possibility."

Suddenly Jack felt a little sick as he realized that that was likely when they had followed Eoghan there. He knew they must have seen Jack going into the pub, followed Eoghan for the rest of the day, put two and two together, and knew they would be led straight to—though Jack suspected, that his parents were no longer interested in simply keeping him there to lead but keeping him from leading a revolution against them. Jack knew now wasn't the time to tell Eoghan this, if ever.

Eoghan laughed. "That's all right, Jack. I've been considering the colonies for a while now. Maybe you can introduce me to Harlow's mother. Mike tells me she's a real spitfire."

"Spitfire" wasn't exactly how Jack would have described his interaction with the woman, but Eoghan might have been on to something: a boyfriend might do her some good.

The ship rose through the air as the nervous small talk subsided. No one fired on the ship. Everyone on the ground knew the thing would be bulletproof. Even the laser weapons wouldn't do any good against the ship—they built it to withstand asteroids and radiation. However, Jack was extremely worried about the possibility of an electromagnetic pulse being directed at the ship and disabling it. He quickly hailed the *Ares* to let them know they were coming while informing them about their little issue as well.

There was no pulse, but when the ship was almost twenty thousand feet up, another RAF ship showed up to throw a magnetic "tow rope" over the ship. Eoghan worked furiously to disable its hold, but his control was overridden, and they were being towed.

The two men looked at each other, and Eoghan was the first to state the obvious. "We're fucked, mate."

CHAPTER 40

SHIP FOR BRAINS

Harlow smiled when Jack's message came through—he was on his way. Unease had bloomed inside her chest the moment he'd gone and woke with her every morning since. He was going to see his family, but she knew that meant nothing when it came to politics. Jack had assured her it would be fine, but his eyes said otherwise.

She held her breath as she waited. Carlos sat beside her on the bridge and tried to act unaffected, but she saw his knee bumping up and down.

"What is it?" she asked.

"What do you mean?" He exchanged a look with Evelyn, Jack's personal guard, who was still angry at him for going to London without her.

"Something's wrong. Spill it, damn it. Both of you!"

Carlos exhaled in defeat. They both knew she would hound him until he told her. "The transmission isn't coming from the *Ares* shuttle. It's an old RAF craft."

"Why would he be coming back on that?" she asked.

He didn't want to answer, and it showed. "Carlos!"

She watched him cringe as he launched into it. "The shuttle craft went offline around two this afternoon. The signal he sent a few minutes ago was off an old RAF craft. I thought perhaps there was something mechanical going on with our shuttle, but he would have left it powered up to communicate with the mother ship to help diagnose the problem. It's suspicious. I'm getting some data from the *Ares* now that indicates the RAF craft is being controlled by another ship. I think it's being towed."

"Towed? As in they are pulling him back down?" she asked.

"Possibly... Probably," Carlos said. He began consulting with the bridge crew, who were reading the same information he was. "If we enter the atmosphere in the *Ares* to help him, it will appear a threat," AVM Miller said.

"I told him not to go alone." Evelyn said through gritted teeth. "He knew whoever went might get stuck there after he defied his parents. He didn't want me separated from Seraph. He didn't want to put any of us in that position."

Harlow breathed deeply to quell the panic threatening to take over.

Doc had heard the commotion and joined everyone on the bridge. Harlow glanced at him, and he returned the look of worry.

"We can't just do nothing," Carlos said. "Besides, there is another person on that ship. Someone is likely helping him. They will pay for having the ship and aiding his escape."

"I understand," Miller said, "but I don't know how we help him without engaging. "It would be the opening shots of a war. Jack wouldn't want that." She looked around the room.

What she was saying was not what anyone wanted to hear, but it was true. Even Daniel, the chief engineer, crossed his arms over his chest and looked at his feet.

Harlow felt sick. They had come too far to lose Jack now.

"Can't we just hack into their system and release the tow?"

Daniel answered, "The encryption would take so long to break that he would be on the ground long before I would come close to getting in."

"I could try something," Harlow said. "Daniel, you've told me before that when the *Ares* communicates with me, it seems to work outside its parameters, taking alternative routes to get things done. What if I just tell it what I need? I'm going to try."

Half the bridge crew spoke in unison. "No!"

Doc expressed what they were all thinking. "Absolutely not! We've been through this before. It was bad enough then, now you're pregnant. Jack will have all our heads if you get hurt."

She knew Doc didn't want another black eye from Jack.

"Listen, I won't take the serum. What I'm suggesting is that we use the weird machine that Aldric had that changed my brain waves. That doesn't affect the baby and shouldn't fry my brain either. We took the machine, right? We still have it, don't we?"

"We do," Doc said. "But that thing gave you memory loss. You've fought so hard to get your memories back."

"Damn it! We're wasting time, and I don't want my memories if Jack isn't here. Getting him back is all that matters. Besides, I've proven I can remember. How long will it take them to tow him back? A few minutes? If we don't do this right now, he'll be on the ground and taken God knows where. You all know we will try to save him, and that will definitely mean lives lost." Harlow didn't wait for anyone to respond but ran down to the new chief science officer's workspace where she guessed Aldric's device was kept. Doc was on her heels.

"Are you going to help me or not?" Harlow asked.

"You're going to get me killed," Doc said. He walked to the machine and got it online anyway.

While Doc set everything up, she went to the clear glass panel where the ship interfaced. She placed her palms on the glass and whispered a prayer. "Oh please, let this work." She went through the commands in her mind that Doc would give the ship once they hooked her up. She couldn't say for sure how he would word it or what programs he would need to run, but she assumed he would need to request that the ship overwrite whatever program was towing Jack's RAF ship. Harlow felt a little strange and gasped as energy moved through her palms. She lifted her head and turned to Doc.

"Doc! Ask Miller or Carlos what kind of program the RAF craft runs on. "Nebulus? Flightsong? Starmark? Which one?"

"I'm right here, Harlow," Carlos said. "The RAF vessels run a Flightsong program."

She hadn't realized Carlos had slipped into the room. Her vision was narrowing. She simply nodded and turned her attention back to the *Ares*. "Flightsong," she whispered. The strange energy ran up her arms but didn't hurt. She also noticed that she was lucid, unlike all the other times she'd spoken with the ship. "Release the tow on the captive ship. Bring it home," she commanded. It wasn't exactly the ones and zeros language the ship spoke in, but she knew the *Ares* understood what she wanted. She felt the *Ares* lock on to the RAF signal and break the hold pulling it back to Earth. She only hoped that the vessel was in good enough shape to hold the EM bubble steady that made trips back and forth to Mars quick. She couldn't imagine the seven months it had taken her ancestors to reach the Red Planet. The *Ares* told her the moment that space and time began traveling up and over the EM bubble the old RAF vessel was encased in. She left her hands where they were a moment longer and whispered, "Thank you." The tunnel vision disappeared and to her surprise, there was no residual headache to contend with either.

Doc rushed over and placed his hand on her shoulder. "Are you okay? I've got the machine ready."

She turned to him and smiled. "I'm fine, and we don't need it. The *Ares* hears me without...without anything!" AVM Miller had entered the room as well. Her eyes were wide with a smile to match.

"What. The. Hell?" Carlos said with his mouth agape.

"You're telling me!" Harlow said.

Doc pulled her eyelids up to check if her eyes were dilated, but she pushed his hand away. "I'm fine. I swear it. Don't fuss!"

Doc held up his hands in surrender.

Carlos ran over to the interface and tapped the glass with a fury. "Well, I'll just be damned. They will be here within the week. Doesn't look like they are being followed either."

Harlow shrugged. "I might've disabled the ship towing them while I was at it."

Carlos turned to Harlow with a huge smile, opened his arms, and she fell into them with a sigh of relief. "Nice job, mi hermana. You saved my best friend."

Six days later, Harlow, Carlos, AVM Miller, Evelyn, and Doc had made their way to the docking bay to meet the RAF ship. Jack got off the ship without saying a word, walked up to Harlow, and got directly in her face. "What. Did. You. Do?"

A giant smile made its way across her face, and she held her hands up in surrender. "I didn't hook my head up to anything, babe."

"Harlow, it's not funny," Jack said.

"It's true. She didn't," Doc said.

"Then someone explain to me how I went from being towed by another RAF craft to being towed by the *Ares*? You shouldn't have been able to hack into their program."

"Jack, I didn't have to do anything but speak to the ship. That's it. I swear. You're here. That's all that matters. I'm sorry it didn't go well," she said in a softer tone. She knew if they had chased him down, it wouldn't have gone well with his parents and that had to hurt.

He looked at her with warmth and love. "I know what I need and where I need to be." A soft smile lit up his face. She recognized the look of resolve and freedom.

Everyone turned to look as a gray-haired man, perhaps in his fifties, stepped off the craft. Harlow couldn't shake the feeling that she knew the man. She searched her mind, trying to puzzle together where she'd met him.

Jack walked back to the man and placed a hand on his back as he introduced him. "This is Eoghan O'Malley. He's Mike O'Malley's older brother. Mike's got a hell of a surprise coming his way."

"Oh, my God!" Harlow said. "You're kidding!"

"Hell no, lass. Woke up a week ago with no intention of coming to live on Mars. I'm here now. No going back."

"Whatever you need, man. Name it," Jack said.

"Hells bells man; don't tell me that!" Eoghan said. "Careful what you say!"

The two laughed.

"Shall we go tell your brother that you're here?" Jack said.

"Yeah, let's blow that lil' bastard's mind," Eoghan said.

Before the two of them left, Carlos gave Jack a quick smack on the back. "I have to admit I was worried for a while there, Marshal."

Harlow watched the exchange from where she stood at his side. Jack looked down at the ground quickly, then back up at Carlos. "It's not Marshal anymore, just Jack. They have stripped me of my title, Sergeant. I don't yet know how that will change things here on the ship or how many of you will be asked to return home. I just don't know yet."

Carlos nodded. "Aye, Boss."

"Boss? I don't even know that you have an obligation to call me that either anymore."

Carlos smiled. "The coalition has been ignoring us for years now, but you haven't. Maybe nothing much will change, or maybe you can get half the coalition to side with you. I don't know, but you're my best friend, and I believe I know what you would do if it were me. I got your back, Boss." Carlos turned and left.

Jack put his arm around Harlow. "I'm a lucky man."

Eoghan spoke. "You all right, Boss?"

"Would you believe I really am?"

"I'm on Mars for Chrissake. I would believe just about anything."

Harlow watched Jack's world coalesce before him, highlighting what mattered and pulling the rest into the shadows as he let the joy of his new life mingle with the pain of the old until something new emerged, something bittersweet and infinitely worthwhile.

"Come on. Let's go see your brother," Jack said.

"You got it, Boss."

CHAPTER 41

REUNION

Jack and Eoghan stood outside O'Malley's tavern. Jack looked at the man who was taking everything in.

"May I ask why you didn't leave with Mike when he came to Mars? He was here when I arrived seven years ago."

Eoghan threw his head back and laughed. "*I* wasn't running from the magistrate. He was. Besides, I was head over heels with a little English gal. She didn't last, but the pub I opened in London did. It became my new woman. I'll miss her," he said wistfully.

Jack felt sick knowing that he had lost his pub helping him escape. "I'm sorry, Eoghan. Really, I owe you."

"Nah. It's like this: that ship was available to the highest bidder. I was likely to get busted at some point by helping someone flee—that's why I had the ship. I'm just glad it was for a worthy cause. If a revolution is about to break out, and I think it is, I don't want to be on the wrong side of it. It was time."

Jack nodded and looked at the pub. "You ready for this?"

"You can't be ready for this. It's been fifteen years. Maybe he'll let me tend bar, huh? Topless maybe?" Eoghan laughed but didn't budge from the spot he seemed planted in.

Jack laughed out loud. "Oh, dear Lord, Eoghan! You're stalling."

Eoghan exhaled. "Yeah, it's just been a long time."

He started walking, and Jack followed. The two entered the dim lighting of the pub and looked around. It was six in the evening, so the regular patrons were trickling in. The first thing Jack noticed was Harlow's mother, Judith, sitting at the bar having a beer and talking to Mike.

Eoghan stood stock still as he watched his brother. He spoke softly to Jack. "It's one thing to see him on the comm, but it's quite another to see him in person. It's so different."

Jack felt sorry for Eoghan. It was all such an incredible shock. "If things don't go well, I can give you a job."

"I'll keep that in mind."

There was a break in the conversation with Judith. Mike looked up and froze. "Jesus," Mike said. Judith turned toward Mike's gaze.

Eoghan looked at her and nodded in greeting. Mike snapped out of his stupor, walked around the bar, and headed straight over. He pulled his older brother into his arms. "What the hell are you doing here?"

"Running from the magistrate. Same reason you came here, brother."

Jack laughed. "It's a bit more complicated than that."

"Yeah, apparently I'm helping start a revolution," Eoghan said as he swiped at his eyes. "The prince had to get back home and thought I might help. You know, since you and he are such good friends and all."

Mike laughed and gave Jack a good-natured punch in the arm. "Like I'm vouching for this guy. We nearly killed each other."

"Ancient history," Jack said, smiling.

"Well, sit and have a pint. We'll hear all about this escape of yours over a few beers with my friend. Judith, this is my big brother, Eoghan."

Judith smiled at Eoghan, and Jack realized he had never seen her truly smile before. He realized she was beautiful when she wasn't busy being miserable. It was the first time he felt that she and Harlow looked alike.

"Pleased to meet you, Eoghan," Judith said.

The energy that passed between them while Eoghan told their story of the narrow escape wasn't lost on Jack either.

He left the pub that evening with something very interesting to tell Harlow.

CHAPTER 42

THE SEEDS OF REVOLUTION

Jack sat in his office with Carlos and grimaced at the shockingly cold sip of coffee he had just taken. He hadn't realized how long he had sat there mulling over his dilemma—it was a big one. He couldn't take Aldric back to London for trial—the asshole had been working for his family. Hell, for that matter, Jack couldn't go back there himself. He couldn't imprison Aldric on the ship, either. It made the place feel hostile somehow. The man was a murderer. Jack had no problem killing him, but he feared there was something missing in the connection between Aldric, Mikhail, and the Chinese. If Aldric were gone, he might never get the answers he needed.

He shoved the cold coffee out of reach so he wouldn't mindlessly drink from it again. That's when he realized what his only option was: the colony prison needed some serious reform, but it wouldn't be getting it before Aldric arrived. If he tried his smug "fuck you" attitude in there, he would get his ass beat.

"I don't like it, Boss," Carlos said.

"I don't either, but we can't keep him on the ship; it makes Harlow nervous. I get where she's coming from. The *Ares* is our home."

"Mine too, but I like knowing he's somewhere where we can keep an eye on him. You know yourself, there are some shady guards in that prison.

"Yeah, but do you have a better alternative?" Jack asked.

"No," Carlos said. "Have you heard back from anyone in the coalition yet?" Carlos asked.

"The US is silent for now, but Spain has been in contact. They've not agreed to anything definite, but I know that they still harbor resentment over my father not throwing in any resources or boots when the Muslims finally claimed half their land twenty years ago. I think they might agree to form a new coalition if we allow them an outpost here. What I fear is promising land to the first who sides with us and then anyone thereafter wanting a piece until we bring rivalries and old resentments here. I don't know; there's a lot to work out."

Carlos watched as Jack's jaw clenched.

Jack reached up to his chin. "I'm doing it again, huh?"

"Yeah, well, you've got a lot to think about, my friend."

"You haven't heard from your command at all? Not even a blip? A rumor?" He worried profusely about how all this would affect Carlos. He remembered the sting of his father telling him he had been stripped of his title, and he didn't want Carlos to suffer the same loss of identity. He knew Carlos's family had a long-running tradition in the Marine Corps.

"Nothing yet, but I've taken my money out of the holding bank."

Jack knew the US forces there in the colonies kept their money in a type of holding bank so that it contributed to the US economy, but they could use what they needed to live on without converting all of it to Martian units, which were worth considerably less. Hearing Carlos say that was like a punch in the gut to Jack. It meant he was truly going to stick around when the shite hit the fan and wouldn't allow the US government to freeze his account if the Yanks ended up siding with Britain and calling him back. It meant that Carlos intended to go AWOL if the US called him home.

Jack realized he wasn't as stone-faced as he would like. He couldn't pull it off with this man anyway. Carlos had known him for too long.

"Don't look so damn stricken, Boss. I made my choice, and I have peace about it. Besides, the US has been paying us half what the ore is worth, too. The colonists are being taken advantage of by everyone in the coalition. It isn't just your family, and with all due respect, it would actually do you some good to let that sink in. I know that you have a sense of guilt about your family being the first to make their intentions clear about the colonies. They may be the first to say it to your face, but they aren't alone."

"Yes, you're right."

"Yeah, that's why you keep me around," Carlos joked.

Jack smiled. "I knew there must have been some reason."

CHAPTER 43

THE BIG QUESTION

Harlow emerged from the infirmary looking a little green. She had been at Tara's side as she gave birth, and though it was less emotionally difficult than Safia's, it was physically more difficult. Her baby had gotten stuck in the birth canal, and he had to be removed via emergency caesarean. She had a boy and Doc believed the shoulders had given Tara such a difficult time. When Harlow walked out to find Jack, she immediately stared at his massive shoulders and cringed.

Jack looked at her with sympathy and placed his hand on her arm. "You okay, sweetheart? Is Tara all right?"

"Yeah. It's just...he got stuck, and they cut her open."

"That bad, huh?"

"My turn is only three months away!"

He wrapped an arm around her as they strolled down the hallway. "I'm sorry. It'll be fine. I promise. Besides, I have a surprise for you."

They walked into Harlow's old room. She found it full of candles.

"Wow! It's amazing, but why?"

"It's for you. I have a question for you."

Jack sat down on the bed and pulled her into his lap as Harlow's heart started thrumming against her chest. She had some idea of what might be about to happen.

"I kept thinking there would be this perfect time when everything would calm down and settle enough for me to ask you this, but I don't know that our lives are ever going to be that way. I'm not even sure they were ever *meant* to be that way. You and I are revolutionaries. I think we always have been, and that doesn't lend itself to perfection or quiet, but that's okay."

Harlow nodded, knowing exactly what he meant.

"I was worried you would find all this," he said, looking around, "too typical or...I don't know. You're the most unique individual I've ever met, and I can't wait another moment to make sure the entire colony, and whoever cares on Earth, know that you are my wife. Not because you are pregnant, but because every day that I'm with you is a good day, no matter what kind of ridiculousness we have to face."

"We specialize in ridiculous," Harlow said with a lump in her throat.

"We do," he said. "But you still haven't said yes."

"Oh," Harlow laughed. "Yes! God, yes! Hell yes! I love you."

"I love you, too, my little thief." He put the ring on her finger set with a peridot found in the depths of Mars and kissed her deep, long, and hungry before lowering them both to the bed.

. . .

They strung lights from the back of the ship to the poles holding up the reception tent. The night was illuminated like a fairy tale as music came from the tents and poured out into the Martian landscape. Jack and Harlow held each other tightly and danced slowly, though the tempo had long since changed to a faster song, and they simply didn't notice or care. Harlow finally opened her eyes and looked up from the cocoon of Jack's arms.

Archbishop Harding had officiated their wedding, and the entire colony celebrated. Evelyn and Seraph danced and laughed. The children from the village stole sweets from the dessert table while parental eyes weren't looking. Doc Hagen raised his glass in her direction. Mike O'Malley, Aunt Mary, and AVM Miller were at the bar clinking shots together. Harlow smiled at the sight of them. She understood the need for a good stiff drink—though she suspected Aunt Mary might be having a drink even if her entire life hadn't just turned upside down. But all Mike had to do was muster up the courage to go ask Janet from engineering—whose boots Harlow had stolen long ago—to dance. Harlow had it on good authority—via Janet telling her—that she would accept, but the man just couldn't seem to do it. For a few years now, Harlow had known that he had been in love with her. She had even wished she could reciprocate those feelings, but she had only seen him as a friend, a brother. She really wanted him to be happy and thought she might need to stick her nose in their business.

"Oh, dear Lord, Jack. Do you see what I see?" she asked as she pointed toward the far end of the ship, where Judith had just emerged with Eoghan, Mike's brother, and to Harlow's absolute shock she was smoothing down her hair as Eoghan struggled to wipe lipstick from his neck.

Jack laughed. "Good for them!"

Harlow wasn't sure what to think. She had just pictured her mother being alone and miserable forever. Not that she wanted it that way, but she thought her mother did.

"Hey." Jack bent down to meet her eyes. "Are you okay with that?"

"Sure I am. I just never thought she would, you know?"

"Yeah, I'm glad she's happy." He pulled her in close again.

Harlow laughed. "She certainly *looks* happy."

"They aren't the only ones," Jack said. He nodded toward the other end of the tent where Safia and Carlos laughed and held hands while Janet was happy to be holding onto Bella so Safia could get a break.

"I'm glad those two are together," Jack said. "I would be surprised if the powers that be just forget about Bella being a super soldier. She needs someone like Carlos looking after her."

Harlow shuddered. "She's so sweet and tiny. I keep forgetting what kind of power she has."

"I hope her mother never does. If she and Carlos stay together, he won't forget. He's wired to spot a threat."

"Spot a threat," Harlow whispered. Her world suddenly tilted on its axis as a thought hit her. She chastised herself for not thinking of it before.

"You okay?" Jack looked around, wondering what had alarmed his new wife.

"Jack, I didn't just forget my time with you. The time I spent at the compound, especially when I first got there, is fuzzy. I remember not being able to say just how long I had been there. Why would they need me to forget my time there?"

"I didn't know you had forgotten any of your time there. I thought they just made you forget me," Jack said.

Even in the dim lighting, she didn't miss the look on his face at her revelation.

"It didn't occur to me before because I thought my entire purpose in being there was completely different, but what if that was only part of it?"

"Maybe you remembered something, and they had to wipe your memory every time it happened," he suggested.

"Could be, but what if they did something to our baby?" She had the feeling that he knew where she was headed with the conversation and was just suggesting an alternative to protect her from worrying.

"Look, it wouldn't make any sense to empower the child of their enemy," he said.

"Yeah, that's true," she said. She laid her head against Jack's chest as they held each other close and continued dancing. It was their wedding night, and she didn't want to give either of them any reason to panic, but she couldn't help but remember that her captors' plan was to never let her go, and never let her remember. She and the baby would have been under their control. Fear swept through her, and she thought she felt Jack tense up almost imperceptibly. Whatever might have happened, she knew there was no help for it now, but there was hope. Though she couldn't yet access them all, she still had the files her father had placed in her head. She'd seen them when she communed with the *Ares* to bring Jack home.

As they danced, she thought about the paper in her pocket containing advice given to her by a very wise woman, former priest, and mother superior who now sat at the bar doing shots with friends. The paper had sustained her through the darkest of nights on two different planets and two different holding cells: "The deeper that sorrow carves into your being, the more joy you can contain." She knew now more than ever, as threats loomed around them, deeper still was an abiding space for joy.

She held Jack closer and smiled.

CHAPTER 44

MIKHAIL

Mikhail walked through the isolated Martian compound and realized why there had been no contact. No one was there. The last he had heard, Aldric was holding Harlow with the rest of the women. They had perfected a virus and turned God's method of population thinning into a superhuman gift. They had all been doing these women a favor by making their children the forefathers and mothers of a brave new world. The colonists deserved equality and would never get it from that sorry excuse of a prince who thought the common man could bring it about on their own. They needed a plan. Aldric had it. It was noble and true. But now...

He looked at the screen and saw that they had stripped the files. All that progress. He knew that the information had been transmitted back to General Cheung, but he couldn't access it from here.

"God damn it!" He screamed as he ripped a cabinet from the wall and flung it across the room. He knew he had the prince to thank for this, but it was his mistake.

"Never underestimate your enemy," he said to the empty room. "I deserve this."

He tore at his clothing. He was constantly hot after living on Enceladus for so long. It never let up. "Everywhere I fucking go!" He roared.

He knew he had to get a handle on his nerves. Tattered clothing hung on him. He walked down the hallway until he found a room belonging to one of the male employees. Looking through the closet, he found some outfits that were a little loose, but close enough.

His anger flared again as he thought of the prince ruining everything. He headed back down the hallway, picked up his ripped pants, went through the left pocket to retrieve the small vial, and injected himself with tranquilizer. He had given his life to the Brotherhood. Now he was having a hard time functioning in his own life, but General Cheung still had faith in him, his passion, and ability to stop at nothing to create utopia. His faith had only gotten stronger when he had emerged from the ashes and pile of bodies as the *Ares* escaped the atmosphere on Enceladus. His flesh had burned, then quickly frozen. Cheung had believed it was a sign that the gods had spared him to lead the masses of lost people into a better world where all were equal and shared in the wealth, all having enough, all having the same vision, and all working for the greater good just as it should be.

He walked over to the mirror and looked at himself. At sixty years of age, his silver hair was still thick, his eyes still bright and alert, and with the right medication, he could remain calm enough to get the job done. He stared at himself for a good long while and remembered his ancestors, how they had fought for Mother Russia and failed. He would not. General Cheung understood the vision, and now he understood that the mistake of his ancestors had been refusing to join with other countries that had a similar vision, a benevolent dream for their people.

"I will not fail!" He screamed to his reflection as he slammed his fist down on the chest of drawers. He did not know how hard he had hit the chest, nor did he feel the crack that ricocheted through his hand.

"I can set and regenerate that broken hand for you, comrade."

Mikhail wiped the sweat from his eyes and turned to see a man with a deep scar running through his eyebrow and down his face.

"I see you've also given your body to the cause," Eyebrow Scar said. "They've taken our files, but I have the info here," he said, pointing to his head. "They strike us down, but we always rise again. Do we not?"

Mikhail felt hope swell in his chest as he straightened his back and replied, "We rise."

NOTE TO THE READER

Reviews are the best way for authors to attract new readers. If you will kindly post a review of *Stealing Ares* on the website of your choice, and send me either a screenshot or link to your review, I will reply with an exclusive short story set when Harlow first journeys to Earth with a long shopping list compiled by her colonist friends. Desperate to get back in their good graces after siding with Prince Jack, she's determined to get their supplies—by hook or by crook!

Please send your review link or screenshot to
kimconrey@ares-ascending.com

Visit my website at **Ares-Ascending.com** for information
about book signings, blog posts, and more.

Look for book two in the Ares Ascending Series coming soon.

LEARN MORE

Speech and language disorders such as Harlow's and awareness of them are near and dear to this author's heart. It's important to recognize that these disorders do not always have to do with pronunciation, but how information (instructions, conversations) is processed in the brain and the ability to respond. This is especially true with disorders such as MERLD (mixed expressive receptive language disorder) and Apraxia of Speech. For more information about speech and language disorders, please visit: https://www.asha.org/public/speech/disorders/.

Thanks to Kelley O'Hare, Speech and Language Pathologist, for her expertise.

ABOUT THE AUTHOR

Photo courtesy of Cherie Lawley Photography

Kim Conrey is a writer, runner, podcaster, and occasional cosplayer. When she's not working on more books in the *Ares* series, she writes about living with the misunderstood condition of obsessive compulsive disorder. She also volunteers as VP of Operations for the Atlanta Writers Club and collaborates on the Wild Women Who Write Take Flight podcast. Kim lives with her husband, two daughters, and three cats in Atlanta, Georgia.